YOU OWE
ME A
MURDER

YOU OWE ME A MURDER

EILEEN COOK

Houghton Mifflin Harcourt
Boston New York

hmhbooks.com

The text was set in Constantia.

Library of Congress Cataloging-in-Publication Data
Names: Cook, Eileen, author.
Title: You owe me a murder / by Eileen Cook.
Description: Boston ; New York : Houghton Mifflin Harcourt, [2019] |
Summary: On a school trip to London that includes her ex-boyfriend and his new girlfriend, Kim meets risk-taker Nicki, who proposes a diabolical deal.
Identifiers: LCCN 2018014683 | ISBN 9781328519023
Subjects: | CYAC: Murder — Fiction. | Friendship — Fiction. | Dating (Social customs) — Fiction. | Foreign study — Fiction. | London (England) — Fiction. | England — Fiction. | Mystery and detective stories.
Classification: LCC PZ7.C76955 You 2019 | DDC [Fic] — dc23
LC record available at https://lccn.loc.gov/2018014683

Manufactured in the United States of America

3 2021

4500827850

To my friends
who have always been there for me
and offer to bring the tarp, shovel, and no questions
when the need arises.

NORTH AMERICAN STUDENT SCHOLARS FOR CHANGE

Our summer programs are formulated to show the world to your exceptional teen. Designed for high academic achievers with an interest in expanding their worldview, our programs have been called life-changing. Our trips combine the opportunity to view art and architecture and learn about history with a world-class guide, and your child will develop his or her independence and maturity while building friendships that will last a lifetime.

ONE

I plotted murder in the Vancouver airport while waiting at gate D78 for my flight to London.

Based on the expressions of the people around me, I wasn't the only one thinking of how to do someone in. Our flight was delayed and everyone was irritated and restless. The couple at the end of the row were fighting about which one of them had forgotten to lock the bedroom window before they left. Then there were at least a half-dozen people wanting to take out the toddler wearing the SpongeBob T-shirt, who vacillated between shrieking at a decibel normally used to torture dogs and running around slamming into everyone with his grimy hands.

The old guy across from me snarled, baring his yellowed teeth, every time the kid whirled in his direction. You'd think that would freak the toddler out, but it didn't seem to make any impact. Maybe the little boy got his ability to ignore unpleasant things from his mom. She stared down at an issue of *People* magazine, her lips moving as she read, completely ignoring the fact that people in the gate area wanted to club her kid with their roller bags. The only way you knew it was her child was that when he would slam into her, she'd hold out a limp plastic baggie filled with rainbow-colored gummy worms and then drop one into his clutching hand. She was like an apathetic mama bird.

I tilted my head to the side to crack the tension in my neck. I wished I could block things out that well. Instead I found myself continually looking over at Connor. My back teeth clenched, tight enough to crack. Miriam was perched on his lap. I told myself to stop staring, but my attention kept being pulled back. He slid his hand under her shirt and rubbed her back in tight circles. I knew that move. He'd done that to me.

Before he'd dumped me.

Miriam ruffled his hair. He couldn't stand it when I'd done that. He'd push my hand away or duck out of my reach. Connor had gone deaf after a bout of chicken pox as a kid and had cochlear implants so he could hear. He wore his hair a bit shaggy because he didn't like to draw attention to the processor behind his ears. I'd found it fascinating. Not just because it's a pretty cool piece of tech, but also because I wanted to know how he felt going from a silent world to being able to hear. But he didn't like to talk about it, or for me to touch his hair.

Apparently, he didn't have the same hang-up with Miriam. I reminded myself that I didn't care. Connor meant nothing to me now. I swallowed hard.

Toddler SpongeBob slammed into me. His sticky fingers, streaked red and blue from the candy, clutched my jeans. He stared up at me with his watery eyes and then, without looking away, slowly lowered his drooling, slobbery mouth to my knee and *bit me.*

"Hey!" I shoved him hard without thinking. He teetered for a moment and then fell onto his giant padded diaper butt, letting out a cry. I glanced around guiltily, shame landing on my chest with a thud. His mother didn't even look over. The old man gave me a thumbs-up gesture. *Great—that's me, Kim, the kind of person who beats up preschoolers when she's not stalking her ex-boyfriend.* I crouched down to help the kid up, but he pushed me away and returned to running wildly up and down the aisle.

I peered down at my phone, wishing I could call my best friend, Emily. She always knew how to cheer me up. She was spending the entire summer working at a camp on the far side of Vancouver Island. She didn't have any cell service or WiFi, so there was going to be no quick "everything will be fine" text or call. Granted, if I'd been able to reach her earlier in the summer, I might not even have been in this situation at all. Communicating old school—by letters—might be vintage and nostalgic, but it does you no good when you have an emotional disaster that needs immediate BFF interaction.

We'd been friends since elementary school and this was the longest I'd ever gone without talking to her. So far, my summer was proof positive that I shouldn't be allowed to handle things on my own. I fished the last card she'd sent me out of my bag. Inside she'd scribbled, *"I know you can do this! Your trip's going to be amazing!!"* Emily never met an exclamation point that she didn't like. Despite the positive punctuation, I was pretty sure she was wrong on both counts. I felt far from capable, and although the flight hadn't even left, I already hated everything about this trip.

I took a deep breath, counting in for three and then letting it whoosh out. *I can do this.* I wasn't going to let Emily and my parents down.

A few rows over, Miriam laughed, tossing her head back as if Connor had just told the best joke of all time. She playfully punched him in the chest with her tiny little hand. Everything about her was miniaturized. She told everyone she was five feet tall, but she was four eleven at best. She looked ridiculous when she stood next to Connor. He could have put her into his backpack and carried her around like a Chihuahua.

I had to admit Miriam was pretty, other than being freakishly petite. She had long dark hair that could have starred in a shampoo commercial. Her only flaw was that she wore too much eyeliner. She was addicted to the cat's-eye look, accentuating the slant of her eyes. She had a flair for drama; she always made huge gestures, sweeping her arms around, flicking her hair over a shoulder, or talking loudly as if she was constantly trying to make sure everyone could hear her. She was in the theater crowd, so maybe she couldn't help herself.

I never would have guessed Connor would date someone like her: showy. I thought he'd enjoyed that we didn't always have to be talking, but if we did, it was about important stuff: Philosophy. Science. Politics. We met once at the coffee shop in the morning before work and split up the *Globe and Mail,* silently passing the newspaper sections back and forth. He was the only other person I knew besides me who liked to read an actual paper. I'd caught our reflection in the window and thought we looked like adults. Like people who lived in New York or Toronto, with important jobs, a fancy high-rise apartment with lots of glass and chrome, and a membership to the local art museum.

Miriam had no volume control, but she wasn't stupid. I didn't know her well — she hung with the drama crowd — but I wouldn't have thought Connor was her type. I would have seen her liking a guy with an earring and some kind of social justice agenda. She wasn't in the hard sciences but still took a bunch of AP courses. She'd written some paper on Shakespeare that won a national award for English geeks. No wonder I wanted to kill her.

I sighed. I didn't want to kill her, I wanted to *be* her. Miriam hadn't stolen Connor. Someone can't steal what you don't have. He didn't dump me because he'd fallen for her. What had happened between us was complicated. More complicated than I even wanted to admit. He had his own reasons for stomping on my heart. If I was going to take anyone out, it should be him. But no matter whom I blamed, it didn't change the fact that I wasn't looking forward to spending the next few weeks watching the two of them make out in front of me. I shook my head to clear it. As everyone kept reminding me, it would be for only sixteen days.

I closed my eyes so I didn't have to see them, but I could still hear Miriam. Her drama teacher should be proud of how well Miriam's voice carried. She was four feet eleven of all lungs. Her voice filled the entire gate area and spread down the hall like toxic lava. I could tell already that the sound would be like fingernails on a chalkboard by the end of the trip.

The worst part was that I'd pleaded to go. I told my parents if they let me attend, they'd never have to get me another gift. Once Connor had announced he was going—before we'd broken up—I'd been instantly consumed with images of the two of us walking hand in hand through narrow cobblestone streets. The program was advertised as if it were a great educational opportunity, but the truth was, there weren't any real demands. We'd be "exposed" to culture, as though it were a cold we could catch. I didn't really care about the chance to travel, or what I might learn from the sights of London; what mattered was going *with him*. I didn't want him to be away for almost three weeks, doing all these things without me. I loved the idea of starting school in September with the two of us chatting constantly about *"remember the time we were in London?"* until everyone around us was annoyed.

In retrospect, I know he wanted to come because he didn't think I was going. He signed up without talking it over, telling me only after it was a done deal. I pleaded with my parents for days, never admitting that I wanted to go because of Connor and instead laying it on thick how it was a great way to expand my horizons, how amazing it would look on my university apps, and how I'd suddenly developed a fascination with British history, until they gave in.

Then, after things with Connor blew up in my face, I'd begged my parents to let me bail, but they wouldn't budge. They insisted it wasn't the deposit, it was the point. My dad called it a chance for me to "build character." As far as he was concerned, Connor had never been worth my time. He made a snide comment about Connor's overbite, which, coming from a dentist, was some serious trash talk.

My mom had made a dismissive sniff and told me "he's not worth bothering over." She acted as though she didn't like him, but when I'd first told her about Connor, she'd been as excited as me. He was exactly the kind of boy she would have liked at my age, and the exact kind of boy she assumed would never know her awkward daughter even existed. She looked at me differently, as if her ugly duckling had finally hit possible swan status. We went shopping together and got matching hot pink mani-pedis. We'd never gotten along as well as we had for those few weeks.

Then when things went bad with him, my mom acted as if she were the one who'd been humiliated. She might have said she wanted me to go on the trip because it was a chance to travel, but she also wanted me to be the kind of person who held her head high to handle the situation the way she would have done. And I wanted to be that person too — the kind who would have a fantastic time regardless of a breakup and, by the end of the trip, see Connor desperately sorry he'd broken up with me. All while making a pack of new friends.

However, if I was going to go full fantasy, I might as well add in that the queen would invite me to the palace, and Will and Kate would ask me to baby-sit, and Harry and Meghan would offer to hook me up with some minor count or a duke. The truth was, the next few weeks were going to suck.

And I was going to be stuck strapped in directly behind the lovebirds for the entire flight, watching them crawl all over each other in the tiny coach seats. I squeezed my eyes shut as if I could block out the mental image playing on the big screen of my mind. I'd told myself a thousand times since we'd all checked in and I'd heard our seating assignments that I could handle this, but with every second that went by, it was becoming increasingly clear to me that I wouldn't make it. I'd snap somewhere thirty-three thousand feet up and beat the two of them over the head with the in-flight magazine.

Or start crying again. I wasn't sure which would be worse. You would think there was only so much crying a person could do before she got completely dehydrated. I'd told myself I couldn't stand him anymore, so why did my heart still seize and my throat grow tight every time he was around?

I stood up so suddenly that my bag fell to the floor. I snatched it up and strode over to the airline counter. The gate agent didn't look up. She was too preoccupied typing into her computer. Her fingernails, which had a thick layer of bright red gel polish, made a strange clacking sound on the keys. I cleared my throat, but she still didn't stop.

"Excuse me," I managed to get out before she held up a finger to silence me.

She finally finished whatever she was doing and glanced up. "If you're asking about the delay, I don't have any more information. As soon as we get clearance, we'll start boarding." There was makeup creased on her forehead and I suspected she was on her last nerve. She was a walking reminder to never go into a customer service occupation.

I leaned forward even though logically I knew Connor couldn't hear me from where he was sitting. "I wondered if I could change my seat?"

She scrunched up her face. "I don't think—"

"See the guy back there?" I yanked my head in Connor's direction. "That's my ex-boyfriend. We're going to England on a travel program. I'm supposed to sit right behind him." I paused. "For nine hours."

Her perfectly arched eyebrows shot up to her hairline and she looked over my shoulder.

I sensed I was getting somewhere. "He was my first boyfriend." My voice cracked and I had to swallow over and over to keep control. "He dumped me just a couple weeks ago."

Her eyes softened, but she shook her head. "I'm sorry, but I can't—"

"That's his new girlfriend. She used to be my best friend."

The gate agent sucked in a breath and looked over at Connor as though he were something she'd scraped off her shoe.

I felt bad as soon as the words were out of my mouth. Miriam and I had never even hung out before this trip, let alone been friends, but I needed the agent to help me. Desperate times called for desperate measures.

I don't lie to hurt people, or to pull something over on them, but I guess sometimes I . . . make up stories to make myself more interesting. As long as I can remember, I've done it. On the playground in elementary school, I told the other kids that fairies lived in my backyard. In junior high I let everyone think I'd been adopted. I didn't want to lie. I *wanted* to be normal and interesting, but I wasn't.

I hadn't lied with Connor. With him I'd been one hundred percent honest about my feelings, and look how that had turned out.

The agent clacked away on the computer. "Your name?"

"Kim, Kim Maher." I spelled my last name.

"I need your old boarding pass." I slid the limp piece of paper across the counter. She tore it in half as the machine spat out a new one. She passed it over to me with a wink. "He doesn't deserve you. Have a good trip."

The tight band around my chest loosened. "Thanks."

I wove through the crowd clustered around the gate and plopped back down in my seat. I pushed the *New York Times* I'd already read out of the way and pulled out the magazine I'd brought. I hid between the pages, blinking back tears. The gate agent was right. Connor didn't deserve me. It was the same thing Emily told me. But even if I knew it was true, it didn't hurt any less. All I had to do was figure out how to get my heart to catch up to the fact that my head didn't like him anymore.

A girl slid a few seats over to be next to me. "Did she say anything about the delay?" Her English accent made me feel as if I'd dropped onto the set of a BBC historical drama.

I shook my head and quickly wiped my eyes so she wouldn't notice the tears. "No news."

The girl sighed. She pulled her legs up and wrapped her

arms around her knees. She tugged the thin cream cashmere sweater sleeves over her hands. She glanced down at the stack of paper on the chair next to me. "Your *Times*?"

I nodded.

"Did you read the article about the changes to the space program? I saw it earlier this morning."

I jumped slightly in surprise. She seemed like someone who would spot a copy of *InStyle* at a hundred meters but wouldn't know a shuttle from a rocket if she were whacked across the face with one of them. "Uh-huh." I picked up the paper, looking for the Science section.

"I think that's what I like about a real paper," she said. "It's like a knowledge Easter egg hunt. You never know what you're going to find."

I nodded like a bobble-head doll. That was exactly why I loved reading a paper too. "Yeah. Are you into space stuff?"

She shrugged. "Just find it interesting."

I held out my hand. "I'm Kim."

"Nicki." She smiled as we shook. "How come you aren't hanging with the rest of your group?" She motioned to a couple rows over. There were eight of us on the trip and we were all on this flight. A few had busted out cards to play a game on the blue carpeted floor, and the others were clustered around Jamal's laptop checking out his music.

"How did you know —" I got out before she flicked the blue and white STUDENT SCHOLARS FOR CHANGE tag attached to my carry-on. I'd forgotten I was branded. "Ah. I'm not really friends with any of them. There are just three of us from my high school. It's complicated," I said.

Nicki nodded. "Story of my life. I was here visiting my dad, and the reason he lives here, instead of in London with me and my mum, is all sorts of complicated too."

Nicki tucked her hair behind her ears. Her bob wasn't quite long enough, so as soon as she did, the hair fell free and swung forward again. "Sorry, that came out a bit pissy. I just find other people . . . ugh. I don't know. Disappointing." She shoved her hair back again.

"Story of my life," I said, echoing her words. She laughed and it reminded me of scales on a piano.

Nicki tapped the robotics magazine on my lap. "You plan on going into robotics at uni?"

I shook my head. "Not sure. I'm leaning toward engineering, maybe computers."

She waited until an announcement about a flight to Phoenix stopped blaring on the PA. "I'm thinking psychology. I'm interested in research. This is my gap year." She watched the unsupervised toddler fish a booger out of his nose and rub it into his hair.

"What kind of research?"

"Human behavior. I don't have any interest in being a counselor. People blathering about their problems all day would drive me barmy. But I'm intrigued with why people do what they do, why they don't do some things, what they could accomplish, that kind of thing."

I traced the pattern in the carpet with my shoe. Understanding other people was one of the great mysteries in my life. "If you ever figure people out, you'll have to let me know what you discover. Math I can make sense of, but people are more confusing than quantum physics. Give me a robot any day."

She laughed. "Don't give up on humanity just yet. Maybe you haven't met anyone worth figuring out."

The overhead speaker chirped to life. "Attention: Passengers on Air Canada flight 854 to London. Due to aircraft maintenance issues, this flight will be further delayed. We apologize for the inconvenience." The crowd groaned. The screen over our gate flickered and a new departure time, three hours from now, blinked on.

Connor stood and stretched. "Who wants to find a place to watch the Whitecaps game?"

Our group began to gather up their stuff. He was like the pied piper of nerdy people. Everyone was willing to follow him. Miriam walked over toward me.

"Do you want to come?" she offered. Her legs were so small that her size extra small leggings were baggy around her thighs. She must buy her clothing in a kids' department.

"No thanks," I managed to say, willing her to walk away. Or she could disappear completely—I was open to that, too.

"You can't want to hang around here for the next three

hours." Miriam nudged my tote with her foot. "C'mon, we'll all get some fries or something. It'll be fun."

Fun wasn't even in the top ten words that I would think of to describe the situation. "I'm fine," I insisted. It was bad enough that Connor wanted nothing to do with me. It was worse that he started dating someone else right away. It was a nightmare that I was stuck on this trip with them. But her being nice to me was a layer of shit icing on this crap cupcake. I didn't even know how much Connor had told her about what had happened between the two of us. I wasn't sure what I preferred: that she knew and felt pity for me, or that he hadn't told her anything because he didn't think I was worth mentioning. I slouched lower in the seat.

"Leave it — she doesn't want to come. Trust me, no one will miss her with that attitude." Connor strode over and took Miriam's hand without even glancing at me.

I flushed. He was right. I was a walking black cloud of doom. I hadn't bothered to get to know anyone else coming on the trip and now I was going to be miserable *and* alone.

"Gawd, he's a tosser," Nicki said, loud enough to carry.

I wasn't entirely certain what it meant, but it sounded both hysterical and insulting. I burst out laughing.

Connor and Miriam walked off down the hall, the rest of the group following behind them. He glanced over his shoulder at us, and when he saw we were still staring, he whirled back around.

My chest filled with air. I felt like one of those large balloons at a parade — ready to float away. "I don't know what you said, but you're my new favorite person on this planet," I said. I meant it, too. My BFF couldn't be reached except by letter. Emily might as well have been in space for all the help she could give me.

"That guy is a loser." Nicki pulled me from my seat. "I can tell, because as we've already established, I study people. You can pay me back for correctly identifying him as a wanker by keeping me entertained for the next few hours."

"How would you like me to do that?"

Nicki's smile spread across her face. "We're smart women, we'll think of something."

TWO

AUGUST 15
16 DAYS REMAINING

Nicki stopped short outside the duty-free store, causing me to nearly slam into her back. She seemed entranced by the bright lights bouncing off a display of jewel-colored perfume bottles.

"Let's go in here," she said.

"They won't have gum," I noted. "There's another store down just a bit further." I pointed, but she'd already started to weave her way through the aisles. She randomly picked up items: a stuffed bear holding a satin heart, a giant Toblerone bar, and a box of washed-out pastel-colored saltwater taffy. She inspected each one as if she worked for quality control and then put each back down. I trailed after her.

My mouth still burned from the jalapeños I'd had at lunch. Nicki claimed the best thing to eat before a big flight was huevos rancheros. She insisted the combination of protein from the eggs and cheese, along with the spice from the salsa, would ensure a good sleep on the plane. When I pointed out the entrée wasn't on the menu, she'd raised one perfectly tweezed eyebrow. "Ordering off the menu is for the common person," she'd declared. When the waiter came over, she turned on the charm, and before I'd known what was happening, he dropped off two custom plates just for us. And she was right—the huge meal made me want a nap.

Nicki grabbed a stuffed zebra and gave it a squeeze. "Things like this make me wish I had a kid brother or sister. Let me guess, you're an only child too."

My mouth fell open. "How did you—"

"Only children are different. They have to amuse themselves growing up. They're independent, better problem solvers. There's tons of research on it. I could tell by the way you've been talking. You're just like me."

Technically, I wasn't just like her. I never knew what to say when people asked if I had any siblings. "About a half-dozen fully frozen" seemed too flip and required an explanation. Saying I was an only child felt like lying about the existence of my parents' cryogenically suspended embryos. They were my brothers and sisters, just in cold storage in a medical lab.

My parents hadn't had an easy time getting pregnant. Thanks to the fact that my mom was an early blogger, the whole world knew about their struggles. Then after three rounds of IVF, I took. My mom called me MBK on her blog— Miracle Baby Kim. She said she used the initials to protect my privacy, but how private could my life be when she plastered every one of my development milestones in cyberspace for the whole world to see?

Somewhere on the Internet there's a picture of me as a three-year-old, wearing a tiara and giant pink fuzzy slippers, sitting on the toilet with the caption "MBK Finally Masters Potty Training!" The "finally" is a nice touch; nothing I like better than people thinking I was delayed in the hygiene department. My mom's name was all over her blog; it didn't exactly take a Mensa-level IQ to figure out that I was MBK. The truth was, she didn't care how I felt about the blog. What she cared about were all the people who read it and gave her nonstop "you're the best mom ever" feedback.

The year I turned ten, my mom wrote a long blog post where she announced to her legions of fans that she and my dad were officially giving up their efforts to have more children. They couldn't keep up the nonstop cycles of IVF. It seemed Mother Nature didn't have it in the plans for my mom to be the mother she wanted to be, with a minivan and the ability to construct something out of Legos while simultaneously preparing an organic dinner for her large happy family. And while she wanted to focus on her blessing *(Beautiful MBK!)*, she could still grieve for what could have been and she would always see those frozen embryos as her babies. The *Huffington Post* picked up that blog post and ran it on their site. It's one of their most downloaded pieces. They rerun it on Mother's Day most years.

It was around that time that I started to become aware that I was a disappointment to my mom. When she'd imagined having children, none of them were like me. She wanted a daughter who liked to play with dolls and whom she'd punish with a wag of her finger, all while smiling at how adorable it was that I stole her makeup. My desire for tangle-free short hair and passion for books and blanket forts befuddled her. Why didn't I want to skip rope outside with the other girls? Why didn't I let her braid my hair into complicated patterns befitting a Disney princess? Why wasn't I similar to her at all? How could she be a mothering expert when her own kid was so . . . awkward?

My mom was one of the first mommy bloggers. Thousands of people still read her site daily. They comment on her recipes *(Super YUM Crock-Pot Meals!)* and reviews of baby items *(Bugaboo Strollers Worth Every Penny!)*. She's blogged about how motherhood is hard and disappointing, but that doesn't mean it isn't worth it. I can't be the only one who realizes that she's trying to talk herself into that fact. I believe that my mom loves me, I just don't think she *likes* me. If she'd had more kids, maybe it would have made a difference. I guess neither of us will ever know.

Nicki sniffed a bottle of Burberry Brit perfume and then spritzed a tiny bit on her wrist. She held out her arm for me and I leaned in.

"Nice," I said, but she'd already moved on to the next display.

She stared up at the tower of Grey Goose vodka. "Want some for the flight?"

I crossed my arms over my chest. "I don't think even you can talk this place into selling us booze."

Nicki winked and I noticed she was wearing a hint of a shimmery eye shadow. "Who says they're going to sell it?"

My heart picked up speed. I glanced over my shoulder to make sure we were alone. "You're going to steal it?" I asked, lowering my voice. My heart rabbited into overdrive.

"No, *we're* going to steal it," she said, her light brown eyes sparkling. "No one ever suspects the nicely dressed girl with a British accent. They think I'm too posh to sink to thievery."

A swarm of spastic butterflies tried to take flight inside my lungs. I was pretty sure I didn't look too posh to be arrested. "I don't know . . ."

"Up to you."

The chatter from the two clerks at the front of the store as they debated the merits of Ryan Reynolds seemed unnaturally loud to my ears. I bit the inside of my cheek. "What happens if we get caught?"

Nicki's lips curled up, Grinch-like. "Bad things. That's why we'll do it so we don't get caught." Her head tilted slightly toward the bottles of booze. "They haven't put on the plastic antitheft devices yet, and I don't see any cameras."

She was right. Every other bottle in the store had a black plastic disk attached around the neck, but the display of Grey

Goose was naked. I could almost hear the angel and devil perched on my shoulders. One advising me to do the right thing and go on to the next store and buy a pack of Trident like a good girl, and the other telling me that it wouldn't kill me to take a risk now and then. Where had playing it safe gotten me? I wanted to be someone else, anyone else. Maybe if I wanted to change the course of my life I needed to change the things I did. Be someone who did daring things, like Nicki.

"What do we do?" I whispered.

Nicki poked my leather tote bag. "When it's time, grab the closest bottle and drop it in."

"How will I know it's time?"

She tapped me on the nose. "You'll know because you're smart." She turned back to the perfume display and grabbed a small bottle. "I'm going to check the price — my mom loves this stuff." She'd taken only a few steps when her foot hooked into the handles of a brightly colored canvas bag stamped with a maple leaf and the words CANADA FOREVER, sitting on the floor among other similar bags.

I opened my mouth to warn her, but she'd already jerked forward with a loud *oomph*. Her arms flew up as she fell and the bottle of perfume collided with the ground with a brittle smash. A cloud of a citrus and musk scent filled the air. The clerks flew to her side.

I was about to do the same when I realized this was it. My hand jerked out as if it were under the authority of another force and yanked a bottle of vodka off the display, plopping it into my tote. I jammed my elbow over the top of the bag to pinch it shut and hustled to where Nicki was now standing between the two clerks. My heart beat out of control.

"Are you okay?" I asked, surprised that my voice didn't crack with the electric tension filling every inch of my body, zapping down my nerves, lighting me up from the inside.

"I'm okay. I think." Nicki looked down at the broken glass on the floor and her eyes widened. "Oh, I'm *so* sorry."

"You'll have to pay for the perfume." The tall clerk pointed to a YOU BREAK IT, YOU BUY IT sign by the entrance.

Nicki drew herself even straighter. "But I wasn't being careless. I tripped on your bags, which were all over the floor."

The mouth on the tall clerk pressed into a tight line, like a slash across her face. "If you don't pay for it, we have to call a manager."

Panic flashed like a bright white light. I had to do something. I kicked the canvas bags now strewn across the floor. "You *should* call a supervisor. Maybe if you hadn't been so busy talking, and instead had straightened up this mess, it wouldn't have happened at all. You know, if she's hurt, you're liable. My dad's a lawyer — he deals with this stuff all the time." As soon as the words were out of my mouth, I wanted to swallow them back down. I hoped I was right. My dad was a dentist. Any legal knowledge I had was from watching *The People's Court* when I stayed home sick from school. *What had I done?*

Nicki's lip twitched. "Now that I think about it, my back is quite sore. I hit the floor pretty hard." She rubbed the base of her spine.

The tall clerk looked ready to clobber Nicki, but the shorter woman with her hair tied up in a mountain of tiny braids put her hand lightly on the arm of the other. "We're certainly sorry you fell."

Nicki met her gaze. "And I'm sorry that the bottle broke."

The short clerk smiled, her white teeth as bright as the wall tiles. "Well then, why don't we just decide that no harm's been done?" The tension that had been coiling inside me released.

"Are you sure?" Nicki asked. Her eyes were so wide, she looked like an anime character. When the clerk nodded, Nicki reached for me. "We should get back; our flight will be leaving soon."

I nodded solemnly as if I were very concerned about timeliness. Every muscle in my body clenched as I walked over the threshold, anticipating a piercing alarm going off, but nothing happened. Nicki gripped my elbow. "Don't look back. Only guilty people look behind them."

My neck stiffened and I kept moving forward down the hall. The adrenaline that had rushed through my system seconds ago was now bailing ship and I felt lightheaded. My bag weighed a hundred pounds. I half expected every person we passed to develop x-ray vision, see through my tote, and point me out as a shoplifter. Nicki seemed to sense I was barely holding it together, and she pulled me along until we reached an empty gate area. We both started giggling as we dropped into a row of seats.

"I can't believe I did that," I said. I opened the bag expecting the vodka to be missing, a figment of my imagination, but the bottle was there. I glanced quickly at Nicki to see if she was impressed that I'd actually done it.

"Since we're headed to England it would have been more fitting to have nicked some gin, but a girl has to work with the opportunities she's got." Nicki patted the side of my leather bag. "You were perfect. When you said that line about how I could sue them, I wanted to cheer."

I shook my head. "Are you kidding? As soon as I took the bottle, all I wanted to do was run for it. I felt like I was going to freak out at any moment."

She laughed. "But you didn't. Being good at something doesn't mean that it isn't hard or scary—it just means that you keep moving forward when other people quit."

I laughed. "I tend to be a quitter. I'm scared of everything."

"Like what?"

I rolled my eyes. "I could make a list a mile long. For starters, I'm terrified of heights. I won't even go to my grandparents' new condo in Miami because they live on the twentieth floor. Usually when things scare me, I'm the first one to bail. I won't go skiing, kayaking, or anyplace that looks like it will have spiders, and I get hives when I have to go to the dentist and my dad's a dentist."

Nicki wrinkled up her nose. "Now, I get the dentist phobia, but heights? If you're going to be scared, be scared of something good." She laughed. "You were scared to take the liquor, but you did it. That's the difference between ordinary people and extraordinary. Extraordinary people might be afraid, but they do it anyway."

My chin lifted slightly in the air. The shame over stealing was mixed up with pride in doing something risky. I wanted to brag about what I'd done and apologize all at the same time. Most of all I wanted her to keep talking. "I still can't believe I did that," I said. I wanted her to understand I wasn't someone who did things like this. Heck, I wasn't someone who did things at all, but maybe it was as simple as deciding that I didn't want to be that person anymore.

Nicki threw an arm around me and gave me a half hug. "Think about it. I wonder what you might do if you let yourself really go? You know, every accomplishment starts with the decision to try. And then keep trying, even when it's hard." She smirked. "And of course, if life gives you an opportunity, take it before it disappears. Or at least before they put the antitheft device on it."

I packed up what she said and placed it carefully into my memory. It struck me that her advice was important. Not because I wanted to become a master criminal—I felt bad about taking the booze and couldn't imagine doing it again. But . . . I liked that I'd done it at least once. Been like Nicki. Daring. Not afraid. She seemed to have figured out the secret to life. All the brochures for the Student Scholars program had stressed how travel made a person grow. I'd secretly thought it was a bunch of marketing bullshit. How could a change in geography make a difference? But maybe it was possible: I could evolve into someone else. I could almost picture my mom's approval . . . and the blog post she'd write about it.

The public-address system squawked and announced that our flight would start boarding. I couldn't believe how the three hours had flown by. I pulled the bottle slightly out of the bag. "Do you want this?"

"You keep it. I don't know the whole story with the guy and girl back at the gate, but I suspect you need it more than me." She pushed herself up from the seat with a ladylike grunt. "We should get going. I still want to get that gum."

I reached for her arm before she started to walk away. "Thanks. I was feeling really down before."

"That's what friends are for!" She poked me in the side as if I were being silly.

"Well, I appreciate you making me a friend after only a few hours."

Nicki smiled. "Don't you know? I decided we were friends the instant we met."

THREE

AUGUST 15
16 DAYS REMAINING

Most people went to sleep as soon as the flight attendants cleared the trays from dinner and dimmed the lights. A few pulled out those squishy kidney-shaped pillows filled with buckwheat. The guy one row in front of me in a too-tight Darth Vader T-shirt was snoring already. Or drowning in his own phlegm. It was a bit hard to tell which from the sound he was making.

I pressed my forehead to the window. I strained to see anything in the darkness, but all I could make out was my own faint reflection in the thick glass. I knew we were miles up in the air, but it seemed more as if we were under water. Black and cold. Even though it was late and the engines made a white noise hum, I couldn't drift off.

"How did you score a row to yourself?" I jolted, surprised at her voice. Nicki dropped into the far seat. She put her feet up on the middle space between us. She had on thick blue fuzzy socks. She wiggled her toes in my direction. "I'm stuck next to some old lady," she whispered. "She smells like mothballs and greasy burgers."

"Where are you sitting?" I hadn't seen her since I boarded.

"Near the front on the other side." Nicki nudged my knee with her foot. "Can't sleep?"

"Ever have that thing where you can't turn your brain off?" I pulled my sleeves over my hands and swung my legs up into the middle seat, mirroring her.

"All the time. Studies show that the higher your intelligence the more likely you are to have insomnia."

"Really?" Suddenly all the nights I'd lain in bed watching the minutes click by were justified.

Nicki smirked. "No idea. I just made that up — but it feels like it should be true." She rubbed her temples. "I couldn't sleep either. I thought you might be so kind as to help."

"Me?"

"Well, your vodka." Her eyebrows bounced up and down wickedly.

I giggled. "You want to drink it here?" I peered around, but all the flight stewards had disappeared.

"No one is going to care as long as we're quiet. You in?"

I didn't bother to answer. Instead I dived for my tote bag under the seat in front of me. I pulled the bottle out like a magician pulling a rabbit from his hat. Nicki clapped silently.

The first sips were like swallowing lit gasoline. It burned

a trail down to my stomach, but after a few more, the edges started to soften. We talked about everything and nothing for hours. I showed her pictures on my social media accounts of the robots I had built. She told me how much she hated her parents' divorce and her dad's new girlfriend. I gave her the highlights of what had happened with Connor.

Nicki's mouth popped off the neck of the bottle with a *smack*. "Wait a minute. He asked you to drop out of a science contest so he could win?"

I closed my eyes briefly as if I could block out the memory. "It's worse," I said, noticing my voice was slurring slightly. *I should slow up on the vodka.* "He didn't ask. I *gave up* the science award. Told 'em I didn't want to be a part of it anymore, because I knew they would then give it to him since he was in second place."

Her nose wrinkled up. "Why would you do that?"

I waved my hands around. "I thought it would make him love me." I sighed — it sounded even more pathetic said aloud.

It had made so much sense at the time. When I got the initial results, I went over to his house. I thought he'd be happy. He knew how much time I'd spent on my quadcopter. And he'd come in second. The two of us — top of the heap for every high school in Western Canada.

As soon as Connor opened the door, I held the notice I'd printed off above my head, whooped, and threw myself into his arms. But right away I could tell something was wrong. His body was stiff—he held me, but it was like trying to hug a statue.

"What's wrong?"

"Nothing." He shrugged me off as if I were a too-warm coat on a summer day. "Congrats."

I wanted him to touch me again and found myself reaching out to tap his arm as I spoke. "Mr. Schmidt's going to have a bird when he hears. He's never had one student place, let alone two in the same year."

"Yeah." Connor shoved his hands into his pockets. "You didn't have to come here to tell me. They sent me an email too."

This wasn't going how I'd pictured it at all. A sour knot twisted in my stomach. And even though I told myself that I was being paranoid, I was certain he was avoiding my eyes. "Are you mad that I won?"

"No, of course not." He looked past me down the street as if he hoped someone would come along to rescue him. "It's just that I was counting on being able to list this on my college apps."

"You can still list it. You came in second."

"Yeah, sure. Listen, I told my mom I'd do some stuff for her in the yard before dinner, so I should go."

"I can help if you want." I flexed my arm. "I'm stronger than I look."

"No, it's fine," he said. "I'll see you at work tomorrow."

I had to fight the urge to shove my foot in the door so he

31

couldn't close it. "If you want, I can help you with your university application essays. I'm great at those things," I offered.

"No, it's okay. I got it."

"I don't mind, or you could write them and I could look them over. I'm a comma ninja, you know." I was trying to make a joke, but it wasn't working. I realized I was wringing my hands and made myself stop. I knew I needed to quit talking, but the words kept building up in my mouth until they tumbled out in a rush.

He shrugged. "It's all good. It's the kind of thing I want to do myself."

"Are you sure you're not mad about the science contest?" I found myself taking steps closer as he moved back.

"I'm not mad, just stressed. Senior year coming up and all that. I'll get over it."

But I had worried he wouldn't get over it. I told myself that I didn't need a fancy wooden plaque — so why not drop out? The organizers would give him first, he'd be able to relax over his applications, and he'd realize how much I cared about him.

Except it didn't make a difference. If anything, it made things between us more awkward. Until he gave me the talk a day later.

"It's not you, it's me. I still care about you — but."

I hadn't handled the breakup well. *Understatement.* My letter to Emily about what had happened must have sounded really dire and desperate, because Emily begged the camp supervisor to let her use their landline to call me, a strict no-no according to camp rules. But there was nothing she, or anyone else, could say that made me feel better. Not even my mom's blog post on *Dealing with Your Child's First Heartbreak*. And as stupid as I was for giving up my place in the science competition, it didn't escape my notice that Connor hadn't turned it down.

Nicki snorted. "I know his type. They use people. He can't stand the idea that you might be smarter than him."

"I don't know if that's it." I hated that I still had the urge to defend him.

She shook her head so that her hair flew around her face. "Don't do that. Don't make excuses for his shitty behavior. He's a knob who made you feel bad about winning, because he couldn't handle that he lost. I dated a guy like that once. I thought he was one thing, but in the end, he turned out to be someone else. Someone *weak*. He didn't deserve me and this Connor guy certainly doesn't deserve you."

I giggled at her slang. *Knob. Knob. Knob.* I took another long drink of the vodka, letting it warm me from the inside out. She was right. Connor was a knob. And if he didn't want to date me, what did it say about his character that he still let me give up the award?

"I'm mad about the science award, but that's not what really ticks me off. What *really* makes me mad is that I didn't see it coming." The truth of the statement burned stronger than the alcohol. Connor was a dick, but I'd been stupid too, and I hated him most of all for exposing that side of me.

"People like him should have to pay," Nicki snarled. "If someone doesn't stop them, they'll just do it again to someone else. The guy I mentioned? He was married."

I sucked in a breath. "He lied about being married?"

She waved off my comment. "No, I knew. He lied about how he was going to leave his wife. The point is, the weak ones will lie to get what they want."

I mumbled a sympathetic sound. Nicki was only a year older than me, but I felt a million years younger, as though I should be clutching a worn teddy bear. *A married guy?* It struck me as gross, but at the same time . . . more exotic than anything that had ever happened to me.

We spotted the flight attendant strolling down the aisle toward us with a bottle of water and a stack of plastic cups. Without a word, we tucked the bottle of Grey Goose under the thin blanket we'd thrown over our feet.

"You two need anything else?" the attendant whispered, leaning in as we took the cups of cool water from her.

"No, thank you." Nicki waited until the flight attendant had ducked behind the thick navy-colored curtain behind us before turning back to me. "I hate when people wear that much makeup. Who do they think they're fooling? You're old. Accept it."

I looked over my shoulder at the swaying curtain. "I didn't notice."

Nicki sighed. "Women like her remind me of my mum. Putting on a show, trying to cover up who they really are."

"So, you live with your mom?"

She looked down at her hands, her thumbnail chipping away at the pale dove-gray polish on her index finger. "I want to live with my dad, but she won't let me."

"Can't you go wherever you want if you've graduated?"

"Whenever I mention it, she falls apart." Nicki pitched her voice high and whiny. *"Oh, I won't be able to live without you. Your father took everything from me and now he wants my baby girl. I'll die if you go."* She shook her head in disgust. "My dad feels guilty. He says I can't move to Vancouver. He couldn't live with her, but I'm supposed to stay." Her eyes filled with tears that spilled down her cheeks.

"Hey, it's okay." I fished through my tote looking for Kleenex. I didn't find any, so I settled for passing over to Nicki a wrinkled paper takeout napkin that had been buried at the bottom.

"Sorry." She wiped the tears off her cheeks as if they personally offended her. She sniffed. "I'm not even sure I want to live with my dad as much as I don't want to be with her. It just keeps getting worse. I'm always having to clean up after my mum. She'll vomit in bed and not even wake up when she does it. I'm having to make excuses for whatever she's done. If

I stay, I'm miserable, and if I leave, then everyone thinks I'm a horrible person."

"I don't think you're horrible." My chest ached for her. My mom drove me crazy at times, but she would never do anything like that, something that belonged in some kind of teen-issue novel.

Nicki reached over and squeezed my hand. "Thanks."

I glanced down at our clasped hands. A wave of affection for her engulfed me. Emily and I had been best friends since elementary school, our friendship building slowly over countless sleepovers and shared secrets, but I had seemed to connect with Nicki instantly. That wasn't like me. I'd always been the kid with straight As in elementary school but with scribbled notes on my report card about needing to work on my social skills. Nicki was the kind of person who wouldn't have even noticed me, and maybe she wouldn't have if the flight hadn't been delayed, but it seemed as though she really liked me.

Nicki took a deep breath as if shaking off her sadness. "I swear I don't usually just spill all my secrets to a stranger."

My chest expanded with pride that she felt she could tell me things.

"I promise not to tell anyone how much you hate Connor if you keep the truth about my mum to yourself," she said.

I raised my hand as though I were taking a vow. "Hey, what happens on the plane stays on the plane."

Nicki dived down for her purse and pulled out a Moleskine

notebook. She tore several pages out of the back and passed them over. "Let's get all the evil out. You make a list of everything you hate about Connor and I'll make one for my mum. It'll be cathartic."

I flipped the tray down and seized a sparkly blue gel pen from her hand, my fingers tingling with excitement. I wanted to put him behind me and this was exactly the kind of thing I needed to do. I'd had so much to drink that I needed to squeeze one eye closed to see the page clearly.

I scribbled WHY I HATE CONNOR O'REILLY across the top and drew a sharp line under it. "I might need more paper," I said, and Nicki laughed as she started on her own list.

The anger I felt poured out of me and through the pen. I listed everything, from how he licked his finger before using it to turn a page in a book (seriously? *gross*) to how he made this weird fish-lip face when working on complicated equations. As soon as I finished, Nicki took the list from my hand and looked it over.

"He quotes sports stats?" Her lip curled up. "Oh god, does he play that stupid fantasy football stuff too, where he makes up his own teams?"

I snorted, picturing him checking his sports apps on his phone compulsively through the day and talking to his friends about trades. I inhaled vodka into my nose, choking for a second, until Nicki clapped me on the back. "You're right, he is a knob," I said. The tight ball of dread I'd been carrying around for weeks in my gut began to melt away. He wasn't worth crying over.

"The guy deserves the death penalty for being terminally in poor taste," Nicki declared. I giggled. She pointed to the top of my paper. "You should add that."

I scribbled AND WHY HE DESERVES TO DIE under the heading. I paused. My mom would say being that vindictive gave the other person the power. I considered scratching it out, but Nicki was already reaching for the paper.

She folded our sheets in half and tucked them into her bag, then held up her hands as if she'd made them disappear. "Love, the entire world would be better off without him and my mum. Now the list is gone and you can let go of him and the anger."

"I can't let him ruin this trip for me." My voice was low and serious as if I were making a promise to myself. I'd already let him ruin the summer. I couldn't let him keep dragging me down.

"Do you really want him gone?" Her voice was quiet and merged into the hum of the engines, making me lean forward to hear. "We have the perfect solution, you know," Nicki said.

"Solution for what?"

Her eyes glittered like broken glass. "For our problems. I kill your ex. You kill my mum. We both get what we want."

I jolted, shocked at what she'd said, and looked at her nervously. Her eyes glinted with mischief. She had to be joking.

Then she started giggling and I broke down too, the laughter burbling up from my chest. "And we'd both get about twenty to life in prison," I pointed out. "No thanks. I've seen enough prison documentaries to know I wouldn't make it a week. I look like crap in orange jump suits *and* I don't have an ounce of street smarts."

She gasped, trying to get her laughter under control. "But that's why it's the perfect crime. There's nothing to connect you with my mum. You've never even met her. Why would you murder her?" Nicki winked. "No motive—no reason for the police to suspect you. Most murders are committed by some-one the victim knows." She nodded at me. "An ex-girlfriend, for example." Then she pointed at her chest. "Or a daughter with an ax to grind against a loser parent."

All the vodka in my system was slowing everything down, blurring my thoughts, but I could still connect the dots of her plan. "But we're total strangers, so if we did the other person's murder, we'd never get caught." I started to giggle again. "It *is* the perfect crime. You're a genius."

Nicki made an exaggerated seated bow and almost slipped out of her chair. I had to grab her and pull her back by her shirt. I picked up the bottle to toast her with another drink and was disturbed to see how much we'd already consumed. I burped, a hot sour taste in the back of my mouth. I decided against drinking any more. The last thing I needed was to start throw-ing up.

"I love the concept, but I'm no killer," I admitted. I held the vodka out to her, but she waved it off.

"You didn't think you were someone who could steal a few hours ago," Nicki pointed out. "Maybe you sell yourself short."

I swayed in the seat, thinking about what she'd said, about how maybe my biggest problem wasn't Connor or my mom, but me. I didn't like to do things that scared me. I was always more worried about living up to what other people wanted. Trying to be what they wanted. I didn't push myself and then I was mad that things didn't happen. It wasn't that I didn't want to be in the driver's seat, but it didn't make sense when everyone else seemed to do it better.

I wouldn't even have come on this trip if I hadn't been following Connor. Emily was after me to try new stuff. She'd wanted me to apply to the same camp where she was working, but I hadn't been willing to do it because the idea of being responsible for kids made me nervous. But Emily was having a great time. If I'd gone with her, none of this would have even happened. We could have crushed on cute male counselors and ate our weight in s'mores and burned hot dogs.

Nicki stared at the screen in the back of the seat in front of her, the flickering images from an old episode of *The Big Bang Theory* reflected in her eyes. "I'm going to get some more water. Do you want any?"

I nodded. Water and Tylenol were a good idea. Nicki

slipped out of the seat and headed toward the back galley. She slid behind the curtain so quickly it was like a magic trick.

I stretched my legs out into the seat she'd vacated. I blinked slowly, watching Sheldon's lips move on the screen. I chuckled again. My eyes drifted shut.

I'd been dreading this trip for the past few weeks, but maybe it was an opportunity. I could hit the reset button in my life. If I was brave enough to go to England, if I could survive the whole thing with Connor, then I could do all sorts of things. I felt a rush of excitement, like I had when I'd stolen the vodka. A new place. A new me.

FOUR

AUGUST 16
15 DAYS REMAINING

Y ou need to put your seat in the full upright position and buckle your seat belt. We've been cleared to land."

My eyes snapped open. The flight attendant stood at the end of the row looking down at me. I squinted, the sun streaming in through the window, drilling into my brain. I closed my eyes, trying to ignore the red waves of pain crashing against the inside of my skull.

"Sorry to wake you, but we're landing soon," she said. Her red lipstick had bled into the fine lines around her mouth, as if it were growing alien tentacles.

I rubbed my face and nodded. I pushed the firm button in the armrest and sat up. I pulled my sweaty shirt from my skin, letting the cool air lick my back. Nicki was gone, the rest of my row empty. I didn't even know when she had gone back to her own seat. I opened my mouth and grimaced. My tongue felt thick and furry. I must have fallen asleep.

Or passed out.

I was never drinking vodka again. I should have known better—I wasn't a big partier. I paused to take stock of my stomach. It rolled over uneasily. It felt as if there were a thick layer of oil floating on the contents, but they seemed inclined to stay in place.

The air in the plane was dry. I needed water. I also wanted to find Nicki so I could get her phone number. I'd always scoffed at my mom's belief that the universe brings you things that you need, but this time she was right. Nicki had made me see everything differently, jolted me out of feeling stuck and sorry for myself. Writing that list about Connor had drained the toxic feelings that had been building inside me. I was actually excited for this trip now. When I got settled, I'd send Emily a long letter telling her that she'd been right, that there was life after Connor. I would let Em talk me into doing something different for senior year, maybe join the film club or sign up for a ski trip to Whistler. So what if I couldn't ski? I'd learn, or at least I'd try.

My foot fished under the seat searching for my beat-up Converse. I found them and jammed them on, ignoring how tight they felt. I stood, stretching, feeling lighter than I had in weeks, and peered over the heads of everyone in front of me.

"You have to take your seat," a steward called out several rows ahead.

"I need some water," I croaked. "And my friend—"

"You need to take your seat," the steward repeated with a

tone that implied he'd be okay with making me do what he wanted if I wasn't compliant. I plopped back down.

The seat-belt sign blinked off and on with a ping. I buckled up.

A dark shape out of the side of my vision caught my attention and I realized we were much closer to the ground than I'd thought. The plane banked on its side and descended for the final approach. A few minutes later the tires bounced down on the runway with a screech. For a second it seemed we would speed down and off the runway, but with a lurch we began to slow. The seat belt dug into my stomach, pushing the acid up into my throat.

"Ladies and gentlemen, welcome to Heathrow Airport. Local time is 10:08 in the morning and the outside temperature is fifteen degrees Celsius. For your safety and comfort, please remain seated with your seat belt fastened until the captain has turned off the fasten-seat-belt sign."

The announcements droned on. I peered out the window trying to see if the landscape looked different, foreign. I'd never been overseas before and I wasn't sure what to expect. All I could see was the dance between planes lining up to leave and baggage carts weaving in and out of the open lanes. It looked like any other airport, but it wasn't. This was London. My heart skipped a beat, like a record jumping around.

People leaped up as soon as the plane stopped, grabbing their luggage and clogging up the aisle like a human knot. It took forever to file off, and as soon as I cleared the Jetway I picked up speed, trying to swim upstream in the crowd headed toward customs. I wanted to find Nicki. I passed Connor and the rest of our group.

"What's the hurry—you run out of booze?" Connor called out, and I heard a few others snicker.

I ignored him and dodged past roller bags and people stopping suddenly in the center of the walkway to check their phones, but even when I bopped up onto my tiptoes I couldn't spot Nicki. I'd missed her.

The customs hall was packed. A cacophony of different languages fought for dominance as people talked loudly to be heard, but everyone stayed in tidy lines waiting for a turn. I rubbed my neck and caught a sniff of myself. I needed a shower.

I kicked my bag forward as I shuffled one person closer to my turn. The Student Scholars program would be waiting outside the hall to whisk us to an international student residence hall. In the brochure, it looked a far cry from a Four Seasons hotel—but at least it would have a bed. I sent up a silent prayer that they wouldn't do any kind of welcome reception. I wanted a nap and a shower before I did anything else.

That's when I spotted Nicki ahead of me and a few lines over. She waved. I stepped toward her.

A security guard moved in front of me. "You need to stay in line," she said, motioning at the rope that kept us in our section.

"My friend is over there —"

"That line is for UK residents only," the security guard droned.

"Okay, but I just need to get her number."

The guard's mouth pulled tight. "That line is for residents only," she repeated. "You can catch up with your friend later."

I stepped back into place, trying to figure out how I could tell Nicki, charades style, to wait for me outside the hall, but she was already at the customs desk sliding over her passport. The universe might have put her in my way to turn things around, but it clearly didn't plan to keep us in touch. I didn't know her last name or any way to reach her.

Maybe it was better this way. We didn't really have much in common. I felt uncomfortable with the idea that we'd stolen the vodka and risked drinking it on the flight. That wasn't like me. But I wasn't sorry I'd met her. We were strangers, but she'd changed everything for me. I'd come on this trip because I'd felt as if I couldn't let my mom down again and because I was ashamed I'd gotten myself into the situation at all, but it was up to me how I handled the rest of the trip. I wasn't going to waste it.

FIVE

The residence hall had a giant light hanging in the main stairwell, a wrought-iron monstrosity. Somewhere a haunted castle was missing a lighting fixture. I'd expected everything in England to be old-fashioned—fussy floral prints, tweeds, and country plaids. Labrador dogs lazing by stone fireplaces with stern butlers lurking in corners ready to address every whim while silently judging you. But it wasn't that straightforward.

We were staying in Metford House in South Kensington, a large stately brick building that was for international students studying in the city. Inside it was a weird mix of modern art and outdated everything else. The dark green carpet looked as though it had been installed when Queen Victoria was on the throne. The main lobby had wood-paneled walls, but the furniture was a mix of a modern leather sectional and tartan-patterned wingback chairs that looked as if they were from a big-box store. The paintings on the walls all seemed to have been done by a toddler with anger issues. There was a desk across from the front door and then the huge staircase that led up to the rooms.

I stood on the landing for my floor and sniffed. I could smell some kind of air freshener, a spicy and citrus scent that was doing its best to hide the smell of mildew and too many people living in a small space.

As I headed to the lobby, I stumbled and grabbed the banister to keep from pitching down the staircase. The steps seemed too shallow. I felt as if I wanted to take one and a half steps every time I moved.

"Look where you're going," an Irish voice called out as he dodged past me carrying a huge basket of laundry up from the basement.

I moved to apologize, but he was already taking the steps two at a time. I felt out of sorts, as if things weren't quite clicking. Jet lag made sudden sense to me. My body was in London, but my brain was still somewhere over the Atlantic Ocean scrambling to keep up. It was as if I weren't fully connected to reality.

I barely remembered arriving at Metford a few hours ago. We'd been met outside the customs hall at the airport by the Student Scholars representative. Our guide would make sure no one in our group got lost and that we saw everything cultural so our parents could justify the trip as educational. Tasha was tall and willowy and wore her hair in a huge Afro like a halo around her head. I guessed she was in her late twenties, not much older than us, but enough that she had an air of confidence none of us could replicate. She had on a tight-fitting leather jacket, distressed jeans, and what seemed like a thousand silver bangles on one arm. Compared to our group of teenagers — unwashed, jet-lagged, and bleary-eyed — she looked like a different creature. We stared at her as if she were an alien as she directed us toward a large van.

Kendra in our group asked if she could touch Tasha's hair.

Tasha pulled back out of her reach. "Are you a stylist in your spare time?"

Kendra shook her head.

"Then keep your hands to yourself."

I snorted at her reply and Kendra shot me a hot, angry look. I tried to communicate that I hadn't meant to laugh to be mean; Tasha's comment had just struck me as funny. Normally *I* was the one to make a social faux pas. But Kendra's lip curled up as though she'd tasted something bad, and I had the sense I'd burned a bridge with her already.

Tasha smiled at the rest of us. "Now, let's get going."

It felt as if it should have been the middle of the night, but, stepping outside into the parking lot and the warm sunshine, I was shocked to realize it was barely eleven in the morning. Tasha stashed our luggage in the back of the large van as though it were a giant Tetris puzzle, telling us to hold our carry-ons on our laps.

Tasha fired off details about the city as the van careened through the streets, narrowly missing pedestrians, other cars, and looming red double-decker buses. My eyes darted around, trying to take in everything at once, like a starving person at an all-you-can-eat buffet. At Metford, Tasha had taken charge at the front desk, filling in paperwork, collecting our passports, passing out keys to each of us, and pointing to the wall of cubbyholes on the back wall where we would be able to get mail or messages. I stood over my suitcase, swaying with exhaustion.

"Okay, people, listen up." Tasha clapped her hands and a few people jolted back to wakefulness. "I know jet lag's a bitch, but there's only one way to get over it—get on schedule." She glanced at the ancient grandfather clock in the corner of the lobby. "It's just after twelve now. I'm going to give you two hours to get settled, take a shower, and, if you feel like you must, lie down. There's a communal bathroom on every floor. Girls on the odd floors, guys on the even. Your key has your room number on it. Get yourselves squared away and we'll meet downstairs in the library at two for orientation. No excuses." A few people groaned. Tasha shook her head. "C'mon, now. Stiff upper lip and all that. If you sleep now, you'll be up all night. You'll thank me later. Off you go."

I'd napped for as long as possible, waking with only fifteen minutes to spare for a quick shower and to pull on clean clothes. I didn't bother to put anything away in my room, not that there was a lot of space. In the brochure it had looked tiny, but in real life it was freakishly dollhouse small. Each room barely fit a desk under the narrow window against the far wall, a twin bed, and a row of hooks running the length of the room with a shelf above for all our clothing. There wasn't even a closet. The floor was worn brown linoleum tiles. It looked like an attic that you'd find in a Charlotte Brontë novel, one where you kept a crazy relative. I couldn't help but compare it to my room back home: my queen-size bed, an entire wall of bookcases, a giant bay window where I liked to sit and read, and a thick cream carpet that my mom had picked out stretching across the floor.

Somehow this space seemed to fit me better. It seemed to have potential, like a cocoon I could emerge from in a few weeks, different. Better.

My wet hair dripped down my neck as I stumbled down the stairs. In the library the rest of the group were wolfing down sandwiches from the buffet set up at the back. Connor glanced up as I came in and pulled Miriam closer to his side as if he thought I might try to wriggle between them. I turned coldly away. I surveyed the rest of our group and tried to remember what I could about them from the information session a few weeks ago.

Jazmin was the tall Indian girl. Her features were sharp and angular, as if they could cut someone, and her attitude matched. She struck me as someone who didn't have a lot of patience for bullshit but had a huge capacity for sarcasm. Kendra was talking to her. Kendra looked like the *before* picture in every makeover story. Her eyebrows begged for the attention of tweezers and she had the misfortune of possessing a resting bitch face. Or she was terminally in a bad mood; that seemed possible too. The only thing I could remember about her was that she had a perfect grade point average. I knew that because she had told all of us a million times during the information session.

Jamal was constantly in motion, like a toddler with ADHD who had just consumed a bag of Sour Patch Kids. He was also tech obsessed. I suspected he wished for a Batman utility belt so he could keep his gadgets at the ready. As it was, he was weighed down with an Apple Watch, his iPad, a phone, a Fitbit, and a digital camera that looked capable of taking photos from the moon. At that moment I overheard him telling Sophie about the various apps he'd downloaded specifically for the trip and then alphabetized to be easily found.

I smiled shyly at Sophie and she waved back. She was covered by a layer of baby fat — everything about her was round and soft. Someday she was going to take off her glasses and shake down her hair, and everyone would be shocked at how beautiful she really was. Until then, she dressed as if she were a forty-year-old suburban mom with an addiction to Lands' End sensible clothing.

Just before I could walk over to her, the guy next to me held out a fork with a thin slice of disturbingly pink meat hanging off the end. I scrambled to remember his name, and then it came back to me: Alex.

"Any guesses what that is?" His nose wrinkled up at the end. He was thin and lanky, like a stick man made three-dimensional. His skin was a light brown, but his eyes were a bright clear blue.

"Um, some kind of olive loaf?" I suggested.

Alex continued to look at the meat uncertainly, his thick dark eyebrows meeting in the center of his forehead. "I'm not just picky, although I am. I'm also allergic."

"I've never heard of an olive allergy," I admitted.

He looked at me, surprised. "Oh, I'm not allergic to olives. Now, strawberries? Totally different thing. I swell up like a blowfish, get all blotchy."

"Attractive."

He snorted. "That's nothing. If I eat shellfish, I pretty much seize up. I look like a white guy trying to dance."

I laughed. I searched his face, picking apart his features.

"Trying to guess my background?"

I flushed.

"Good luck. I'm a total 'all of the above' kind of genetic pool." He held out the meat again. "But seriously, green olives in meat?" He turned it back and forth as if he might have discovered some type of new life form. "I mean, have you ever been making a sandwich and thought, *Cheese, lettuce, tomato, mayo . . . Ooh, I know — green olives would go great on this? No, wait — even better. Green olives in this.*"

My lips twitched. "I don't really know."

He glanced up. "You don't know if you like olives on a sandwich?"

I shook my head. "No, I meant I don't know why people would want olives in their sandwich." I paused. "Although I suppose if you did, having them embedded in the meat would make it convenient. Easier than slicing them up and having them fall out of the sandwich."

He smiled. "Excellent point. Hadn't thought of that. Gotta admire a packaged meat that's efficient." He popped the slice into his mouth and held out his hand. "Alex, in case you can't remember." When he noticed my hesitation, he wiped his palm on his pants leg to rid it of the bologna sweat before holding out his hand again.

"Kim," I answered.

He smiled again, his eyes sparkling. "I know. A great memory is one of my many assets."

"You're too perky. Did you sleep on the plane?"

"I did — I was up in business class." He blushed, then shoved his hair out of his eyes. I would have killed for eyelashes like that. They were thick and long, as if he modeled for Sephora. "My mom works for the airline," he explained. "She gets all kinds of perks, so she arranged for me to fly up there."

"Was it nice?"

He nodded solemnly. "You have no idea how good. The seats lie flat like a bed and at one point they brought out cookies and ice cream." He held up a hand as in the *stop* motion.

"*Warm* cookies," he clarified. "Although I heard you had a pretty good time back in coach."

I flushed. I'd have to thank Connor for making me sound like a drunk to everyone in our group.

"So, I can't remember—what school do you go to?" Alex asked, kindly changing the subject.

I smirked, enjoying the chance to tease him. "I thought memory was your asset."

He rolled his eyes. "I said I have a good memory, not that it's like a superpower or anything. I can't have *everything* going for me. That wouldn't be fair to the rest of you mere mortals."

"I go to Handsworth. Our guidance counselor really pushes this program. She thinks the independent travel will look good on our university apps. You?"

"Homeschooled." He shrugged. "Explains my weirdness. Poor social skills."

I blinked. I had no idea how to respond to that. I couldn't tell if he was joking. "Oh."

We stood silently next to each other while I desperately cast around for something to talk about. If I didn't come up with something soon, he was going to wander off and talk to someone else who was capable of conversation. I flashed to hanging with Nicki at the airport. She would have taken one look at Alex and instantly known how to connect. He and Nicki would already have been best friends by this point. My mom had some kind of internally memorized list of conversation topics. She could chat up anyone from a cashier to a nuclear scientist at a moment's notice.

It wasn't just that I wanted to have a friend on the program, although I did. And it wasn't that he had a decent sense of humor and, if he was on this program, could be counted on to be bright. The Student Scholars program had sent eight of us, and I had the sense there was going to be a lot of "pair up with your buddy" activities. I wasn't remotely interested in being the odd one out that someone felt stuck with. Looking around, I could see that people were already matching up. I'd talked to Sophie a bit at the airport at check-in, but she was now chummed up with Jamal.

"You like the Ravens?" I said, motioning to Alex's T-shirt, which was emblazoned with the band name. "My cousin is their concert organizer." This was . . . a bit of a stretch, but my cousin did work for a travel agency that had booked the band's flights. Granted, it was only once, but still, shared interests are a great place to start a conversation.

Alex's mouth fell open. He reached for me. "Let me touch you so I can say I touched the hand of someone who touched the hand of someone in the Ravens. That is how much I love that band." He let his fingers rest on the back of my wrist and sighed deeply. "That was amazing."

I jolted at his touch. *Why did I lie?* What were the odds that he would be a band groupie? All I had wanted to do was have something to talk about. I glanced around the room to see if anyone had noticed us. The pairs seemed even more obvious now. I took a deep breath. I had to take charge of my life. I had to do things. Nicki wouldn't be sitting around hoping she wouldn't be left out. "Listen, if we have to buddy up for stuff, I wondered if you—"

"—would be your date?" He flung his arm around me. "I thought you'd never ask."

I felt a blowtorch of heat all over my body. Then I noticed Connor staring. I thrust my chin into the air and let the weight of Alex's arm warm my shoulders. *That's right. I don't need you.*

"Would I want to buddy up with someone who basically *works* with my most favorite band ever?" Alex shook his head in disbelief. "Good luck getting rid of me now."

His passion for the Ravens was starting to freak me out. He was going to want me to score him tickets or a backstage pass. "My cousin's not, like, their manager or anything—he just did some of the travel planning," I said, trying to ramp back my lie.

Alex misread why I was hedging. "Don't worry, I won't hit on you just to get close to them." He smiled. "I can come up with better reasons to do that."

My face went stiff. *Is he making a joke?* He was smiling. A tiny chip out of his front tooth made him seem younger. He shoved his hands into his pockets and didn't meet my eyes.

"Plus, you solved the great olive loaf mystery, which means you're also going to be handy to have around on this trip," Alex added. "Having a partner who's an excellent problem solver strikes me as a good plan here in a foreign land. But now a serious question that will determine the course of our future relationship: Star Wars or Star Trek?"

I paused to consider the options. "I'm more a *Serenity* kind of person."

The corners of his mouth twitched. "Ah, so you aim to misbehave."

I found myself smiling back. "I think I do."

Tasha came into the room, clapping her hands above her head. She'd stripped off her jacket so that she was in just a fitted white T-shirt. Her arms looked as though she belonged in an action movie. "All right, people, put your bums in a chair."

She waited until we were seated around one of the scarred tables. "I know you went over the ground rules before coming, but let me touch on the most important one." She paused until we each met her eyes. "This is not a democracy. I'm in charge of the eight of you. Maybe you thought, *No parents, no teachers* — that you had it made." She shook her head. "Forget it. Think of me as your queen while you're here." She smiled. Against her dark skin her teeth looked almost fluorescent. "What I say is law."

"Don't do what she says and off with your head," Alex whispered to me out of the side of his mouth.

Tasha swiveled in his direction, her gaze pinning us both into place. "Exactly," she said.

Alex's eyes widened. "How —"

"—did I hear you?" Tasha said, cutting him off. "I hear everything. I hear things you haven't even said yet. Things you haven't even thought—that's how good I am. You're not my first summer scholar group. During the school year I teach kindergarten. If I can keep command of twenty tiny children with marginal bladder control, I can certainly take charge of all of you. We're going to have fun while you're here and I'll make sure you see all the sights and even learn a few things so you can consider this educational. My suggestion is that you don't test me by breaking the rules. In return, I'll make sure you have a great trip and get home safely. Deal?"

The eight of us nodded slightly in awe. Sophie took notes in her tidy, almost typewriter-perfect handwriting.

"Great! Then let's get you moving. I thought we'd take a walk around Kensington Gardens. It's just a few blocks from here. Get the blood moving, take a gander at the neighborhood so you have your bearings, and we can swing by the Tube stop on the way back and get all of you set up with an Oyster card. That's like your ticket." She motioned for all of us to stand. "You'll need a partner for the next few weeks, so buddy up."

Alex and I high-fived.

"Okay, let's stick together. London's a big city, after all."

People shuffled to their feet, gathering up their stuff. Jamal stuffed various gadgets into pockets and slung his giant, paparazzi-worthy camera around his neck.

"It's raining," Sophie pointed out, peering out the window.

Kendra wrinkled up her nose as if personally offended by the weather. That girl was going to have some serious wrinkles by the time she hit thirty. Her whole face was a frown line.

Tasha rolled her eyes. "You call that rain? Love, here in England we call that a healthy mist. Hardly worth getting out the umbrella. Why do you think all the British have such great skin? Moisturizing with Mother Nature." She patted her cheeks and went over to the library door, opening it wide, gesturing for us to go ahead. The walk was clearly not optional.

Alex cocked his elbow at me. "'So here is us, on the raggedy edge,'" he said, quoting my favorite movie. "To a new adventure."

My heart rate accelerated. This was it. Day one, new me. I linked my arm through his.

After we passed Tasha and were out in the hallway, Alex leaned in. "I'm pretty sure she's ex-military. Possibly a lesser-known Marvel superhero."

"She can probably kill you with nothing more than a paper clip and her pinkie finger," I whispered back.

Alex snickered. "She only needs the paper clip for extra style points."

We stumbled out of the residence and onto the sidewalk. The sound of traffic crashed in on me. A red double-decker bus careened around the corner and every other car seemed to be honking. I looked up and down the street, taking in the stores and restaurants that seemed to be packed in tighter than on the streets at home, as though the city were too large for the space. People of every shape, size, and color wove together on the sidewalk, moving in a coordinated fashion. My heartbeat skipped and I felt as if there were an electrical current in the air.

This was it. I was really in London. I was still trying to put my finger on how it was different from Vancouver. It was larger and everyone seemed to have an accent, but it was more than that, as if the history of the city were peeking out at odd places, catching me off-guard. You'd see a Starbucks nestled up to a building that was at least two hundred years old. It wouldn't have shocked me at all to see Shakespeare or Harry Potter ducking into a storefront or pub. London was a place where magic was possible; mystery crackled in the air, filling in the spaces, setting me alight.

This was my chance. I glanced down at my arm still linked with Alex's. A warmth spread through my chest.

"Check it out—there's a Thai place over there." Alex's nose twitched. "Thai is my favorite. Want to grab something after the walk?"

Did he mean just the two of us? "Um, sure." A small Thai flag fluttered above the restaurant window. "I bet whatever they have beats olive loaf."

He wriggled his eyebrows. "Everything beats olive loaf."

I laughed, realizing I was hungry and my hangover was gone. I'd been in London for only a few hours, but so far, I loved it.

SIX

I shivered and pulled the hood of my rain jacket down farther. Summer in England was a flexible concept.

"Let's check the Wakefield Tower." Alex looked down at his map and then scanned the area. We were on a scavenger hunt through the Tower of London. Tasha had combined our group with some of the other study abroad programs staying at Metford, but what had seemed like a large group on the bus was now lost in the sea of tourists all over the grounds.

I touched the walls as we walked, trailing my fingers along the wet stones, trying to wrap my head around the idea that the castle had been there since 1066. My mind would start to calculate how many years had gone by, how many people had touched the same wall, and then my circuits would overload. I'd turn a corner, or duck under a low doorway, and there would be a flash where I'd think I could almost see into the past. History, and the dead, seemed closer in this space. The air in the building was thick with the breath of the millions of people who had passed through it.

"You guys having any luck with the last clue?" Sophie asked.

Alex shook his head and Kendra scowled. "They shouldn't have made it so hard," she declared. "Everyone still has jet lag and now we're supposed to figure this stupid thing out." She crumpled up her paper before stalking off to join Jamal, who was madly scanning information on his phone, trying to Google his way out of this situation.

"It's just supposed to give us a reason to see everything," Alex pointed out to Sophie, who was still standing nearby. "There's not, like, a grade or anything."

Sophie nodded. "I know, I told her." She shrugged and motioned to Jazmin. "C'mon, come with Jamal and me — we're going to check out the chapel again." The three of them wandered off.

Tasha had created elaborate clues with the other group leaders, and dozens of us had swarmed over the site in our matched pairs looking for the answers. They were tricky, more riddles than clues. Pretty much everyone was down to one last question that no one could figure out. There'd been a promise of a prize for the winners, which was rumored to be a pair of theater tickets to one of the big musicals in the West End.

"The rest of you shouldn't even bother trying — we've got this one," Connor had crowed on the bus on the way over. Miriam jabbed him in the ribs as though it was a joke, but I could see the competition burning in his eyes. He wanted to win. Badly.

As I watched him, I'd realized something. A month ago, I would have thrown myself off one of the tower walls if it would help him win. A day ago, I would have pushed him off, if it meant keeping him from winning. Now I didn't really care either way, and that made me feel like skipping. He'd been like a toxic fever, but it was breaking.

"That's it!" I called out. Alex jerked around and came back to where I stood. My brain had been thinking about Connor on one level, but on another it had put the riddle together. I pointed to Traitors' Gate.

Alex's forehead wrinkled. "I don't get it."

I looked down at the sheet. "Listen to the clue again. 'This is the place where they say there was a cry of innocence and pleading, but rather it's a fake Judas doorway.' We thought it had to be something in the chapel because of the Judas reference, but what if we're looking at it wrong?" I lowered my voice in case anyone else was listening. "Remember Tasha's lecture about Anne Boleyn this morning over breakfast?" There might not have been homework in our program, but they were determined to teach us a few things. We couldn't move an inch without Tasha spewing out random facts about history or art.

"Yeah," Alex said slowly.

"How she was brought here by Henry the Eighth, and when she came, she —"

"—fell on her knees and declared she wasn't guilty," Alex completed for me, his blue eyes flashing. "A pleading of innocence."

"And how everyone used to say she came in through Traitors' Gate"—I motioned to the gate over my shoulder—"but historians now say this wasn't likely because she was a queen, that they never would have brought her this way. And what is another word for *traitor*?"

Alex's face broke into a wide smile. *"Judas."* He grabbed me and spun me around. "You're a freaking genius."

Warm waves of satisfaction ran through my chest. I'd figured it out. The question that had been driving everyone else crazy for the past hour hadn't bested me. I felt the rush I got when I knew the answers in class. Maybe the ghost of Anne Boleyn figured I deserved the answer since we'd both been overthrown by a guy who moved on pretty quickly to the next model. She would have moved on too—if they hadn't cut off her head.

"No big deal." I waved off the praise.

"Are you kidding? I think they should put up a plaque here: *This spot is where the divine Kim Maher solved the unsolvable.*"

I liked the admiration in his eyes. He really was impressed. He didn't rush to point out what questions he'd figured out or make it seem as if it hadn't been that hard. He was honestly happy for me.

"You got the question about heraldry right," I pointed out.

"True." Alex seemed to be pondering. "It's possible we're an unbeatable team."

I smiled, liking the sound of that.

"Let's go find Tasha and the other leaders," Alex said, grabbing my hand.

An electric shot ran up my arm where we touched and I noticed he didn't let go. We wove through the crowds of tourists. That's when I spotted her.

Nicki.

I stopped in place. *Is it her?* She'd turned so all I could see was the back of her head. I pulled away from Alex.

"I'll be right back," I called to him over my shoulder.

I swam through the people, trying to reach Nicki. What were the odds in a city of nearly nine million I'd bump into her? Nicki walked toward the White Tower in the center of the complex. "Excuse me," I mumbled to people as I tried to catch up with her.

"Nicki!" I called out.

The woman stopped and turned, looking around as if she'd heard her name, but I still couldn't see her directly. Then she started moving more quickly toward the chapel.

I picked up my pace. I didn't want to lose her. The center courtyard was jammed with people. I couldn't see her anymore. *Shit.* I jumped up, striving to see over the mass of humanity. She might have gone inside. I stepped closer to the door for the

Martin Tower, and a large man wearing a cowboy hat grabbed my arm.

"Hey, we're all in line!" He pointed to where a winding snake of people behind him all waited to get in to see the crown jewels.

"I'm not trying to cut — I'm just looking for my friend."

He snorted, indicating his disbelief. "Sure, sweetie."

I felt my nostrils flare in annoyance. Before, I would have mumbled an apology. But not anymore. "I'm not your sweetie." I spun around so I could keep looking for Nicki.

"You tell him, darling," a Southern voice called out.

I spotted Nicki. She must have somehow doubled back, as she was now walking toward Wakefield Tower and the exit.

I picked up my pace. If she left the complex, I'd never catch her.

A tour group surged forward, cutting me off. I slammed into the back of an elderly man, who stumbled. Another guest grabbed his arm so he wouldn't fall.

"I'm so sorry," I said, horrified at what I'd done.

"No running on Tower grounds," a Yeoman Warder bellowed at me. He was dressed in the dark blue and red livery, the red crown crest across his chest. His voice was loud and bounced off the thick stone walls.

"I'm sorry," I apologized again. Why did I have to be so uncoordinated?

The old man waved me off with a smile. "No harm done."

I glanced back toward the gate, but Nicki was gone. If it had even been her in the first place.

"There you are," Alex said, jogging up. "You okay?"

I motioned toward the entrance. "Yeah. I thought I saw someone I knew." I felt a pang of loss. It would have been nice to see her.

"We should go. Tasha's getting everyone together. We're supposed to be on the bus in a few minutes."

"Why? We haven't even done the Yeoman Warder tour yet."

"That loud guy in our group? Connor? He fell and did something to his knee, or ankle, so we've all got to go back."

Connor was normally super coordinated. The kind of guy who never caught a ball with his face instead of his hands. Being clumsy was my skill. He must have jet lag to have stumbled. Alex saw something in my expression, but he misunderstood it. He held up a hand. "No worries, I made sure we turned in our sheet. We were the only group to get all the answers. The tickets are ours."

"What show?"

Alex bounced on the balls of his feet. He moved fluidly, like a cat. "Two seats, *Phantom of the Opera,* for this weekend!"

"You didn't strike me as the kind of guy who would be into musical theater."

"You have no idea of the things I'm into. I'm a complex man of the world, you know." He cocked his elbow out for me to take. "M'lady, may I have the pleasure of your company for an evening at the theater?" He dragged out the last word with a thick fake accent.

I linked arms with him. "Why, I would be delighted."

"Then it's a date," Alex declared.

Another jolt of electricity ran through my body.

It was just a saying. I'd been head over heels for Connor only a few weeks ago. It wasn't as though I was going to fall for someone else so quickly just because he was smart and funny.

And good-looking.

I glanced over at Alex's face. His wide mouth was pulled back into a smile. I found it infectious and I smiled back.

SEVEN

S ee all of you at Westminster in thirty minutes," Tasha
called out the next morning as we entered South Kensington Station. Everyone nodded. Kendra and Jamal peeled off
to grab some coffee at Café Floran, while the rest of us headed
straight in. Tasha had made sure before we left Metford that
we were all clear on where we were going and the meet-up
point, knowing that in the packed stations it would be nearly
impossible to stay together.

The South Ken station was the definition of chaos with the
District, Piccadilly, and Circle lines coming in and out. Tourists and locals swarmed the stores that ringed the entrance of
the station, grabbing bottles of Coke, copies of *Time Out* or the
Times, or candy bars for their trip.

This was only my third day in London, but I was starting
to feel like a local. I knew how to tap my card on the turnstile

and could dodge between people and baby carriages to thunder down the escalator, knowing exactly what train I needed.

"You want a bottle of water?" Alex asked. I nodded and started to fish through the pockets in my shorts for some pound coins. He waved me off. "No worries, I got this." He loped over to the closest newsstand.

"I need to talk to you." Connor came up on my side. He was limping, his ankle wrapped with an elastic bandage due to his fall the day before. No doubt he was milking it for all the sympathy he could get. Connor jerked his head toward Alex standing in line. "Does he know?"

I felt my back teeth grind. "You've been really clear. There's nothing between us, so there's nothing for him to know."

"The two of you were pretty snuggly last night." The residence hall had converted the cafeteria, which they called the canteen, into a movie theater for a night. It had been a triple bill of the first three *Alien* movies.

I flushed, thinking of how close Alex and I had sat together. We'd both jumped every time an alien leaped out from a hiding place, our hands bumping in the popcorn bucket.

"If you're dating him just to make me jealous, there's no point," Connor said.

My mouth filled with bitter spit. "Not everything is about you."

Connor leaned closer. "Don't act like that isn't something

71

you would do. He seems like a nice guy. Maybe I should tell him what he's in for with you."

I backed up. "What does that even mean? Look, things didn't work out. Whatever. You've moved on. I'm moving on. Just leave me alone."

Connor laughed. "So now you're all 'moving on'? This despite the fact that you freaking followed me here. Now you're stringing this guy along to get my attention. That's sick."

Alex was handing over his money at the booth. The last thing I needed was for him to hear all of this. Who the hell had pissed in Connor's corn flakes this morning? He hadn't talked to me in weeks and now he had shoved his nose into my life?

"Leave me alone—that's what you wanted, so do it. Fuck off," I hissed. Kendra and Jamal stopped in front of us, Kendra's eyes widening at my language. Great. Now everyone could wonder what had happened between the two of us. I forced my face into what I hoped would pass as a pleasant expression and waved to the two of them. Jamal shrugged and they headed down to the platform.

Connor shook his head. "We're not done." He whirled and limped to the escalator.

"Here you go." Alex handed me a cold, sweating bottle of water. He noticed I was staring off at Connor. "What's with him?"

I bit the inside of my cheek. It wasn't enough that Connor

had broken my heart—now he wanted to ruin whatever was starting with Alex. "Nothing. He's—"

"Excuse me, miss?" I turned to see an elderly couple, each wearing white sneakers that made it look as though their feet had been consumed by giant marshmallows, their outfits complete with zippered fanny packs. The elderly man held open a well-thumbed Rick Steves guidebook marked with brightly colored Post-it Notes. "Do you know how we get to Buckingham Palace from here?"

I could have kissed him for the distraction. "You'll need to take the District line." I pointed to the overhead sign, grateful that I knew the answer. "You'll get out at St. James. It's just a short walk from there. We're taking the same train so we can show you part of the way."

Alex and I slowed our pace so they could follow us down the escalator while the woman kept up a nonstop description of how they were visiting from Indiana, their delayed flight, and how it was impossible to get the kind of yogurt they liked here. I enjoyed her patter—it meant I didn't have to try to explain anything to Alex.

The platform was packed with people, making the space hot and humid, like a steam bath. An announcement blared overhead. There was a delay at the next station and the crowd built quickly. I turned to the American couple. "If we get separated, you just get on this train and you get off for the palace just a few stops down."

The two tourists nodded, but I could tell they were already engrossed in the people around them. I half expected the old guy to snap a picture of the goth girl standing near him with the safety pin through her eyebrow. He kept leaning closer and closer as if to inspect it.

"Keep an eye on them, will you," I whispered to Alex. "They look like the kind who could wander off."

"Look at you, guardian angel to the elderly," Alex teased me, and I jabbed him in the side with my elbow.

More people poured onto the platform, making all of us shift farther down. I lost sight of the couple. Alex was tall enough that I could still see him. He jerked his head to his right, letting me know he still had them in view.

Miriam barked out a laugh, her voice cutting through the noise of the crowd. She and Sophie were talking animatedly by a vending machine. Connor stood near the edge of the platform, inspecting the posters against the far wall across the tracks, advertising everything from vodka to the ballet. He was still glowering, his bad mood all over his face. Miriam must not have wanted him around either, with that attitude. I stared at the back of his head, willing him to keep his mouth shut around Alex.

A whoosh of cool air rushed through the tunnel and the squeal of the incoming train could be heard as it came closer. The hum of the crowd grew louder as everyone started shifting forward. There was a sharp jab in my calf and I spun around. A guy holding a large umbrella was behind me, the metal tip of the umbrella pressing into my bare leg.

"Do you mind?" I asked.

"Sod off," he said, his voice hard to hear over the loud squealing of the approaching train and the announcement reminding everyone to stay behind the line. Then there was a loud, wet *thump* and the train braked hard, the wheels screeching on the tracks.

Someone screamed and that set off a wave of panic in the crowd. Half the people pressed forward, while the other half moved back toward the stairs, uncertain as to what was happening, afraid it might be a terrorist attack. I stumbled and the crowd pressed in around me, keeping me from falling.

Another person started chanting. "Oh god, oh god . . ."

I took a few steps and found myself near the front of the platform. A transit employee rushed toward me.

"Everyone get back!" he yelled, waving his hands. "Don't jump onto the tracks!"

Why in the world would anyone jump onto the tracks? The people inside the train were pressed up against the glass looking out at us, as if we were creatures in the zoo.

Alex was suddenly at my side, grasping my elbow. "What happened?"

"I don't know." My voice was tight. That's when I spotted it on the ground. A blue Nike sneaker. It sat there, its tongue flapping forward as if someone would come along at any moment and slide a foot inside. A sneaker Cinderella.

The transit employee jumped down onto the tracks and crouched over something. A large woman in a red dress moved to get a better look. She stepped back quickly, her girth swaying before she bent over and threw up on the platform.

"Jumper," a voice said behind me. It was the man with the umbrella. He shook his head.

The meaning of his words struck me. Someone had thrown himself in front of the train. Hot, sour bile twisted in my stomach as the reality of the act washed over me.

"Jesus, now we're never getting out of here," the guy said, his voice dripping with disdain. He hitched up his pants. "Best bet is to walk up to the next station. It'll take forever to clean the mess off the rails; they won't be getting trains in or out of here for at least an hour," he declared to those standing near him. He wove his way back through the crowd toward the stairs. Others followed his lead, trailing after him.

"Connor?" Miriam called out.

I searched up and down the platform, spotting people from our group, seeking Connor among all the faces. I flashed back to the image of the shoe. *Doesn't he have shoes like that?*

"Connor?" Miriam's voice was growing shrill. Sophie's eyes were wide and she waved madly when she spotted Tasha farther down the platform. Tasha shoved her way through the crowd and peeked over the side of the platform and then pushed Miriam away from the sight.

"Don't look," Tasha commanded. "Student Scholars!" she yelled. "All of you — back up to the stairs. We are leaving. Now!"

Our group clustered together and moved as one mass. Tasha had Miriam around the waist and seemed to be half-carrying, half-dragging her.

I had to look. It was as if I were tethered to the front of the train and slowly being pulled closer. I peered over the side of the platform.

My brain scrambled to make sense of what I was seeing, to put it in order. It was all wrong. A mannequin assembled incorrectly. Arms and legs, but not in the right places. One leg torn completely free. There was blood splashed up the wall. His face was turned to the side, but I could still see one brown eye looking forward. Connor, but no longer Connor.

All the sound in the space turned to a high-pitched whine, like a mosquito army in my head. My underarms were clammy and I could feel a slick of sweat breaking out on my forehead.

Alex was in my face saying something, but I couldn't hear his words. I needed to get away. I tried to run, but the nerves that ran to my legs seemed to be short-circuiting. I took a few stumbling steps and then fell.

EIGHT

I felt like a puppet that had had its strings cut. I collapsed to the floor. Alex dropped down next to me. There was a strange smell in the air, like hot metal. Coppery, like burning pennies. I struggled to get up. My legs kicked out and my hands slid across the filthy tile floor, which was gritty under my palms. I was desperate to get away, but my body wouldn't obey. Reality felt broken and choppy, as though I were missing frames in a movie.

"Whoa, take it easy, you've had a shock." Alex put his arm behind me and helped me sit up. He passed me his water, but I waved it off. There was still a loud buzzing in my ears.

"Connor," I said.

"Yeah," Alex said, not able to meet my eyes. He looked pale and shaken and I wondered if he'd seen it too. Not *it*. Connor.

"You ready to stand?"

I nodded. There were more transit cops on the platform,

78

but everyone else had vanished. My glance shot to the edge. The shoe was still there. I began shaking. Alex slipped his arm around my waist and stood, pulling me up with him.

"If she's okay, you need to clear out of here," one of the transit cops said. "Did she hit her head?"

"No," Alex said. "She didn't pass out, just collapsed." He pulled me closer, his lips almost touching my ear. "I told Tasha I'd get you back to Metford. Can you walk?"

I nodded, but I wasn't sure that I could. My limbs didn't seem connected in any logical way. My legs felt as if they were different lengths, and the bones that should have held me up were like rubber, threatening to give way at any moment. Alex led me to the escalator, putting me in front of him so that I wouldn't fall back down.

I stopped short as soon as we exited the station. It was bright and sunny; the clouds had blown away. People were walking around the sidewalks with purpose. One woman was laughing into her phone, a loud donkey-like bray — *ha-haaaa-ha-haaaa*. I put my hands over my ears and closed my eyes, trying to get things to make sense. Alex led me over to a park bench and I sank down.

"I'm going to get you some ginger ale." Alex sprinted off.

Connor was dead. There was no doubt in my mind. I winced. The last thing I'd said to him was "Fuck off."

Alex dropped into the seat next to me and spun the cap off a bottle. "Here, drink this." He pressed the soda into my hands.

The fizzy burn of the ginger filled my mouth and for a second I wasn't sure I could swallow it. "Thanks," I managed.

Alex rubbed his palms on his jeans and then shrugged. "I have no idea why I got ginger ale. That's what my mom makes me drink when I feel sick."

The sugar in the drink seemed to be cutting through the fog in my head. I no longer felt as lightheaded. "Sorry, my body just sorta gave out there," I said.

"It was pretty bad," Alex said. "You're probably in shock."

"What happened?" I asked. "I mean, did he just fall?"

"I don't know. I was watching that older couple and then I heard the scream." He shook his head as if he wanted to clear it.

I drained the rest of the bottle. I felt the need to explain. Alex didn't even know that I'd dated Connor. "You know, Connor and—" My voice cracked, as if the words were too sharp to get out.

"Hey, don't worry about anything right now. Let's just get you back."

As we walked toward Metford, I told myself what had happened between Connor and me didn't matter. It didn't change anything. Chiming in to make sure everyone knew we'd once gone out was nothing but a grab for attention. A way to make a tragedy about me. Even Connor deserved better than that.

* * *

The Metford desk clerk pointed us toward the library. Sophie passed each of us a mug as we came in.

"The cafeteria made up a bunch of tea for us." She nodded to the mugs. "Near as I can tell, they put about a pound of sugar in it. Something about the hot and sweet is supposed to be good for this kind of thing. There are cookies, too." She bent over to refill Kendra's cup.

What kind of thing is this? I sipped the tea and winced at the heat that seared my tongue like a branding iron. "Thanks."

"Is Miriam okay?" Alex asked.

"Tasha took her upstairs."

"Jesus, what would make a guy do that?" Jamal asked. "If you want to take yourself out, that's one thing, but why with a train?" His movements were jerky—he kept jamming his hands into his pockets and then taking them out, rocking back and forth on his feet.

"You don't know what happened," Jazmin said. "This is bad enough without you making guesses. Maybe he just fell. Accidents happen."

"Or maybe someone pushed him."

Everyone turned to face Kendra, who had folded herself into a tiny ball in the corner of the sofa. Her mouth was pursed into a tight circle.

"What did you say to him?" Kendra continued. She was addressing me.

My hand started to shake. "What are you talking about?"

"You guys were fighting at the station."

"No, we weren't," I lied.

"I heard you. So did Jamal."

Jamal started as if shocked to find himself drawn into this scene. "Um, I didn't hear much."

"You heard Kim tell him to fuck off," Kendra spat.

I winced. Everyone around Kendra and me had backed up a step as if we might explode. I scrambled to say something other than the truth. "He accused me of cheating on the scavenger hunt yesterday. He was mad that he didn't win."

"The guy could be a real asshole," Jamal added. Jazmin punched him hard in the shoulder. Jamal rubbed it, looking confused. "What? He could."

"There's no reason to speak badly about the dead," Sophie chided him, but at the same time patting his arm tenderly. "Everyone's upset, but we're supposed to be a team. Let's not say anything we'll regret when we don't even know what happened."

"Kim knows," Kendra said. "You were the person closest to him when it happened. You must have seen something."

I shook my head, feeling the panic return. "I didn't see anything!"

Alex took a step closer to me and I had to fight the urge to fall into him, to let him physically support me. "I was right there and I didn't see what happened either," Alex said. "It was packed on the platform and things happened fast."

"What do we do now?" Jazmin asked.

Jamal shrugged.

"Tasha will be back down in a bit," Sophie said. "Until then we should stay put."

"Screw that." Kendra stood. "I need to get out of here." She stomped out of the room, shooting daggers at me as she passed. She clearly thought I was somehow to blame. I drew back, like a turtle into its shell, and Alex placed a steadying hand on the small of my back.

I should have stayed there with Connor. With his body. I'd just run away like the others. Even though I'd been mad, he deserved better than that. He shouldn't have been left alone. I should have stayed so that people would have seen him as a person, not just a mess to be cleaned up. I owed him that for how I used to feel.

"Don't let Kendra get to you. She's just freaked out," Alex said.

"Dude, we're all freaked out," Jamal said.

Sophie tugged her shirt into place. "Okay, who wants some more tea?"

I could see her trying to force a sense of normality back onto our lives, to roughly stitch together who we had all been this morning to the raggedy torn edge of who we were now. I appreciated that she was trying to make things right, but I wasn't sure they ever could be again.

NINE

The following morning, our group met in the cafeteria, but no one was remotely interested in eating breakfast. Jazmin picked at some toast. Jamal and Alex had taken food, but their scrambled eggs were turning into rubbery blobs, the baked tomato bleeding red watery liquid on their plates. I kept checking the door, but Miriam still hadn't come down. Other students would glance over at our table and then look away. No one wanted to sit near us. It was as if our tragedy might be contagious and they wanted to give us a big berth — but not so much space that they wouldn't be a part of the drama. I wanted to hurl my silverware at them to make them stop staring. What had happened to us wasn't entertainment.

I closed my eyes and when I opened them I saw Connor. He sat alone at a table in the back. I blinked, but he was still there, watching our group. I wanted to point him out to the others, but I was paralyzed. It had all been a horrible mistake.

84

He was okay. There would be some explanation of what had happened.

Except there was none. I'd seen his body. I couldn't *stop* seeing it. This wasn't real. But Connor was looking at me, his mouth in a grim tight line. His expression was one I knew all too well—disappointed and exasperated. He'd worn it when he told me that I needed to stop following him around. When I begged him to give us, to give me, another chance, even though I knew he wouldn't. It was the same look he'd had yesterday when he accused me of using Alex to make him jealous. He looked disgusted with me.

A thick rivulet of dark blood started to run from his hairline down the side of his face. It was a rich red. Then another, and another. I blinked and he was gone.

A night of almost no sleep was getting to me. I felt less connected to reality. At one point last night I'd woken up to realize I was standing in front of the sink in the community bathroom and didn't even know how long I'd been there.

I pinched the bridge of my nose. The smell of bacon repulsed me.

"How's Miriam doing?" Jamal asked.

Jazmin shrugged. "The residence arranged for a doctor to come last night. She gave Miriam something to put her out."

"I saw Tasha around midnight, just sitting in the lobby. She had to talk to Connor's parents and tell them what happened." Jamal pushed his eggs around on his plate.

"Are they coming here?"

Jamal put his fork back down. "I dunno. There's no real reason for his parents to show up. It's not like he's missing or anything. I would guess the police will ship . . ."—his Adam's apple bobbed in his throat—"the body back."

Everyone's voice was hushed, as if we were in a church. I closed my eyes, willing the image of Connor out of my head. It kept popping up like a horror show jack-in-the-box. All night I'd start to fall asleep and then would jolt awake thinking of him, picturing his skewed eye looking up at me.

Alex squeezed my hand under the table. He thought I was upset because of what I'd seen. He didn't know about my history with Connor. No one here did, other than Miriam, and I wasn't even sure how much she knew. Part of me wanted everyone to know. It warred with my other half that wanted to bury the information as a secret.

Kendra stabbed at the eggs on her plate but never lifted her fork to eat any. She seemed focused on simply destroying them.

Tasha slipped into the room. Her hair was pulled back with a scarf. She wasn't wearing any makeup and her skin looked ashy. We all sank lower into our seats, watching her as if she were a bomb technician and the room were at risk for exploding if we moved too quickly.

"Okay, I know everyone had a rough night," Tasha said.

"How's Miriam?" Jamal asked.

Tasha rubbed her palms on her jeans. "She's about as well

as can be expected. Sophie's with her. Miriam's talked to her parents and they're on their way."

"Is the trip canceled?" Kendra asked. I iced over. It hadn't occurred to me that they might cancel the trip, but now that Kendra said it, it made sense. Connor was dead.

I hadn't wanted to come, but now that I was here, I didn't want to go back.

"The program has decided to go ahead with the trip but will refund partial fees if anyone wants to return to Vancouver." Tasha tossed back her coffee as if it were a shot of whiskey. She winced at the heat and then wrapped her hands around the chipped white mug. "Changing your flight will depend on what kind of ticket you have and on which airline; you might have to buy another ticket if you want to leave early. Talk to your family before you decide anything."

"What if we want to stay?" Jamal asked. He chewed his fingernails. The flesh around what was left of the nails was shredded and red. He glanced up and down the table, taking in how everyone was staring at him. "I mean, Connor and I weren't, like, friends or anything."

Jazmin wrinkled up her face. "Nice. You know it's not all about you, right?"

Jamal threw his hands up in the air. "I know. I'm just saying that I don't see what the point would be of going home. I feel bad the guy decided to kill himself, but it has nothing to do with me."

"We don't know if Connor killed himself," Tasha said, cutting short Jamal's rant. "It might have been an accident. There's nothing to be gained by getting peeved at one another. There's no right or wrong way to handle this."

Jamal glared at Jazmin, vindicated. I refused to look over at Kendra. I wondered if she'd told Tasha about the argument Connor and I had had at the station.

"To answer your question, if you want to finish the program, that's fine. Most of the fees, dormitory charges, and activities were all prepaid. I'm here for the duration." Her voice was flat. She didn't sound thrilled about the idea. "So, anyone who wants to continue, we will. I'm going to encourage you to talk to your parents, if you haven't already. The program heads have already reached out to your families, by phone if they could reach them and otherwise via email, so they know what's happened. There wasn't much on the schedule today, but the optional tour to Hampton Court is nixed. I'm going to meet with each of you one-on-one to check in and see how you're doing and what your plans are. If anyone's struggling, we've arranged for you to have access to a local counselor. Now isn't the time to bottle this inside. If you're having trouble, you need to tell me." Tasha pushed her sleeves up, her arms strong, the muscles defined under her dark skin.

"So that's the plan. I'm putting a sheet by the door with times to meet with me. Sign up and then come to the library for your scheduled slot. Otherwise you're free to do whatever you want today. I've arranged for the van to take anyone who wants to go to a nondenominational service this evening. We'll pick up our regular schedule tomorrow to see the Victoria and Albert Museum. Any questions?"

I held my breath, waiting to see if Kendra would say anything, but all the fight seemed to have leaked out of her.

No one spoke, so Tasha stood, and that seemed to be the cue everyone was waiting for to be released. I signed up for my time, the pen dragging on the paper, and then hauled myself back upstairs to my room to call my parents.

The phone rang forever before my dad picked up. "Kim? What's wrong?"

I heard my mom pick up the extension. "Kimberly?"

"Nothing's wrong," I said. That wasn't true — everything was wrong — but I wasn't entirely sure how to put it into words.

"Then why are you calling?" Mom asked.

I pulled my phone away from my head and looked at it. Her response made no sense. "They told us to call," I said eventually. "Tasha said you guys know what happened, that they told you." My voice cracked.

"It's okay, pumpkin, it's just that it's one in the morning here. When you called, we thought something else might have happened," Dad said.

I winced. I'd entirely forgotten about the time change. "Sorry."

The sandpaper sound of my dad rubbing the stubble on his

chin came through the phone. I could picture him sitting at the edge of their king-size bed, the mountain of throw pillows my mom liked clustered at his feet like begging dogs. "How are you coping?"

"Okay." The image of Connor's body flashed across my brain in neon colors.

"Do you want to come home?" Mom asked. I could imagine her in her purple Ralph Lauren floral nightie, her hair sticking up as she held the phone from the guest room.

I tried to answer, but my throat had squeezed shut. I wanted her to want me to come home, to meet me at the airport and fold me into her arms and tell me everything would be okay. I wanted her to make the decision for me.

"It's fine if you do," Dad said, filling the silence. "I know this must be very hard. Your mom and I know you really cared for Connor despite everything."

"I don't know what to do," I said, pushing the words out.

My mom sighed. "Oh, honey. I'm so sorry you're going through this. I think the best thing you can do is move forward and finish the trip."

"What happened is a tragedy," Dad said. "And it's going to be extra difficult on you because of your history with him." I nodded even though my dad couldn't see me. History. That's what it was — past tense. "Hopefully they'll have some answers for his parents soon. It sounds like they don't know the whole story."

"With what the program costs, you'd think they would have kept a better eye on all of you," Mom chimed in.

I didn't bother pointing out we were old enough to not be tied together like a set of kids from a preschool. Tasha had been paying attention, but she couldn't be everywhere.

It *had* to have been an accident. He'd been at the edge of the platform. Connor was usually pretty coordinated, but he'd been off ever since we got here. Maybe he wanted to get a closer look at a poster and his foot slipped. Or maybe he hadn't heard the train; if he had his cochlear implants turned down for some reason, he might not have realized he was leaning too far forward until it was too late. It would have taken only a second.

Part of me wanted to tell my parents about the fight I'd had with Connor just before he died. I felt guilty that the last time I'd spoken to him had been so nasty. All of it had been horrid. I'd wished him dead for weeks and now I wanted to take it back. I felt sick that I'd ever been that spiteful, even in my head. What if I had put that negative energy out into the universe in some way? I'd wanted karma to take him out.

Then a thought exploded in my head, zapping away the fog that had filled my head since the night before.

It hadn't been karma. I sat down hard on the bed.

"I should let you go — it's really late," I said, cutting off my mom and whatever she had been saying.

"If you need us, you just call," Dad said before I clicked off the phone. I dropped it on the floor, not trusting myself to say anything else. My brain raced in circles.

It wasn't just that I'd wished Connor would die after what he'd done to me. I'd talked to Nicki about killing him. But it had been nothing but a joke.

Right?

TEN

AUGUST 19
12 DAYS REMAINING

I t was ridiculous to think Nicki had murdered Connor. We hadn't been serious; it was just a drunk conversation where we blew off some steam. It was the kind of thing that people say all the time. *I could just kill that guy.*

Even thinking about Nicki as a possible suspect in a homicide was stupid. It was taking one piece of information and embroidering it into a full-blown fantasy. It was the kind of overly dramatic thing I'd expect Miriam to do. Sure, Nicki was a bit wild, but it's a huge leap from stealing some booze to committing a murder.

It had been a mind game, thinking of a perfect crime. Something to keep us occupied on a long flight. Nicki didn't have any reason to kill Connor. People don't push someone in front of a train because someone else they had met once didn't like him. Why would anyone risk life in prison for a stranger? It was illogical.

But crimes weren't about logic. What did they say? *Crime of passion.* It was all emotion.

I paced back and forth between the door and the window, making tight circles in the small space, looking out at Harrington Road. It was raining and people streamed down the sidewalks, their umbrellas bobbing along like black oily bubbles. I was obsessing because my dad had put his finger on something that I hadn't been able to face—how I felt about Connor's death.

I felt guilty.

Guilty that I'd ever slept with him.

Guilty that I'd let myself fall for the idea of him.

Guilty that I'd spent significant amounts of time imagining bad things happening to him. I wasn't that kind of person, or at least I didn't want to be.

Guilty that I'd said so many mean things about Connor to anyone who would listen, including a total stranger I met in an airport.

I chewed on the inside of my cheek. I wished I had some way to get in contact with Nicki. It would be a bizarre conversation, but I would feel better if I could call and just check. *You didn't do anything, did you?* I kicked myself for not thinking to get her phone number before the plane landed.

Another thought zapped through my brain and I grabbed ahold of it as if it were a lifeline. Nicki hadn't gotten my number either. She wouldn't even know how to find me, or Connor!

My mouth went dry. Unless she'd followed me somehow? How much had I told her that night on the flight? I'd thought I'd seen her at the Tower of London, and that was the same day Connor had almost fallen down the stairs. He'd told everyone it was an accident, but he could have been tripped on purpose. Maybe he wasn't suddenly clumsy on this trip — maybe someone had done something to him. My heart thundered in my chest.

I shook my head, trying to scatter the thoughts that were Ping-Ponging around inside of it. My phone chimed, reminding me that it was time to meet Tasha. I caught a glimpse of myself in the mirror. My hair was sticking up and there were dark circles under my eyes. I went down the hall into the bathroom and ran the cold tap and then pressed a wet paper towel to my face, letting it soothe me as I took long, deep breaths. I pulled my hair back into a stubby ponytail and jerked my shirt into place.

As I walked down the hall toward the library, I saw its door open and Miriam slipped out. She looked ragged. I paused, not sure what to say. As she drew near, she took me by the elbow and pulled me into a hug.

"Connor was an asshole, you know. He never deserved you." Her words were soft and whispery in my ear, like an insect's wing, despite the hard edge of what she was saying. Her breath tickled my neck and the tiny hairs stood up.

I pulled back slightly. Had I heard her right?

"Be careful what you tell them." She let go of me and walked quickly away.

My heart jumped up into my throat. *Does she know about Nicki?* I couldn't get the words out. Miriam was already most of the way down the hall. Sophie appeared; she must have been waiting for Miriam in the lobby, for she was suddenly glued to Miriam's side, making soft clucking, comforting noises.

I turned and tapped on the library door and Tasha called for me to come inside. I stepped into the room and then stopped in my tracks, my hand clutching the door handle like a bird's claw. There were two police officers in the room.

"If you're busy, I can come back later," I offered.

"No, it's fine. This is DI Sharma and DI Fogg." Tasha looked up from her papers and realized that I was still locked in place. "They're the detectives looking into Connor's accident," she said. She waved me forward. "Everything's fine—they're just collecting information."

I nodded and willed my hand to let go of the door handle. *What does Miriam know, and what did she tell them?* I walked over to the table, my gait jerky and stiff. I sank into the seat. Maybe I should mention Nicki to them, just in case. They could find her. They were the police, that's what they do—find people. But they might think I sounded crazy, that I had talked about Connor with this girl I met on the plane and we'd sorta made a murder deal, but I hadn't meant it. All Miriam had said was to be careful. Did that mean to tell them everything or nothing? I bit my lip, the sharp pain bringing me into focus.

"How are you bearing up?" Tasha asked.

"Okay," I mumbled.

"Did you know Connor O'Reilly very well?" Detective Fogg asked, pulling on his thick dark beard.

"Not really." As soon as the words were out of my mouth, I wanted to catch them and shove them back down my throat. I didn't know why I'd said that, other than the last thing I needed them to do was dig into my past. This was probably what Miriam was trying to warn me about—talking without thinking. My fingers knit themselves together under the table. "I mean, I knew him. We go to the same school, and we worked together this summer, and we used to be . . . closer. But no, we weren't friends." That, at least, was the truth, even if it was vague.

"Have you had much interaction with him on the trip?" DI Sharma asked.

"No." The word came out in a long rush, like a sigh.

Detective Fogg looked down at his paper. "Kendra said she heard the two of you having an argument."

My fingernails cut into my palms as I clenched my hands under the table. "It wasn't really an argument. He made a nasty comment about a scavenger hunt we did the other day. I told him to fuck off." My voice started to shake. "I didn't mean anything by it. I didn't want anything to happen to him."

Tasha reached over and patted my hand. "Hey, it's okay. People say things they don't mean sometimes."

"Had he said anything to you about being upset or bothered by anything? Any reason he might be depressed, or feel overwhelmed, stressed, that kind of thing?"

I shook my head. "I wasn't the person he'd talk to if he was upset."

"Were you aware he and his girlfriend had broken up?" Detective Sharma tapped her pen on her notebook.

The air in my lungs iced over. Then I realized they didn't mean me, they meant Miriam. "What?" I looked over at Tasha.

She took a deep breath. "Apparently, Miriam told him that morning that she felt they'd be better suited as friends."

Miriam had dumped Connor? That explained his lousy mood that morning. Had she somehow found out about what had happened between him and me? "I didn't know," I said softly. My feet itched to run upstairs and find Miriam. I had to know what had happened between them.

Tasha sighed. "No one did. As you can imagine, Miriam's a bit distraught given what occurred."

DI Fogg snorted as if he didn't quite believe she was that unsettled. When he noticed the rest of us had paused to look at him, he cleared his throat and gazed down at the pad of paper in front of him.

"Miriam insists she and Connor parted as friends. She didn't think he was that upset; she said he never wanted to get serious," Tasha said. "I saw him myself yesterday morning and he seemed fine—maybe a touch irritable, but he certainly didn't seem despondent. I suspect that's why he said something nasty to you—he was in a bad mood. But a bad mood isn't the same thing as clinically depressed. His parents are certain he's not the type to do anything . . . drastic."

My brain scrambled back to the day before, trying to slow down the events and see them freshly with this new information. Maybe he blamed me for the breakup. If Miriam had heard about what had happened between us, she might have taken my side. He would have hated that; he liked to see himself as a hero. He had a way of making sure unpleasant things weren't considered his fault. I pinched the inside of my arm, cutting off that uncharitable thought.

"Hard to know what's in a teen boy's head," DI Fogg said.

The female detective laughed. "Hard to know what's in a grown man's mind, for that matter."

The two of them smiled slightly and I had the sense they worked well together. Like an old married couple who finished each other's sentences and laughed at jokes they'd already heard a million times.

"Fair enough," DI Fogg said before turning back to me. "Is there anything else you can think of to tell us?"

If I was going to mention Nicki, now would be the time. *This is likely nothing, but I feel I should tell you I contracted for Connor's murder just a few days ago—but it was all a joke. Ha ha ha.*

There was no way I could say that. It would make me sound crazy. Or guilty. Or both.

"Kim?"

I jerked and realized that Tasha was talking to me.

"Sorry. I can't think of anything else."

Tasha squeezed my hand. "Okay, you're outta here. Go take a walk in the park or something. It'll do you all good to get some fresh air. Enjoy your theater tickets tonight. It'll be a chance to get your mind off things. You and Alex earned them."

I nodded my agreement and slid off the chair. I'd forgotten about the play.

"If you do think of anything, you just let us know." DI Sharma held out a business card.

I didn't want to take it, but I did anyway. The thought that Nicki had pushed Connor was ridiculous and illogical. He either tripped or was way more upset about the breakup than he'd let on. There was no way she'd done this. She couldn't have.

As soon as the library door clicked shut behind me, I bolted up the stairs, my feet sliding on the worn carpet. The door to Miriam's room was wide open. The bed was stripped, the sheets in a ball at the foot of the bare mattress. The hooks were empty of Miriam's things.

"She left," Jazmin's voice said. I spun and saw Jazmin leaning against her own open door. "Her parents came and picked her up."

I blinked. "She's gone?"

Jazmin looked at me as if I were slow. "That's what I just said. Her parents took her to some hotel around here. I guess the police don't want her to leave the country until they figure out what happened. Her dad was seriously pissed the cops talked to her before he and the mom got here. That dude looked ballistic."

I stared into the empty room as if Miriam might still be there someplace, maybe hiding under the desk. "Yeah. I can imagine."

I turned to go back to my own room. Now I wouldn't get any answers.

ELEVEN

I hadn't wanted to go to *The Phantom of the Opera*. Confusion and sadness were like a thick blanket keeping me from moving, but Alex and Tasha had insisted. I'd trudged to the theater, resenting being forced to go out, but they were right. Once the show started, everything that existed outside the walls of the theater ceased to matter. I wasn't in London anymore; I was in the tunnels below Paris.

As the lights came up, I kept clapping, my hands stinging. People shuffled toward the exits and I had the urge to scream that they should all sit back down. I wanted to hit rewind and see the show all over again. I wanted to stay here where things seemed to make sense. The emotion of the play had hit me like a punch in the gut. I'd cried through most of the second act, sucking in lungfuls of theater air filled with the smell of dusty curtains and wood polish.

Alex placed his hand lightly on the small of my back after a few minutes as the rows emptied. "You ready?"

I nodded. I half expected him to drop his hand, but he kept it there as we walked out. It was warm and steadying and I found myself pressing back against him. I wanted to stay in this moment.

He motioned to a place across the street as we walked out of the theater. "Want to get something to drink before we go back?"

The pub was full of the after-theater crowd and we had to wedge ourselves in. The evening had cooled, but the bar was steamy with all the people packed inside. We couldn't get a table, but there were two stools next to a counter along the far wall. "Grab those and I'll get us something," Alex said.

I peered around, trying to take it all in. Every so often it would strike me: I was in London, seeing plays and going for drinks. The British accents of the crowd around me almost sounded like a song. It felt like a completely different life from the one I had at home. I wished I could call Emily and tell her about it or hold up the phone so she could hear it for herself.

Alex came back with two pints of beer and raised them aloft like a victor before putting them back down. "I asked for them as a joke, but he didn't even want to see ID."

It felt somehow right that we had real drinks. As though

the evening called for it, as if we were older in this reality. We clinked glasses. "To the show," I said as a toast. I took a tentative sip. The hoppy brew was room temperature. Alex sipped it slowly.

"They don't serve it cold," he said.

"Why?"

Alex shrugged. "Maybe they developed a taste for it this way back in the 1600s, prerefrigeration." He took another sip. "For what it's worth, it's growing on me. I also ordered us some Scotch eggs. The bartender says they're awesome."

"What are they? Eggs in plaid kilts?"

"Not a clue, but I figure we should go native." Alex passed me a paper napkin and motioned to my face. "Your makeup is messed up a bit."

Oh god, I probably looked like a raccoon. I licked the napkin and wiped under my eyes, trying to clean up the kohl liner that had streaked from my tears. "Better?"

He stared into my eyes, inspecting me, making me flush, and then nodded.

"I guess I shouldn't go to plays—I can't handle them," I said, trying to make a joke.

"For me it's the SPCA ads they have on TV. You know the one where Sarah McLachlan sings?" He shook his head sadly. "Gets me every single time."

I managed a weak smile.

"You okay?"

My throat tightened. "I guess. It's just, you know, every-thing in the past few days and then the play was so emotional."

I wanted to tell Alex about Connor. About what had hap-pened between the two of us and how that now made every-thing more confusing. I was still mad at Connor for how he'd acted with us. And then I felt guilty for being mad because now he was dead. And then there was also this heavy level of regret that things between us would never be better.

"Yeah," Alex said. The waitress dropped down a plate in front of us. Two dull gray orbs rolled around the center. Alex poked one of them cautiously with a fork, cut the sphere in half, and then sniffed the bite before putting it into his mouth. "Huh—hard-boiled eggs wrapped in sausage, I think." He chewed. "Not bad." He pushed the plate toward me. "I have to say, for the first play I've ever seen, that one was pretty good."

I put my glass down, surprised out of my depressing thoughts. "Really, you've never been to a play before?"

"Nope."

"But you seemed so excited, I figured you must be some kind of musical theater nut."

"I'm always excited to try new things." Alex turned so his knees faced mine. His elbow rested on the counter beside us. He looked perfectly relaxed. His dark hair curled over one eye. He looked like a friendly pirate.

"You mean that, don't you?"

He nodded. "Sure."

I paused to consider what he'd said. "New things freak me out. I tend to stick with what I know I like." I took a big drink of beer to avoid how awkward I suddenly felt. "That's lame, I guess."

He glanced over. "No, it's not. It's just what you feel. Why would liking new stuff be better?"

I shifted on the hard seat, avoiding his gaze. "Because it is." I struggled to explain what seemed to me a basic truth. People who tried new things were exciting and daring. They were the opposite of me. "Everyone knows that."

Alex waved off what I said. "Who cares what other people think?"

"Most people," I pointed out. "Me." I winced at the truth. I cared too much. I hated every single post my mom put up, imagining what people thought. People I didn't even know. The general public passing judgment on every mistake and heartbreak. I'd been dreading what it would be like when Connor and I got back to school and he told everyone what had happened.

I swallowed hard. I guess that wouldn't be a problem anymore.

"Does it seem weird to you that Connor is gone?" I asked Alex. "That he could be alive one day and then dead the next?"

"I guess that's partly why I want to try new stuff all the time. I figure I'll regret more of what I don't do, versus stuff I do that doesn't turn out. Like, this play was fun. Some other stuff I've tried sucked, but I survived."

"What kind of stuff sucked?" I asked, curious.

Alex ate another bite of the egg. "I ate a cricket once on a dare. That was gross."

My nose wrinkled up in disgust. "I could have told you eating bugs was a bad idea."

Alex chuckled. "Yeah, maybe. Although millions of people do it." The smile fell off his face. "And I asked this girl out once. She was in a writing group at the library with me and I thought . . . I don't know . . . I thought she would say yes. She clarified right away that I thought very wrong."

"Sorry," I said softly.

He shrugged. "Yeah." He took a drink.

"A guy broke my heart right before I came here," I blurted out. I couldn't say Connor's name yet. I wanted Alex to feel for *me*, not Connor, who was now more sympathetic because he was dead. My throat was tight and I was suddenly sure I was going to start crying again.

"Ass-hat," Alex said. His insult shocked me and I almost spit out a mouthful of warm beer. He smiled at me. "His loss."

"Technically, I'm the one who got dumped. I don't think he saw it as a loss."

"If he didn't see that you're brilliant, beautiful, and have a killer knowledge of sci-fi movies, then it's his loss. But that's my point — sometimes you try stuff and it blows, but sometimes new stuff turns out pretty cool. Like the play — that was good."

"Yeah." He'd called me beautiful.

"You say you don't like new stuff, but you do it. Like coming to England — that was something new."

I fiddled with my glass. "After he broke up with me, all I wanted was to crawl into bed and never come out again."

Alex nudged me softly in the side. I could smell the beer on his breath, yeasty, like warm bread. "But you didn't. You came. And it's turned out okay, so far, right? I mean, we're here. We've seen this great show and now we're hanging in a pub in London having a pint. And you tried the egg — that took some guts."

I shifted again on the stool. He was right. "I guess."

"See? And who knows how it might go from here." Alex raised his glass.

The corners of my mouth turned up. I clinked glasses with him and we sat there, our legs touching.

TWELVE

We went to the Victoria and Albert Museum in the morning. Miriam was with her parents in a hotel. We'd been told they planned to leave as soon as they got clearance. The rest of us had chosen to stay for the remainder of the program. And as if by agreement, none of us mentioned Connor or Miriam. It was as though they'd never been a part of our group and things were business as usual. It helped that they had been paired up with each other, so our remaining buddy groups stayed the same.

I'd sent Miriam an email. I needed to know more before she left, but so far, I hadn't heard a word in response. I told myself it wasn't that she was avoiding me — she was likely busy with her parents and wasn't checking email. But I couldn't tell if she had been trying to warn me or threaten me, and I had to know.

The V&A museum seemed to be the giant junk drawer of

England. A several-acres-size storage room. Dozens of galleries with dishes and ceramics, from every time period and every style a person could imagine; rooms of key collections; statues tucked into stairwells as though the curators had run out of room; antique clothing on faceless mannequins; tapestries; and even a giant bed that was famous for some reason that I'd already forgotten.

It had been fascinating at first. I'd press against the glass cases, reading the small tags for the various items. Alex and I took turns pointing out random artifacts to each other, but after an hour, the displays began to blur. Jamal had found that one of his apps had a behind-the-scenes story for almost *every* object. There was simply too much: it was like an antique-store version of an endless Ikea. A headache built up behind my eyes, as if my brain were trying to push its way out of my skull to escape the deluge of information. My feet dragged on the slick floor. The crumpled map in my hand showed that we still had a long way to go before we'd crossed off everything Tasha wanted us to see.

Alex turned around and noticed I wasn't right behind him. "You okay?"

"I'm not feeling very well," I admitted.

"You look a little pale." Sophie's eyebrows drew together in concern.

Alex steered me to a wooden bench in the middle of the room. "You want me to get you some water?"

"No, it's just a headache. I haven't slept great the past couple of nights."

That was an understatement. The nightmares I had about Connor kept jerking me wide-awake in the early dawn hours and then I wouldn't be able to fall back to sleep. Or I'd be pacing my room, not even sure if I was awake or sleepwalking.

"I've got some Tylenol." Sophie dug through her bag, handing items from it to Jamal so she could search better.

Jamal looked down at the pile of things growing in his hands. "Is there anything you don't have with you?"

Sophie looked up. "Nope, I've got pretty much everything covered. I've also got some Band-Aids, and Gravol if you feel a bit pukey." She hunted a bit further and then pulled out a tiny bottle of Tylenol. "Bingo."

I took the pills from her. "Thanks."

"Well, you know what the British think: a cup of tea can fix just about anything. Go down to the café and grab a cup, and we'll meet up with you there after we cross all this off." Alex held up the work sheet where we initialed each item we'd seen.

"Are you sure? You'll be stuck doing the rest of it."

"How often does someone with my build get to be a hero?" He motioned to his thin frame. "Plus, then you'll be grateful and feel like you owe me something." He wiggled his eyebrows and I laughed, feeling my cheeks heat up.

Jamal barked out a laugh and high-fived Alex. "Nicely done, man."

Sophie shook her head, dumping everything back into her bag. "Tea *is* good for a headache—it's the caffeine." She motioned toward the exit. "I'll make sure we don't leave without you."

"Go on, go get some tea, feel better," Alex said.

"If you're really sure," I said, already standing.

"Stop trying to keep me from being gallant."

I squeezed his hand in thanks, waved to Jamal and Sophie, then wound my way back to the main floor. I paused in the door of the café. I'd expected a sterile cafeteria, but the space was opulent, like an extra room in *Downton Abbey*. Decorated pillars held up the impossibly tall Morris-tiled ceiling with a bank of stained-glass windows at the back.

The hostess found a small table for me near the wall and I ordered a cup of Earl Grey tea and a scone. I pressed my hands to the cool white marble tabletop, feeling the tension in my neck leaking away.

This was exactly the kind of place I usually disliked. I took after my dad, having inherited his desire for clean, streamlined spaces, zero clutter, everything with a purpose. One of my favorite places was the school lab. I liked the chemical smell, vaguely metallic and sulfuric.

My mom was the opposite. She described her style as "Parisian distressed chic," which near as I could tell was shorthand for an overabundance of shit. She loved piles and piles of throw pillows with scratchy fabrics and trim—and beads.

She had collections of things squatting on tables and bookshelves: glass bottles in different shades of pink, tiny ceramic birds, vases, vintage cameras, and absolutely everything that was breakable. I moved through my own home on high alert. I had a constant phobia of bumping into a spindly table and sending a display of fragile teacups to the floor, which, given my coordination (or lack thereof), wasn't unlikely.

This was different. The café was an explosion of color and light. Everything in it had a purpose, but also existed to be beautiful. The tall ceiling, for example, not only let in light but also made it feel easier to breathe. The couple seated next to me got up, leaving their copy of the *Times* at the table. Once they were gone, I nabbed it before the waitress could throw it away.

I felt my limbs loosen in pleasure. The beautiful room, the hot tea and not-too-sweet scone, and now a paper. I've always loved newspapers. I know almost no one reads them anymore, and there's no doubt that it's easier to find what you want online, but there's something special about newspapers. The smell of the ink and the thinness of the paper make the stories seem more vulnerable, but because they are a real physical thing, and not pixels on a screen, they are also more permanent. I chalked up my old-fashioned affection to the fact that my dad also loved newspapers. On the weekends, he got both the *Globe and Mail* and the *New York Times*. He'd leave sections scattered around the house, Business folded up on the kitchen table, the Arts section by the sofa in the living room, and the Book Review — his favorite — by his bedside. My mom was always trying to get him to subscribe to the digital versions, but he said he didn't know what he wanted to read until he turned the page.

I sipped the tea, breathing in the steamy bergamot. The rest of the café drifted away as I skimmed stories on everything from farming subsidies in East Anglia and EU policy on immigration to a recipe for roasted beets and a biography piece on a British film star I had never heard of. The sheer pleasure of the moment — not needing to be anywhere, the heat of the tea seeping through the china, and allowing the words to drift me along — was perfect. The black newsprint marched across my vision, tidy lines of information like a military parade flowing through my head. I broke off small pieces of the crumbly scone, liberally coated in thick cream and raspberry jam, and popped them into my mouth. My headache had slipped away. I felt myself pulling together at last, the loose threads tightening back into place.

That's when I saw it.

It was a small article. Hardly more than an inch or two buried deep in the first section: POLICE SEEK INFORMATION ON DISTRICT LINE DEATH.

It took me a beat to realize that the death they were discussing had to be Connor's, based on the date and location. They didn't use his name in the article; they called him a tourist.

Accidents happened all the time in the Tube. This one merited an article because the police had seen something on the CCTV camera. The direction of the camera meant they hadn't had a clear shot, but according to the paper: "The victim suddenly lurched forward in front of the train, falling headfirst, despite the fact that it appears he'd been standing still prior to the fall. The angle of his fall, combined with the speed, indicates that there is the possibility he may have been pushed. Authorities are requesting any witnesses to come forward so they can determine if this was an accident."

The headache that had drifted away slammed back. It was like being hit with a metal baseball bat across the forehead.

I glanced around, expecting people in the café to be staring at me with horror and disgust, but no one seemed to notice me at all. I carefully tore the small article out of the paper, wincing at the ripping sound.

I'd known it deep down all along.

Connor had been murdered.

I didn't say anything about the article to Alex or the others when they came to meet me. Alex wolfed down the last few bites of raspberry scone I hadn't been able to finish. My stomach had atrophied into a tiny tight ball, and the sense of peace I'd had for just a moment had exploded. How long until everyone knew Connor may have been pushed? It was possible the police were already back at Metford asking more questions. I was going to have to tell them about Nicki this time, but they'd want to know why I hadn't said anything before.

I thought back through what Miriam had said and tried to fit it in with this new information. She couldn't have done anything to Connor. I'd seen her for myself; she'd been at the very back of the platform with Sophie when it happened. But if she knew about our breakup, there was the chance she might think I had something to do with Connor's death. Perhaps she thought she was protecting me.

I trudged back to the residence with our group. The weather was perfect — sunny, but with a light breeze. It put everyone in a great mood. Sophie and Jamal decided to go into Kensington Park and rent bikes while Kendra and Jazmin were going to head to Oxford Street for shopping. I begged off, pleading my headache. Alex offered to come back to my room with me, but I told him to go biking with Sophie and Jamal. I needed to be alone to figure out what to do.

Maybe I should call my parents and tell them exactly what had happened. This was murder, after all, and I might need a lawyer. You hear stories all the time about people getting blamed for crimes. There was that girl in Italy a few years ago — they sent her to prison. Then when that missing girl in Michigan was found dead, everyone thought it was her boyfriend until a psychic figured out it was her dad. Someone who was innocent could seem guilty in the wrong light. My brain was whirring in circles without alighting on any one path.

I fired off a phone call to Miriam, but she wasn't picking up. I walked toward the central staircase in the lobby before I realized one of the front desk girls was calling my name. She waved a white envelope over her head like a flag. "This was in your mailbox."

I took the envelope. The paper was thick. It felt expensive, as if I'd been issued an invitation from Buckingham Palace. I turned the envelope over in my hands. It was blank—there was no return address or anything.

I slid my thumbnail under the flap, tearing it open. A small scrap of newspaper slid out. My hand reached down into my jean pocket. The article I'd ripped out in the café was still there, crinkling under my fingers. I knew it hadn't leaped from my pocket to the envelope, like a magical ball disappearing from one hand to appear a second later in the other, but here was another copy of the same article. This one not torn out, but clipped with sharp straight lines from the paper.

There was a strange rushing in my ears, as though I were under water listening to waves crash against the shore. There was a message scribbled in red ink across the paper.

You're Welcome

I ripped the paper into smaller and smaller pieces until there was just a sprinkle of black and white confetti on the floor, trying to obliterate the words and what they meant. The clerk behind the desk was saying something, but her voice sounded like a high whine.

Someone took my elbow, his face too close. His mouth moved too, but I couldn't hear him at all, though I could smell the onions on his breath.

I wanted to explain that I was fine and for him to leave me alone, but black dots rushed around the edges of my vision and then there was nothing.

THIRTEEN

AUGUST 20
11 DAYS REMAINING

A pile of candy bars rained down onto my bed, thanks to Alex.

"I brought you basically one of everything. There's a Dairy Milk, Lion, Galaxy Caramel, Crunchie, and something called a Wispa, which looks weird to me, but the clerk swears by it. And if you're not feeling chocolate, I also got wine gums and some kind of toffee."

I picked through the pile and went for the Dairy Milk. I peeled back the wrapper and broke off a piece, letting the chocolate melt in my mouth. "Thanks," I mumbled. I motioned toward the candy and Alex grabbed the Wispa.

"I figured you could use the sugar. Is Tasha going to arrange for you to see a doctor?"

I shook my head. "It was my own fault. I wasn't feeling well and I didn't eat."

Alex raised his eyebrows. He'd seen me chow down on a bowl of yogurt and granola this morning.

"Look at this." I passed Alex the article I'd torn from the paper.

He read it quickly. "The police think someone might have pushed Connor in front of the train?"

I nodded.

"Damn." Alex stared down at the paper.

I swallowed. "The thing is, someone sent that to me." I didn't mention the note she'd left on the copy I destroyed. That message required too much explanation.

"I don't get it."

"Someone left that for me." I picked at my thumb, whittling the nail down. "It was in my mailbox in an envelope. No name or return address or anything."

"That's messed up." Alex dropped the paper as if it were poison. "Did they send it to anyone else in our group?"

I shook my head rapidly. I hadn't checked, but I knew I was the only one.

"Why would they leave it for you?"

"I used to go out with him." My hands twisted in the bedcovers.

Alex blinked. "You dated Connor?"

"Remember when I told you that someone broke my heart before I came here?"

Alex glanced toward my door and then shut it before

sinking down onto my bed. "I thought he was going out with Miriam?"

"He was. He and I . . ." How did I even begin to explain how things had gone down? "When we stopped seeing each other, he started going out with her." I sighed.

Alex motioned toward the paper on my bed. "So, is this person trying to make some kind of connection between you and the accident because you went out with him?"

I nodded. "I think so, or maybe that they're the one who did it." I held my breath waiting for his reaction.

"If you think that, you've got to go to the cops."

"I can't. I didn't tell them I dated Connor when they came to ask questions. They're going to think it's weird I lied."

"Why didn't you tell them?"

I felt myself deflate. "I don't know. Connor acted like we didn't know each other on this trip, so in some ways it was easier to pretend we didn't." I glanced over at Alex, trying to explain. I stood up and started pacing.

"At first I thought I couldn't breathe without him in my life. But things between us were never right and we broke up. Once I was here, I realized that I could get over him, but then he died, and I felt like shit, like with all those bad thoughts I had *wished* him out in front of the train, and did you see him? Jesus, Alex, that train, it ripped him apart. I saw him — his arm was hanging on by this strip of flesh, his leg was off all together, and parts of his insides were all —"

Alex grabbed me by the shoulders and I realized I was sobbing. "Hey, hey, take it easy. Take a deep breath."

"I can't . . . I—"

"Shhh." He pulled me close to his chest. He smelled clean, like soap and cotton warm from a dryer. His arms were wiry and strong. I inhaled his scent and felt my heart slow. "It's going to be okay." His voice flowed over me like smooth honey.

My head pressed against Alex's chest, his heart coming through to me like a muffled bass drum. I matched my breathing to his. We stood that way in the middle of my room for what felt like hours.

"Better?" he asked softly.

"Yeah."

"Okay." He pulled me down so I was sitting next to him on the bed. "We're going to figure this out."

My heart flip-flopped. He'd said *we* would figure it out. Together. We. "What do we do?"

"We don't freak out. We've been assuming this person sent you this for a bad reason, but maybe they just wanted you to know."

I sucked in a breath. "I have an idea who it might be. I met this girl on the plane. She's from here. I told her all about Connor." The only other person I could think of in all of England who even knew I had been with Connor was Miriam, and why would she send me this, when she could just come see me or return my call if she wanted to tell me something?

Besides, I knew Miriam hadn't sent me this article. I just knew.

Alex nodded. "That's a place for us to start. What's her name?"

"Nicki. I don't know her last name or where she lives or anything." I motioned toward the window. "It's not exactly going to be easy to narrow it down in this city."

"We'll think of something."

"You said your mom worked for the airline, right?" I picked at the duvet cover, not meeting his eyes.

"Yeah."

My words came out in a rush. "She could pull a list of who was on the flight, couldn't she? I can't believe there would be a bunch of people named Nicki on it. If she got us a last name, it gives us something to go on. We could check her out, and then if something about her is weird, or if she sent the article for a bad reason, we can take what we know to the cops."

Alex was shaking his head before I'd even finished talking. "No way. My mom, the airline . . . that stuff is super private. You can't just ask for a list of people."

"All we need is her last name, not her credit card information or anything."

"We'll find another way." He ran his hands through his hair. "Look, even the police have to get all kinds of special clearance to get a passenger manifest—my mom's not going to break that rule for you."

I bit my lip. "But she'd get it for you."

He looked away.

"I have to do something. I can't go to the police with nothing. All they're going to hear is that I used to date him, that I was on that same train platform, and that I admitted he broke my heart weeks ago. No way will they think I got over him. They're going to think I did it. They'll lock me up and consider the case closed." I couldn't tell Alex all of it, that if the police knew *everything,* they'd have even more reasons to point fingers in my direction.

Alex shifted uncomfortably. "I get why you're freaked out, but I don't know. This is a stretch. I don't see what this Nicki girl has to do with Connor's death."

"You could tell your mom you met Nicki and liked her, that you want her name so you can find her."

He rolled his eyes. "First off, no way my mom is buying that story. I'm not the kind of guy who starts chatting up girls on a plane. Second, even if she did buy the story, she isn't going to give me someone's name so I can go all creepy stalker on some passenger on the flight."

Hot tears streamed down my face. Alex leaped up and brought back the box of Kleenex from the desk. "Don't cry," he pleaded. I wasn't sad—I was frustrated—but I didn't know how to explain it. Alex groaned. "Hey, it's going to be okay. I'll think of something to tell my mom so I can ask her."

I threw my arms around him. The hug that started with a rush of gratitude began to feel like something else. Charged, an awareness of each of our bodies, every sliver of space that they touched lit up with neon light. At the same moment, we both sat back, suddenly aware that we were alone in my room.

Alex stood up, digging his thumbs into a seam on his jeans. "Have some candy and take a nap or something. I'll email my mom and see what I can do."

"I really appreciate it."

He blushed. "No problem."

But it was a problem. I knew he didn't want to ask her, that he was doing it just for me. That both thrilled me and made me sad. I linked pinkie fingers with him. "Thanks," I said.

Alex leaned in and kissed me quickly on the side of the mouth. It could have been just a friendly thing, but we both knew it wasn't. It was more than that; it held a zap of connection, like a completed electrical circuit. We stared at each other, the air between us crackling with energy. I wanted to step forward into the space between us and pull his head to mine, this time to kiss him properly, but I was scared. "Okay. See you later," he finally said.

I nodded and he backed out of the room.

"Later," I repeated. I closed the door behind him and leaned against it.

I was going to find Nicki. It was going to be okay. She would tell me she had nothing to do with this. Miriam would call me back and say she hadn't meant anything, she'd just been upset. I checked my phone, but there was still nothing from her. I felt a flash of annoyance but forced myself to take a deep breath. All of this would go away, leaving me and Alex alone. Together.

FOURTEEN

I fished through the bin of scarves. I wasn't the kind of person who was known for wearing accessories, but the colors had caught my eye—really, everything in Covent Garden was designed to attract attention. Our group had split up, with everyone weaving between the aisles, checking out everything from clothing to handmade chocolates. Each stall was different from the one before, populated by people calling for your attention. Tasha had tried to get everyone interested in the history of the place, but we were more intrigued by the jewelry stalls than her stories about Henry the VIII stealing the land from the church, or how the area used to be a seedy red-light district. She gave up and told us to meet back at the entrance in an hour.

"Three fer price of two," the woman running the scarf stall said to me. "I get 'em from India, mostly. Here, let me." She rummaged around and pulled out one with swirling turquoise, blue, and green paisley. "This would go with your skin tone."

I took it from her fingers and held it up next to my face, considering it in the tiny mirror she'd suspended from wires on the side of the stall. The scarf did look nice.

"Lean in." She reached over and with a few quick movements had it tied around my neck. "There you go, right as roses. Make you a deal for one, just a fiver."

I glanced at my reflection. I looked different. Older, maybe. Vaguely French. The trip was changing me. I'd come for the wrong reasons, but despite everything it seemed as though the trip was turning into exactly what I needed.

"I'll take it." I handed over some cash, patting the scarf around my neck.

"I have to talk to you." Alex appeared beside me. He grabbed my elbow and began leading me away. He waved off the offer of a receipt from the clerk.

"I wanted her to show me how to tie this," I said, but he'd already guided me toward a hallway that led to the bathrooms.

A group of senior tourists, all wearing HI, MY NAME IS . . . nametags, passed us, and Alex paused until they were gone.

"I heard back from my mom."

I waited for him to say more, but he was silent, arms crossed over his chest. His bony elbows made sharp triangles in his sweatshirt. My stomach shifted uneasily. "Was she mad that you asked for Nicki's last name?"

"No. I mean, sorta, but that's not the problem. I don't know how to tell you this."

My gut went into free fall. "Just tell me."

"There was no one named Nicki on the flight," Alex said softly.

I blinked, trying to make sense of what he'd said. Of course Nicki had been on the flight. "Maybe Nicki is short for something," I suggested.

"There was no Nicole, or Nicola, or Colette, Nikol, Nykia, Niko, Niks." Alex listed off the names in a flat monotone. "There was no single female traveler on the plane with any *N* name."

"But that's not possible," I protested. I hadn't *imagined* her.

"I don't know what to say," he said.

"That's the name she gave me," I insisted, feeling prickles of panic. She had been there.

It felt as if my brain were spinning on a hamster wheel, going faster and faster. I hadn't told him the details about my conversation with Nicki about Connor. I had no idea how to bring up the subject. What would he think of me if he knew I had said that stuff, even as a joke? I seized on the only evidence I had. "What about the newspaper clipping? Why would she send me that?

"I was thinking about it," Alex said. He wouldn't meet my gaze. "Maybe this has nothing to do with the girl on the plane. Is there a chance it was just random? I mean, nothing was written on the envelope or anything. So maybe someone at Metford saw the article and meant to put it in Tasha's box, but it ended up in yours instead. You've been assuming the two things are connected, but maybe they're not."

I stared at him in disbelief. "I didn't make this up," I said. I wished I hadn't destroyed the copy she'd written on, that would show definitively that meeting her and the article were connected, but then he'd want an explanation of what the message meant. But the article with her note had been real. I remembered tearing it into a million pieces.

"I wasn't saying that you did," Alex rushed to explain. "She totally could have sent the note, but maybe it's just a coincidence. If she did send it, that's some pretty whacked-out shit."

"Yeah." I wasn't sure what was worse, that he thought I was cracking apart and delusional or that I was being trailed by a psycho.

"I think we should talk to Tasha about your worries. She'll know what to do."

I leaned forward. "No. Absolutely not."

"C'mon, Tasha seems pretty cool! If nothing else, she can get the clerks at Metford to keep an eye out for this Nicki girl. If she did drop off a clipping and she's crazy, you don't want her wandering around Metford. That place is easy as hell to break into. The only security they have is that one guard who is possibly older than this place. You can pop the locks for the rooms with a credit card, for crying out loud."

"Or Tasha might tell the police about me dating Connor. No way. I don't want to be dragged into that investigation."

"You're not going to be dragged into anything. Anyone who meets you for ten minutes is going to know you wouldn't hurt anyone."

I forced a smile on my face, but it felt plastic and fake. He didn't know the full story. "I know, but maybe you're right. It might just be a coincidence that the article showed up. Before we make a move, let's see if anything else happens first."

Alex shifted uneasily. "Are you sure?"

"Totally," I said with confidence I didn't feel. "Hey, I'm going to grab a souvenir to bring back to my grandma. Will you run ahead and tell Tasha I'll meet up with you guys later? I want to stay and look around longer."

Alex hesitated. "Are you sure?" he asked again.

I nodded enthusiastically and gave him a joking push. "Go on, I'll catch up with you in a little bit." I waited until he melted into the crowd before I slumped against the cinder-block wall. The cold seeped through my T-shirt. I needed to think. I placed my palms against the wall as if I were holding on to reality and without it I might float away.

I closed my eyes tightly. I hadn't made up Nicki, or screwed up her name. That's what she'd called herself. I had sat next to her. We drank that vodka together—she wasn't some elaborate manifestation of my imagination. She was real. She'd killed Connor and she'd sent me that note to make sure I knew it.

I was nearly panting. I focused on slowing my breathing

down so I didn't end up having a panic attack. The knot of the scarf had grown tighter. Now it was less of an accessory and more of a noose. My fingers yanked at the fabric for relief, and once the knot was looser I inhaled a greedy breath.

I tried to look at the positive side of the situation. If I'd gone to the police first and they were the ones to discover there had been no Nicki on the flight, it would have been worse. The cops would have thought I was lying and that would make them wonder what I was up to, especially when they heard about my past. Alex might imagine no one would suspect me of anything, but that's because he was a nice person.

Maybe I should go home. Call my parents and tell them I'd changed my mind. If I left London, Nicki couldn't do anything to me. I turned the idea over in my head, debating my options. My phone rang. I went to click it off, but the display showed Miriam's name.

"We have to talk," she said, not bothering with a hello.

I cut her off before she could say more. "Not on the phone. Tell me where to meet you."

She was silent for a beat. "I'll text you the address. Meet me in the lobby."

The Ampersand Hotel was in Kensington, not far from Metford House but about one million times nicer. There was a doorman who swept the door open in front of me as if it were magic. The lobby was done in cool gray and white tones. The furniture, wallpaper, and crisply dressed front desk staff all oozed money and opulence.

Miriam stood as soon as I came in and walked past me. "Follow me downstairs — they've got a place we can talk."

I trailed after her down the winding staircase. There was a hall leading to a restaurant, but she turned so we were in an empty office center where guests could print out documents and get a bit of work done.

Miriam put her hands on her hips, as if she were irritated with me, but I could see something different in her eyes. She looked scared. "We need to talk."

"What did you mean the other day when you said he didn't deserve me?"

She sighed. "It's nothing top-secret. I meant that Connor is a dick . . . was a dick." Her voice cracked. "I didn't want you to feel bad about what happened to him."

"If he was such a dick, why did you date him?" I asked.

She wouldn't meet my eyes. "I don't want to get into all of this."

I lightly touched her elbow. "I need to know." Now my voice cracked.

Miriam's hands twisted in front of her. "I was only pretending to be his girlfriend."

"What?"

She sighed. "Look, Connor went out with a friend of mine at another school, and then after they broke up, he sent naked pictures of her to everyone. Then I heard about what he did to you from a guy I know who is in his crowd. I checked around. He does this stuff all the time, treats girls like they're a joke. You're lucky he didn't have pics of you on his phone, because if he did, they'd be spread all over the Internet."

Goose bumps prickled over my skin, and they had nothing to do with the blasting air conditioner. In fact, Connor had begged me to let him take pictures. It was only my own insecurity that had kept me from saying yes.

"I decided to get him back," Miriam said, her voice soft and low.

I sucked in a breath. "You killed him?"

Her eyes went wide. "What? No! I let him think I liked him. I kept stringing him along, telling him I didn't feel 'safe' for us to be intimate but that he could show me he was someone I could trust. If he let me get pictures of him first."

"And he fell for that?"

Miriam shrugged. "I'm an actress." Then her tough-guy stance broke and she started to cry. "It wasn't supposed to be like this. I just wanted to teach him a lesson. I told him that morning that this time he was the one who got played. I might have made it sound like I would post his naked pictures." She paused, biting her lip. "I wouldn't really have done it. It was just a threat, something that could keep him from doing this to anyone else, to make *him* scared for a change."

"He really treated all the girls he dated that badly?" Her

whole scheme — pretending to like him, getting pictures, then blackmailing him — I don't know, it seemed so over-the-top. But then, Miriam was over-the-top. This was so perfectly something she would do.

"He broke my friend's heart. *Humiliated* her. I did it for her. I thought she'd find this funny when I told her, you know? Something we could laugh about. I had no idea he'd jump in front of a train." Her lip shook.

"There's a chance Connor was pushed," I said slowly. I didn't like to see Miriam blaming herself when I knew deep down his death had nothing to do with her.

She stared at me, astonished. "Are you sure?"

"I'm not sure of anything, but there was mention of it in the paper. Camera footage or something that makes it seem like a possibility."

"I wonder if he did something shitty to someone over here?" Miriam asked herself. She peered out into the hallway as if she thought we might have been followed. "I wouldn't put it past him to have been sneaking around on me with some British girl. Maybe she took things into her own hands." Miriam's eyes were wide.

Ideas tumbled around in my head. Connor was a player, but we hadn't been in England that long when he died. Would he have had time to meet and seduce some British girl? But on the other hand, Nicki *had* been visiting Vancouver. Miriam thought there was a chance Connor had met a British girl here, but maybe he'd met her back home before he ever left the country. It was possible Nicki had picked me out at the airport because she already knew who I was and my connection to Connor. She'd acted as if she was mad at Connor because of what he'd done to me, but it might be that it was about how he'd treated her. She might have had her own motive to murder.

If he had treated Nicki badly, then perhaps she sent me the note as a confession. I'd taken it as some kind of threat, but maybe she was reaching out for help. She thought I would understand after what he'd done to me. If she was desperate, then I couldn't just leave her. Maybe I could convince her to go to the police. If he'd threatened to show pictures of her, then there would be extenuating circumstances. She needed to know that we weren't the only two he'd treated like dirt.

"I'm sorry I didn't return your calls right away. I was try-ing to figure out what to do," Miriam said, breaking into my thoughts. "The police want to meet with me one more time tomorrow and then my parents and I are flying home. I'm going to tell them the truth about what I did. Faking it to Con-nor, I mean. I wasn't sure if you wanted to come with me and say what happened to you. If you don't, that's okay too." She'd wrapped her arms around herself, and she looked so small, like a lost elementary school student.

"No. I think it's a bad idea. Listen, just keep to the story that you told the police, that you decided to break up because you wanted to be friends or whatever. There's nothing to be gained by telling them the truth—it just confuses things. You didn't do anything," I reminded her. "You were way back on the platform. Sophie will back you up. Stick with your story and let me handle it."

"But what if there is some British girl that pushed him? It doesn't seem fair to leave this all on you."

"I don't think Connor had time to meet some British girl. You were always together."

Miriam chewed on her lower lip. "I guess."

I had no idea how long Nicki had been in Vancouver before I met her at the airport. They could have met, could have had plenty of time to have a relationship. "You know if you talk to the police it's just going to complicate things, and you don't need that."

"Still. I feel like I should."

The desire to tell her what was going on was like an explosive pressure inside of me. Miriam was smart—maybe she could help me figure it out, but I always did that, let other people take charge. "I'll be fine. I'm almost sure it was an accident. What you did had nothing to do with what happened."

"Are you sure?"

I channeled what my mom would say. "You did something where you have regrets, but that means it's a learning opportunity."

Miriam nodded, her eyes watery with tears. "God, I've learned so much."

I hugged her. We hadn't been friends before, but now I felt connected to her after all of this. "Me too." I glanced down at my phone. I knew I should go. I needed to meet up with Alex and the rest of the group. Miriam hugged me again and then practically skipped out of the room. I could see she was already feeling lighter. She'd wanted someone to tell her that she didn't have to confess to the cops and I had given her that. She was free.

Then the answer of what to do next came to me in a whoosh and I almost fell back into my chair. I'd been so worried about how to find Nicki, but I'd been focusing on the wrong thing. It was like writing software. You can think the problem is one thing and spend hours trying to fix it, before you realize the real problem is several lines of code up. Fix that and everything else falls into place. I didn't need to find Nicki — she would find me. And I already had an idea on how to encourage her to do it sooner rather than later.

But I needed to figure out what I would do when she showed up.

FIFTEEN

AUGUST 22
9 DAYS REMAINING

I snapped another shot of Trafalgar Square, trying to get the huge column in the center of the photo, and then glanced around. The place was thick with tourists despite the wind whipping around, swirling up tiny tornadoes of loose trash. I tapped the arm of a Japanese tourist and held my phone up, miming in an exaggerated fashion that I wanted him to take a picture of me.

"Sure—where do you want to stand?" he asked in perfect English, making me feel instantly embarrassed. I wished I could have taken the picture myself, but I was there alone and needed enough background that you could easily tell where I was. That was my plan: upload the pic to Instagram and hit the location tag. The square was iconic and situated almost in the center of the city.

If Nicki wanted to find me, I couldn't have made it any easier, short of holding up a giant sign with an arrow pointing directly to me. Especially since I'd taken every privacy setting off all my social media accounts. If my mom found out, she'd have a cow. She saw me as exactly the kind of person who would fall for some Internet catfish and end up in a teen sex slave ring. But it wasn't some online fake Romeo I was trying to attract. If Nicki was looking for me, she'd have no trouble now.

"Can you get me with that?" I passed the tourist my phone and struck a pose in front of one of the four large metal lion statues that circled Nelson's Column. I didn't bother to clamber onto one of their backs the way other people did. This wasn't about capturing the perfect vacation moment.

Once I had the picture, I posted it, not bothering to doctor it up with filters, and added the caption: *loviN quICKIe visit to trafalgar :)*. Hopefully, the heading would draw Nicki to me. The capital letters spelled out her name, and I was counting on the idea that the smiley face would let her know I didn't mean her any harm. It struck me that with her love of puzzles, she'd spot the clue right away, but it wouldn't stand out to anyone else. It's not as if social media posts are known for great spelling and grammar.

I jammed my hands into my pockets and paced the large square, scanning faces as I went. This had to work. I had no other way to reach her.

I walked around for more than two hours, checking my phone for the time every few minutes. Nothing. There was no way to know if she'd even seen my post, or been too busy to come, or felt like leaving me to hang a bit longer simply to prove that she was in control. I had to decide how much time I was going to give this plan before I acknowledged it hadn't worked and I had wasted the whole day. I could tell that people in my Student Scholars group thought it was weird I didn't want to hang out with them. I couldn't keep slipping off to do my own thing.

A woman wandered around, offering to read people's palms. Her teeth were stained — they looked like antique piano keys — and her hair hung in greasy strands. I watched her closely. I was pretty sure she was using the excuse of wanting to tell people's fortunes to get close enough to pick their pockets. I wished she did have psychic abilities. Then I could ask her what to do about Nicki.

Eventually I plopped down onto the cement stairs that led to the National Gallery, sitting alone in the crowd of people who had also stopped to sip a coffee, relax, or wolf down a snack. I scrolled through my phone to look busy. I'd have to try something else. Maybe I'd put up a post about where I planned to visit tomorrow.

A text popped up from Alex: Want to grab some Thai?

I fidgeted. I didn't know how long this quest to find Nicki would take. Busy now, maybe later?

I hit send and hoped he wouldn't think I was blowing him off. I could tell he was worried. I'd caught him this morning at breakfast looking at how I'd picked at my fingernails.

Meet you at Thai place at 4. Everything okay?

Just checking some stuff out.

This isn't about that girl, is it?

I chewed my lip. I wasn't sure how to answer. I didn't want to lie to him. At least not any more than I already had.

Did she contact you again? Then less than a second later: Kim? Tell me you're not trying to find some weirdo stranger you met on a plane.

Don't worry, everything's okay, I texted.

Hands slapped over my eyes. "Guess who?"

I choked off a scream and rocketed up from my position, almost dropping my phone. *Had she seen what Alex had written?*

Nicki laughed, throwing her head back. "You should see your face."

"You came," I said.

"Of course I did—you invited me." She held up her phone, wiggling it back and forth inches from my nose.

"You sent me that note." I'd planned for my voice to come out stern, but it wobbled. "I need to know what you want."

She nodded. "Let's go get something to drink and sit down where it's not so hot. I can't sit in the sun. I burn too easily.

There's a cute place just a block or so away." She headed off without waiting to see if I followed.

Nicki wound her way through the crowds on the sidewalk. Most people in the square were wearing shorts and T-shirts with sneakers — perfect for sightseeing. Nicki had on a loose black boho dress, gladiator sandals, and giant sunglasses. She was like a different creature from the rest of us. I hated myself for admiring her.

She turned down a street and ducked into a pub. I caught the sign above the door: MR. FOGG'S GIN PARLOUR.

When I stepped inside, it took a second for my eyes to adjust to the dim light. The wait staff were dressed up like they were on a break from a steampunk cosplay event. Every inch of the walls was covered in Victorian-style flags and knickknacks. I felt off balance, as if I'd wandered into a Disney film. I half expected to see an animated character behind the bar mixing drinks — maybe a toad with a cravat and a pocket watch. Nicki had already swooped in and nabbed a table from a couple who had gotten up. She waved me over.

"Two gin and tonics," Nicki said to the waiter, who glided up just as I dropped into the seat.

He touched the brim of his top hat. "Any preference on gin?" Nicki glanced at me, but realizing I didn't have a clue, she answered. "We'll take Monkey Forty-seven." She turned back to me. "It's my favorite."

"Nice choice." The waiter gave us a crooked smile, making his waxed handlebar mustache tilt. "We've got steak and kidney pie on special."

I wrinkled up my nose at the idea of eating kidneys. "No thanks," I said. He tipped his top hat at us and then moved off.

Nicki pushed the tiny glass bowl of nuts toward me. "Want one?"

I shook my head. "Why are we here?" I asked.

She glanced around as if half-surprised to find us wedged into the corner table. "I like this place. Besides, it's loud — no one's going to pay us a bit of attention and we can chat." She leaned in. "Plus, no extra eyes." Her glance darted up to the ceiling. "So many of the corporate pubs have security cameras now. It's almost impossible to walk around this city without being recorded. They keep making it harder and harder to be sneaky."

"Were you sneaking around with Connor?"

Her right eyebrow arched. "Beg your pardon?"

"Did you and Connor go out? Back in Vancouver? I know he was seeing a British girl." I crossed my fingers under the table and hoped she wouldn't realize that I was bluffing. I needed to come across as stern, get her to admit what she'd done so we could figure out what to do next.

Nicki gave a dismissive sniff. "He may have dated someone, but I can assure you, it wasn't me."

I searched her face, trying to tell if she was lying. "Your name isn't Nicki."

Her face broke into a huge smile as if I'd just told her she could have a pony for her birthday. "Clever girl! Well done, you. How'd you figure that out?"

"There was no one on the plane with that name." I realized I was sitting at the very edge of the wooden seat and slid back. I needed to give the appearance that I was under control. "I checked."

Nicki nodded at the waiter, who placed our drinks down and disappeared. She took a sip, pulling out the sprig of rosemary that had been placed inside and sucking on the end. "Lovely. Gin is all about the botanicals, you know. Change them up and there's a completely different flavor. This brand has won all sorts of awards."

"I don't give a shit about the gin," I snapped, blowing my effort to look relaxed.

She raised one eyebrow as if I'd disappointed her, as though I were a puppy who'd peed on her floor. "I'm simply trying to introduce you to something new. That's what you said you wanted. Tackle fears, experience new things. Isn't that the point of travel, after all? Meeting people, expanding your horizons." She waved her hands to encompass the bar, then leaned forward. "Now, tell me, however did you get the plane manifest? What are privacy laws for if they're passing that kind of information around?"

"I know someone at the airline." I didn't mention Alex's name. I didn't want Nicki to know who he was.

She nodded slowly. "My father always used to say: 'Never underestimate the value of a good network.' Being able to call on the right people makes all the difference."

"So, what's your real name?"

"Does it matter?"

I took a sip of the drink to have something to do with my hands. The mix of spice, pine, and bitter washed over my palate. The cocktail tasted strong, like what it might be like to suck on a car air freshener. "It matters to me."

"Names are weird, aren't they? They define a person. I mean, if you hear that a girl's named Gertrude, you get a picture in your mind of what she's like, don't you? Much different than a Penelope. So, given how important names are, isn't it rather silly that your parents choose them? You're basically an unformed blob when you're born. They select a name based on who they want you to be, not what fits you. It seems to me that a person should get to pick their own name once they reach something like fourteen or sixteen. You know who you are at that point. I always saw myself as a Nicki, much more than what my parents came up with." She took another drink, the ice tinkling against the glass. "You're another perfect example. I wouldn't picture you as a Kim. Too pretty, not serious enough for you. Kimberly." She drew out my name, somehow managing to fill it with extra syllables.

I'd never liked my name either, but I didn't want to give Nicki the satisfaction of knowing she was right. Kimberly had been my mom's favorite name and it didn't fit me at all. "What sort of name do you think suits me?"

Nicki clapped her hands. "Oooh, this is fun." She rubbed her chin, regarding me very carefully. "I think it should be a touch old-fashioned—you're an ancient soul. Not too girlie, but not butch, either. Irene, maybe." She shook her head, dismissing the idea as quickly as she'd said it, and then whacked her hand down onto the table, making our drinks jump. "I've got it. Ada." She waited for me to respond. "You know her, right? Ada Lovelace? She was a countess way back in the 1800s, a mathematician."

"I know who she was. She was one of the creators of Babbage's Analytical Engine."

Nicki nodded. "The first computer, when you think about it. How perfect is that for you?" She looked proud of herself. She cocked her head to the side. "Yes, you're definitely an Ada. I'd change your name if I were you. You'll be a completely different woman as an Ada." Her hands flitted through the air. "It will alter your entire destiny."

Meeting Nicki had changed my destiny enough already. "You still haven't told me your real name."

She sighed. "You're focused on the wrong things."

I lowered my voice. "And would the right thing be that you murdered Connor?"

"Of course not—that's already done and dealt with. No point in chatting up that topic."

I blinked.

Was she completely insane? I assumed she'd deny it, but she didn't. She acted as if it were no big deal, as if we were discussing what we'd had for lunch, or the score of a football game. There wasn't anything in her voice that hinted at panic or desperation. "Then what should I be focused on?"

"How you're going to kill my mother."

My ears began to ring and I could hear the rush of blood inside my head, drowning out the voices of the other people in the bar. "What did you say?"

"You owe me a murder."

I choked on my drink and put it down quickly.

She leaned back, regarding me. "Oh, come on, now, you're acting like we didn't have an agreement. Is that why you asked if I dated him? I told you, then there's no point—a person shouldn't have a motive. Don't you remember? You wanted to get rid of Connor, and I need to be rid of my mum."

"I *never* agreed to that."

Her hands were flat on the table as if we were having a business negotiation. She spoke slowly as though I were a small child. "Yes, you did. We had quite a nice long chat about the whole thing. It really is the perfect plan. You can't go and back out now that I've done my part. You *knew* this would happen."

What she was saying hit me. *Oh my god, this is all my fault.* I was having a hard time breathing; it was like sucking air through a tiny cocktail straw. My lower lip started to shake.

Nicki rolled her eyes. "Jesus, pull yourself together. You're disappointing me. I thought you and I were alike, that we *got* the way the world worked. The boy was a total waste. You're acting like I took out the Dalai Lama. I can assure you, the last thing the world needs is one more boring, self-entitled teen guy."

"How can you say that?" I shook my head rapidly as if I could toss her words out of my ears. "I'm nothing like you." I'd wanted to be like her when we met, how she was so confident and brave, but all of it was just a pretty, plastic veneer over her ugliness.

Nicki sighed and leaned back. "Check out the gentleman over there."

I turned slightly, catching the patron's reflection in the mirror above the bar. He was in his early thirties, with floppy brown hair that was supposed to look casual but probably took a lot of effort and expensive product to get that way. He was wearing a suit and what looked like a thick gold watch.

Nicki continued. "I'm guessing he works in finance—he's too well dressed for tech." She looked him up and down. "Family money too, I imagine. That suit is Savile Row."

"So what?"

"Do you remember the woman in the square? The one hustling for money, saying she could tell the future?"

"What does she have to do with anything?" I asked.

"Do you think she's worth the same as the guy at the bar?" Nicki leaned forward in her seat.

"She may not have the same amount of money, but of course she is."

Nicki picked out a cashew from the nut bowl and popped it into her mouth. "Really? What do you base that on? Tell me what she provides. Not tax dollars — I can guarantee she's not declaring what she makes or steals. She doesn't work in a job that helps people or moves the economy forward. She doesn't create art or music to lift the human spirit." Nicki scoffed. "Hell, she didn't even smell good."

The contents of my stomach rose up in revolt. "That's a disgusting thing to say about someone."

"No, that's the truth. Some people are simply more valuable to society. I'm not saying she's worthless, just that she's not worth *as much*. Pretending that everyone is the same so we can all feel better is foolish. We talked about this at the airport — about how we're smarter than other people. I thought you got it."

"Being smarter than someone else doesn't make us better." My passion wasn't about being politically correct, it was about what was right. Deciding some lives were worth more than others was . . . repulsive.

"Of course it does." She leaned forward again, elbows on the table. "Imagine you need to have surgery and the hospital offers you two doctors. One's a specialist with thirty years of experience and a degree from Harvard. The other is a new grad from some mail-order medical school and doesn't even has his zipper up when he comes out to meet you. Which doctor would you select?"

"This is stupid," I said.

"No, I'm making a point. You'd choose the experienced doctor, right?"

"Yes, but that's not the same thing as judging people by race or gender."

Nicki threw her head back in annoyance. "I don't give a fig whistle about race or gender — I'm talking about *value*. Connor was of very limited value — he was shallow, vain, and a wanker. And even if you don't want to admit it, the scientist in you knows it's fact. Some things are worth more, and so are some people. Deep down you think you're better."

"No, I don't." I pinched the bridge of my nose. "And even if I did, that doesn't mean you can just" — I made myself lower my voice — "kill someone you don't see as useful."

"Well, certainly not everyone. Just the ones in my way." Her voice was light, as if she were discussing a church social.

"Connor wasn't in your way!"

She pointed at me. "No, he was in yours. My mother's in my way, which brings us full circle to what we started to discuss. You owe me a murder." Nicki tucked her hair behind her ears, the curls springing free. "She drinks all the time — I think it will be fairly easy to make it look like an accident, but you need to pick a time when I have an airtight alibi. The police will look at me otherwise — I'm dripping with motive."

I pushed back from the table so quickly that the chair made a loud squealing protest. "I have to go to the bathroom." I bolted toward the back of the pub, following the tiny WC signs.

The door to the restroom banged open and I was relieved there was no one else inside. I bent over the toilet, certain I was going to puke, but nothing came up except sour spit. After a minute, I went to the sink and splashed cold water onto my face.

She was completely insane. I'd thought it was bad enough that she might have killed Connor to get back at him if he'd hurt her, but to kill him for no personal reason at all was sick.

I stood looking in the mirror, trying to figure out what I should do. I suddenly had the perfect idea. I'd get a photo of her, and then I could at least show it to Alex. Maybe that would prove that she existed, and we could somehow connect her to the newspaper article she had sent me.

I burst out of the bathroom and nearly plowed into a waitress carrying a large tray. I dodged around a group of people clustered at the bar, holding my phone out in front of me as if it were a stop sign, ready to snap the picture. Then I froze in place, my arm sinking slowly back down to my side.

Our table was empty except for our two drinks, the condensation on the glass puddling around them. My jacket still sat on the back of the chair, but Nicki was gone. I looked around, searching the faces of the packed pub, but she wasn't there.

"She took off," I said softly.

"Here you go." A waitress placed a bill down onto the table.

"Did you see the girl who was sitting here?"

She shrugged. "No, sorry."

I shoved past her so I could see the bar. "Where's the guy who was our waiter? Dark hair, mustache?"

"Simon? His shift's over. He left."

I wanted to grab her by the shoulder and shake her. "I need to talk to him." He'd seen Nicki — maybe he'd even overheard some of the stuff she'd said.

The waitress smirked. "Sorry, love, I happen to know he's got a bit on the side already."

"I don't want to *date* him — I have to ask him a question!"

She wiped her hands on her apron. "You can leave a note if you like, and next time he works, he'll get it."

I dropped into the seat. There was no point. "Never mind," I mumbled.

She tapped the bill on the table with her long fingernail. "You want another drink or would you like to settle up?"

Nicki had left me with the bill. The gin she'd chosen was expensive, too. I slapped bills onto the table. Of all the things I imagined spending my summer job savings on, this wasn't it. I had to be smarter next time we got together. I had to get proof so someone would believe me.

She'd be back. That was the one thing I was certain of — she felt I owed her. She wasn't going to give up, but neither was I.

SIXTEEN

AUGUST 22
9 DAYS REMAINING

My favorite computer teacher, Mr. Donald, always said when you've got a brutal math question, start with defining the problem.

I reminded myself of this as I sat on a park bench watching people stream past. This was by far the most complicated problem I'd ever had to solve. It wasn't exactly shocking that I felt overwhelmed, but if I was going to get out of this, I had to stop acting like some kind of drama queen and instead tackle this the same way I would a tricky math problem.

I'd picked the wrong person to sit next to on a flight. I wasn't a psychologist; I had no idea what the fancy term was for her diagnosis. It was enough to know she was clearly batshit crazy. She'd killed Connor and now expected me to murder her mother and seemed to have zero idea how insane all of that was.

I went through my options. The most obvious solution was

to go to the police, but I still wasn't convinced that they would believe me, versus thinking I was somehow messed up in Connor's death. If they poked around into my history, combined with finding out that Miriam had been blackmailing him for being a pig, I was going to look like a suspect. Miriam had been standing far away, but I was close enough to have done something, maybe on behalf of both of us. And unless Nicki confessed, there was nothing to connect her to me or Connor.

Going home seemed to be my best bet. I sent my mom an email asking her to check into tickets. I got a long email back almost immediately that could be summarized as *You can come home if you absolutely feel you have to, but I think it would be a mistake.* My hands twisted in my lap. I didn't know how to explain why I needed to come home so badly without disclosing everything. My mom already thought I was a screwup—if she knew the whole story, she'd be disappointed on a whole new level. She'd be thinking about how she'd never gotten herself messed up with a psycho when she was my age and how she knew my frozen zygote siblings likely wouldn't have done this either. I could already picture the blog titles: *What to Do When Your Child Befriends a Killer* and *When Your Kids Mess Up, It's Not Your Fault.*

I closed my email and toyed with the idea of setting up some kind of sting operation to capture Nicki. I'd arrange to meet her and get her to confess while I recorded the conversation. I played with the record function on my phone. Hmm. It might work. I'd take that to the cops and then they could go after her.

I'd have to lead her into saying something incriminating. She also might guess what I was up to, and if she discovered me recording her, it wasn't going to go well.

Then the solution popped into my head. It was so simple I didn't know why I hadn't seen it before. I laughed out loud and yelled, "Working the damn problem!" An elderly woman passing by gave me a worried look and crossed to the far side of the sidewalk. I didn't even care. I felt like skipping.

I'd been so worried about how to get Nicki to confess, but I was focused on the wrong thing. My issue wasn't what she'd already done, or that I had met her at all. My *real* problem was what she was trying to make me do. All I had to do was refuse.

No. I'm not going to murder your drunk mother. Fuck off.

What could she do if I refused? It's not as though there was a signed contract. She couldn't take me to court to force me to kill someone. And as long as I was careful to never be alone with her, she wouldn't physically attack me. She couldn't go to the police and say I hadn't kept my promise—she *was* guilty of a murder.

Hopefully she'd realize that I wasn't like her. Maybe she would just go away. Search out a fellow psycho who would do what she wanted. And if she did approach me again, I'd refuse. I couldn't change what she'd done to Connor, but at least I could keep the situation from getting worse.

I took the steps two at a time up to Metford's front door, feeling lighter than when I'd walked out hours before. I had just enough time to clean up before meeting Alex. I was hankering for some spring rolls.

I crashed back down to earth as soon as I entered the lobby. Tasha was sitting on the sofa with Alex, their faces both drawn and serious.

Tasha stood when she saw me. "Kim, I'd like to talk to you."

Alex scurried off to the stairs without looking me in the eye. *What had he told her?*

Tasha motioned for me to sit across from her in one of the chairs. "You want a cup of tea?"

What was it with the British and their compulsive need to have a cuppa every time something stressful came up? "No thanks."

Tasha leaned back in her seat, the bangles on her arm clinking as they slid along her wrist. "Anything you want to tell me?"

What Tasha didn't know was that my mom was a pro at this game. She'd gotten me to confess to a range of things before I'd learned to shut up until I knew exactly what information she already had. I shook my head. We stared silently at each other.

Tasha ran her hands through her hair. "Why didn't you tell me that you and Connor used to date?"

Alex, how could you? My heart rate tripled. If I had been

hooked up to an EKG, it would have been beeping out of control. "It didn't seem important."

One of her perfectly tweezed eyebrows arched. "You didn't think it was important to mention that you'd been in a relationship? Not even when the police were asking about him?"

"We weren't *still* dating."

"All the same, seeing what happened to him, losing someone who was important to you must have been devastating."

I bit down hard. I had to be careful what I said. "It was, but I didn't want to talk about it."

Tasha nodded. "Uh-huh. Alex is worried about you. He says you've gotten a little obsessed about Connor's death . . . about trying to figure out what happened. He thinks you're convinced it wasn't an accident."

Had he told her about Nicki? "I'm not obsessed." I crossed my arms over my chest. "I feel like you're accusing me of something."

She leaned forward. "Listen, I'm on your side here."

"I don't have a side," I insisted. "I'm just upset. Not because we used to date, but because it's horrible. Maybe I should have said something, but like I said, I didn't want to talk about it."

"What about this person who you think sent the article?"

I clenched my teeth. "I don't know who did it."

"I have to tell the police about this. I think Alex is right and the article was likely someone's idea of being helpful, but we need to make sure the authorities have all the information."

I wanted to beg her not to, but I knew it wouldn't work. Tasha wasn't the kind of person to be swayed by some tears. "Okay," I said. I pushed up from the chair and walked to the main stairs without looking back. I was right—there wasn't much to talk about where Connor and I were concerned, but it wasn't going to look like that when the cops started poking around.

SEVENTEEN

AUGUST 22
9 DAYS REMAINING

A lex stood up as soon as I came into the Thai place a few minutes after four. He shifted uncomfortably as if he didn't know what to do with his hands and feet, like a puppy that was a mix of adorable and awkward. "I ordered you a Diet Coke."

"Thanks." As soon as I sat down, I started picking at the paper napkin, tearing thin pink strips off and letting them drop into my lap. The smell of curry and spices hung in the air like a fog.

"I'm glad you came. I wasn't sure you would." I didn't answer. Alex took a deep breath as if he were about to jump off the high dive. "Look, I'm sorry I talked to Tasha. And I get it if you're mad and don't want to speak to me ever again, but I had to. I was worried about you."

"You don't have to be worried." My heart zinged to hear that he cared. I realized I wasn't angry at him. I ignored my reflection in the mirror across the restaurant. I didn't want to see the dark circles under my eyes. I moved my hand, knocking the napkin shreds onto the floor. "I'm fine."

Alex's eyebrow twitched, but he didn't call out my lie. "What you feel about Connor is normal. He hurt you, and now he's dead, and that has to be hard—"

"You have no idea," I said softly, then pinched my mouth shut to keep myself from saying more than I wanted. Alex winced. The waitress dropped a plate of steaming spring rolls onto our table, breaking the tension.

"No shrimps," she said, without waiting for Alex to ask. The waitress was used to his allergies by now.

I waited until she walked away. "Sorry. I know that I'm stressed and acting weird and you were trying to help, but this could get me in real trouble."

"It's not going to."

"What if the cops think *I* did something to Connor?"

"They won't."

I shook my head. It wasn't that simple. I had a motive for hurting Connor.

"They can't think you did anything. You have an alibi." He grabbed one of the spring rolls and dropped it quickly onto his plate. "They're really hot," he warned. "I told Tasha that you and I were standing right next to each other when

Connor fell. They can't accuse you. I'm your witness that you're innocent."

Alex hadn't been next to me. The crowd on the platform had separated us by at least five or six people. I'd been closer to Connor than to him. Then I realized the impact of what he'd said. "Why would you lie for me?"

He blew on his food. "Because I know you didn't do anything to Connor. That's not a lie. All I'm doing is making sure they don't focus on the wrong thing."

My heart seized. I couldn't believe he'd done that for me. He really believed in me. Enough that he'd lie for me to keep me safe.

Alex leaned forward. "What the cops should worry about is why someone sent you that newspaper article. She contacted you again, didn't she? That's why you took off today."

"No." Technically I wasn't lying. I'd reached out to Nicki — she hadn't contacted me. I wanted to tell him. I ached to share what she'd said, but I couldn't trust him to keep it to himself. "I thought I'd figured out a way to find her."

Alex dipped the spring roll in the sweet-and-sour sauce. "But what would you have done if you'd located her? Even if she didn't do anything, she's clearly got issues — why else send you that thing? She's fixated on you for some reason. Someone like that can be dangerous."

"So, you believe me that she exists?" My voice came out so

small that it was almost lost in all the crashing and banging of pans that came from the open kitchen.

He put his fork down. "Of course. I didn't mean to make it sound like I didn't believe she existed — I just wasn't sure she was the one who sent the article." He stared down at the table, then shook his head before reaching over and touching me lightly on the hand. "I really want to help and I feel like I screwed this all up."

I kicked him lightly under the table. "It's okay. I'm not mad."

"Really?"

"It's impossible to be mad at a man wearing that T-shirt." I waved my fork toward his chest. The design read: *There are 10 kinds of people in the world, those who understand binary and those who don't.*

Alex looked down at his shirt. "I figured if anyone was going to like a coding joke, it would be you."

"I appreciate you offering to be my alibi. No one's ever looked out for me like that before." I realized it was true. My parents worried about me, but what they were really worried about was what people would think of the job they were doing as parents. Alex cared about *me*. He thought I was worth it, and that made me begin to trust in myself. "You're my knight in shining armor."

Alex blushed, the freckles sprinkled across his nose disappearing in the flush. "I always knew all those years of role-playing games and watching Lord of the Rings movies would pay off."

The waitress came over with a plate of pad thai. "You share?" We nodded and she dropped the plate in the center of the table.

"I'm not sure it was the games," I said.

"They taught me how to act brave."

"You don't *act* brave," I said. "I think you just *are* brave."

He smiled. Then he reached across the table and took my hand and squeezed it.

EIGHTEEN

I was still thinking about Alex and his hand squeeze as I thundered down the stairs, hoping that my clothes were done in the washer so that I could quickly put them in the dryer and wouldn't be late to meet Sophie. I'd been blowing off everyone except for Alex and I didn't want to lose my connection with the rest of the Student Scholars. Sophie seemed the easiest way back in.

The machines in the basement had minds of their own when it came to locking our clothing inside and spinning it around for an indeterminate amount of time before finally declaring their job done. Everyone in our group had tried to figure out if the washers had a cycle that could be a determined length of time, but the machines were totally random. Sometimes they took forty minutes; other times they boiled your clothing for hours, refusing to open no matter what button you pushed. This wouldn't be too much of a problem, except if you weren't there when your washer dinged its completion, someone else would drag your stuff out and leave it in a damp heap on the questionably clean folding table.

"There you are. I was beginning to think you'd abandoned your things."

I froze in the doorway. Nicki sat cross-legged on top of the table. Sunshine from the narrow window near the ceiling behind her made it difficult to see her features. She uncrossed her legs, looking like a spider getting up to move in on something caught in her web. She paused on the edge for a second, then jumped down.

"You know, you've got to be careful. Places like this, there's always some weird knicker sniffer who will steal your panties." She winked.

I slowly reached down and patted my pocket. I didn't have my phone with me. I'd left it upstairs. Nicki smiled at me as though she knew what I was doing. So much for recording her.

"I went ahead and put your stuff in the dryer. My treat." If she was waiting for me to thank her, it was going to be a long time. "So, I have something for you."

I took a step back, avoiding whatever was in her hand. "Whatever it is, I don't want it."

She didn't seem bothered that I refused to take what she'd brought. Instead she just laid a tiny square of paper onto the table. "It's the address. Where you'll find my mum."

I swallowed before speaking, doing my best to remain

calm and remember my strategy. "I'm not doing anything to your mom."

"My thought is that you could kill her later tonight," Nicki said, as if I hadn't even spoken. "I won't be home, plus she started drinking early. She had a pitcher of mimosas going, saying friends were supposed to come over, but really it was just an excuse. She's already tipsy and it's not even noon." Nicki rolled her eyes. "She thinks if she serves things in fancy crystal it means she can't be an alcoholic. She'll keep it up all day, which means by tonight she'll be ready to pass out. She'll be dead to the world." Nicki giggled. "Well, not *dead* dead, but close enough for it to be easy for you."

"I'm not breaking into your house."

"Don't worry, no breaking in is required. The door by the back garden doesn't lock. It's been broken forever. I suspect it will be the first thing the police notice when they come for her body. An unlocked door in this city?" Nicki shook her head as though she couldn't fathom her mom's stupidity. "It's basically inviting trouble."

She moved around the laundry room as if she were a general doing an inspection. "I can draw you a map of the house if you like, so you can find your way around without too much trouble. Look out for the third step on your way upstairs—it creaks. Hopefully you can make the whole thing look like an accident—that would be the best. I'll leave it up to you. She takes a bunch of medication. If she's totally out, you could drop a bunch of pills into her mouth—she'd swallow them without even knowing she's doing it. Make sure you give her enough. I can't have her waking up a few hours later with a wicked headache and having sicked up all over everything."

Nicki bit her lip. "I think the easiest thing is to go upstairs and then make some kind of noise to lure her out onto the landing. When she's by the stairs, give her a big shove. She's got no balance when sober—I suspect when drunk she'd go ass over teakettle down those steps.

"It's not like anyone would be exactly shocked that she fell. Last month she walked into a doorjamb and broke her nose. She tried to convince the doctor that she'd been running for the phone, but he didn't buy it. The woman sweats Hendrick's, for god's sake."

The smell of detergent mixed with the mildew in the basement was giving me a headache. I shook my head to clear it, but Nicki thought I was disagreeing with her.

She raised both hands as if surrendering. "If you don't want to do it that way, that's fine—it's totally up to you. I'm simply trying to give you options. But remember, we've got neighbors, so you'll need to keep things quiet." The dryer buzzed and she opened it up. She pulled a few items of mine onto the table and tossed my jeans back in. She dropped in a few more coins, and with a lurch, the machine started up again.

"These things never get everything dry." She started folding my clothes—tight, tidy shapes, as if she worked at the

Gap. She took the tiny slip of paper with the address on it and placed it into the pocket of one of my shirts, patting it softly as though she were tucking in a small kid.

"You are completely unhinged."

Nicki threw her head back and laughed as if I were joking. She held up my dark gray fleece. "I'd suggest wearing this. This morning I swapped out the bulb in the light above the back door for one that's burned out, but our neighbor on the one side lights up their place like it's a West End theater marquee. They aren't too nosy — they're used to my mum banging around in there, crying and whatnot — but they do keep an eye on things. Don't slink around — if they see you being sneaky, they'll call the cops. You know how paranoid old people can be. Don't worry about the place on the other side of us — it's up for sale and empty."

I yanked my fleece out of her hands. My heart was thudding so hard I was surprised my shirt wasn't billowing out with the effort of my heart trying to push past my ribs. "I don't know how else to tell you this. I am *not* doing anything to your mom." Even as the words left my mouth, I could imagine all of it in my head. Stepping into their backyard, the gate clicking softly behind me. Nicki's house would be dark. I'd creep up the stairs, remembering at the last minute to skip the third. Then I'd stand over her mother, the smell of stale booze hanging like a fog in the room as I held a pillow above her face, steeling myself to press it down, crushing the air out of her.

Nicki cocked her head to the side. "But you promised."

I grabbed my stuff on the table, then stepped past her to stop the dryer and grab the rest of my things. I didn't care if they were still damp. She scared me. "I didn't promise anything," I told her.

Nicki blocked my way. Adrenaline flew like a sharp arrow to my chest. "Why are you acting like this?" she asked.

"I don't want to see you ever again." My voice sounded shrill in the empty room. If she attacked, I'd scream. I kept reminding myself there were people upstairs. Someone would hear me. Somehow Alex would hear me.

Nicki's mouth tightened; she looked almost as if she was about to cry. "I don't understand."

She seemed sincere, but I wasn't sticking around to explain. I moved past her out into the hall, half expecting her to grab me, but she stepped aside. My hands shook, barely able to hold on to the wad of clean laundry. "Leave me alone."

I bolted up the stairs, but I could still hear her behind me. "You know I can't do that."

NINETEEN

AUGUST 23
8 DAYS REMAINING

I refused to think about Nicki the rest of the day, as if she were a demon that couldn't be summoned unless I said her name. I knew I would have to do something about the situation, but I didn't want her in my mind. I concentrated so hard on blocking her out that by the afternoon the only thought in my head was baked goods. I tapped on the glass case in my favorite coffee shop, pointing at a croissant.

"Get the chocolate one instead — they're better."

I recognized the detective's voice right away.

"Make it two of the chocolate," the detective said to the clerk. "My treat."

"You don't have to do that," I said. I held my tote tightly as if I thought she were going to yank it away from me.

"No problem. I thought we might go back to Metford and have a chat."

"I'm supposed to meet up with friends in just a bit," I tried, knowing even as the words left my mouth that she wasn't going to let me go that easily.

"This won't take long."

"They're supposed to meet me here. I don't really have time."

She sighed. "Okay, we'll talk here, then. Have a sit." She motioned to two stools along the bar by the window.

The barista called out my name and passed me my latte, the heat of the paper cup searing into my hand. I wanted to run for the door, but instead I trudged over to where the detective was waiting. My feet felt as though they were encased in lead boots. Dead girl walking.

The rest of our group piled in, laughing. I hadn't been lying, unfortunately. Kendra nudged Jazmin and everyone glanced over. Alex took a step toward me, but I shook my head. I had to handle this on my own.

They all acted as if they had a keen interest in ordering their coffee and considering the contents of the bakery case, but they leaned toward us, trying to hear what we were saying. I shot a glance at the lot of them, willing them to leave, but they didn't. I bit back annoyance that they were finding my drama their entertainment.

"I'm Detective Sharma, by the way, in case you forgot." She broke off a corner of her pastry and popped it into her mouth. Her hair was pulled back so tight it looked painted on, as though she were a doll. We were still in the chummy stage of the discussion.

I sipped my latte. "Tasha told you about Connor," I said as quietly as I could. She nodded. "And you're wondering why I didn't tell you I dated him."

"Nah. I got some theories on that."

My hand jolted, causing me to slop a bit of my latte on the wood counter. Her comment was unexpected. "Oh."

"It made perfect sense to me why you didn't say anything." Detective Sharma nudged the plate with my croissant closer to me. "You'd broken up, this horrible thing happens, the last thing you want is to volunteer any connection. Now, I happen to love the police department, but that's not a feeling shared by everyone. Most people avoid us if they can." She smiled and tiny slivers of croissant stuck to her lips, like flaking skin. "That's human nature. I looked through my notes and checked with DI Fogg. You never lied to us. You didn't say you dated him, but we didn't directly ask."

Air filled my lungs. "That's right, I didn't lie." I repeated that loudly so the crowd at the register couldn't miss it. Alex nodded encouragingly.

"Sounded like the bloke broke your heart."

I shrugged. "It was pretty bad, but you know, things happen, you gotta move on . . ." I trailed off. I didn't even know what I wanted to say. She waited for me to voice something else, but I stared down at the counter, counting the rings in the polished wood.

"They say young love is some of the strongest."

"Yeah," I mumbled. "It was never really love. Tasha told you about the newspaper clipping."

"You don't have it anymore?"

"No. I threw it away."

Detective Sharma nodded. "And it didn't come with any kind of note, or return address or anything?"

"No."

"There's not really anything we can check on. But I wanted you to know we looked into your history with Connor." She smiled again, licking her lips free of crumbs, and I suddenly had the sense that she'd been leading me somewhere, the real reason she'd come to find me.

I made a noncommittal noise. I was starting to wish I had agreed to go back to Metford so we could have had this discussion in private.

"I also talked to your parents."

I closed my eyes. *Uh-oh.* The espresso machine screamed, blowing steam into the air.

"Your mom was very keen to make sure we knew what a great kid you are." Detective Sharma took a long sip of her drink. "She didn't think much of Connor."

I bet she'd had plenty to say. One thing you could say about my mom was that she wasn't someone who had a hard time sharing her feelings.

"Now, it's not that unusual for parents to not be that fond of someone their kid is dating. You know what they say, *No one is good enough for my little girl.* But do you know what I found most interesting about what she said?"

My throat was tight and I had to push out the "no," so quiet that Detective Sharma leaned in to hear me.

"What was interesting is that she said you never dated Connor O'Reilly."

I heard Alex gasp behind me just before his cup of coffee hit the floor.

My mom always went on and on about being a writer, as if she were the female blogging equivalent of Hemingway. The Jane Austen of the Internet. Most of the time Mom stuck to blogging, but every few months she'd cycle through a phase where she decided she was meant to write a novel. She would either start a new one or pick up one of the projects she'd been dragging around for years.

She had to have the right atmosphere. Her office was full of smelly candles, crystals, and a big antique typewriter, an Underwood, that she'd found on eBay to use as inspiration. It was less like a real working space and more like a Pinterest post of an author's office.

My dad would get this pained expression when she'd start talking about writing her book, as if he wished he were a traveling dentist and could get out of town until the whole thing blew over. Both of us always tried to pick up more chores around the house to give her some extra time to work on her book, but if she ever saw a dish in the sink, she'd still break into tears and stomp off, declaring that no one took her seriously as an artist.

My mom's muse was a real bitch.

But one thing that she always said stuck with me: *Each word makes a difference.*

Take the term "dating."

It's certainly not the *only* way you can describe that type of interaction. It wasn't the perfect way to describe my relationship with Connor. Even I knew that — but I wasn't a writer like my mom. I didn't have any other words to express what had gone on between us. It was so convoluted I didn't know how to understand it myself, let alone communicate what had happened to anyone else.

"How did you and Connor connect?"

I was brought abruptly back into the excruciating present. The smell of coffee, so alluring only moments ago, was now making me nauseated.

"We worked together — summer job," I mumbled.

I had fallen hard for Connor, which was a bit unexpected considering I'd known him for years. Our lockers were near each other, and sophomore year we'd even been lab partners. I have no memory of my heart going pitter-patter as we dissected our fetal pig or mastered how to use the ancient microscopes.

We hung out in different crowds, but we had similarities, too. Smart, not popular, but not unpopular, either.

Detective Sharma looked down at her notebook. "That was the Science Center, correct?" She waited for my nod. "I bet that beat waiting tables."

"Yeah. They do a summer camp for kids. We were responsible for setting up experiments for the campers, creating balloon-powered boats and making their hair stand up with the plasma globe, that kind of thing."

Detective Sharma tossed the final bite of croissant into her mouth and then brushed off her lips. "Was it love at first sight?"

"No." I couldn't bear to look over at Alex. I could feel the other Student Scholars listening intently and my skin crawled. "We connected at a party."

I hadn't planned on going—I didn't even know why I told Connor that I'd be there. It wasn't my kind of thing, but with Emily out of town I was bored and lonely.

As soon as I got there, I wished I hadn't gone. I felt awkward and out of place. The fact that I worked with Connor didn't make me a part of his crowd. I kept drinking red Solo cup after red Solo cup of punch that seemed to be equal parts juice and vodka.

Detective Sharma smiled, but it didn't reach her eyes. "So, you knew him from work, but the sparks flew at this party?"

I nodded. I had been pretty far gone when Connor finally

showed up and sat next to me, but what had really set my head spinning was when he leaned over and kissed me. Just like that. One minute we were talking about what we thought of our boss, and the next second we were making out.

There was no way I was telling Detective Sharma the complete truth. I didn't want the words in my mouth. I had had sex with Connor that night. Just like that. And just like that, I'd fallen for him . . . or at least for the idea of him, for whom I wanted him to be.

I would ache when I saw him at work, as if every atom in my body were tearing itself free to be closer to him. When he was near, I would close my eyes and inhale his smell. Pulling it deep inside myself, breath after breath, growing lightheaded with the scent.

"We got together at the party," I said simply. The barista called out Sophie's name, but I didn't look over. I could tell the entire group was hanging on my every word, and I refused to give them the satisfaction of knowing I cared.

"But the relationship didn't really take off."

"I guess not," I murmured. We had gotten together a few more times over the next week. But it wasn't until later that I realized we rarely did anything other than make out. But I refused to see it — it was as if by being with him I was going to be this totally different person. The kind of person that Connor dated. I didn't let myself realize that he was never worth my attention.

I shrugged. "He was suddenly busy all the time. He was *avoiding* me. The more he tried to distance himself, the harder I tried to make things work." I left out that it was around then that he announced he was going to England. And when I gave up the science award.

"I understood that he indicated that you were too serious for him, it had just been a lark, a bit of fun. That he needed his space and didn't want a girlfriend."

Or at the very least he didn't want me. My teeth clenched. Connor had said he was sorry if he'd given me the *wrong impression*. He was so calm about it. As if it were no big thing. As if he hadn't reached in and pulled my heart from my chest and tossed it into a garbage disposal.

"From Connor's perspective, we'd never gone out. We'd been coworkers with benefits. That wasn't how I saw things. I was hurt."

"At the time, he described you as more than hurt. He implied you were a bit obsessive."

I winced. I couldn't really deny it. I had stalked him at work between camp sessions, following him from his staff locker, just a few steps behind, trying to catch a whiff of his cologne or overhear him talking. I'd finish my work early so I could watch him with his campers. I'd show up at the coffee shop near the center and act as if I was surprised to find him there.

In retrospect, I get that my behavior was creepy. But no one seemed to understand that what he'd done felt just as wrong — to have that closeness with me with no intention of it meaning anything. He wasn't simply rejecting *me,* he was taking away the future I wanted. I couldn't face reality. I became convinced that he was just stressed with the start of school coming and that if I could only hang in there, we'd work it out.

Detective Sharma shifted, smoothing a single loose hair into the bun at the back of her head. "He told his parents?"

"In July. I guess like a month ago now. They called the Science Center, who called my parents. We had a meeting where I was told to leave him alone." You don't really know humiliating until you're stuck in your boss's office with your parents while your supervisor and the human resource person tell you that you're engaging in stalker behavior that is "not acceptable."

The only person who seemed more embarrassed than me was my dad, who could have gone his entire life without knowing that I had any kind of sex life at all. These were the kinds of parenting issues that he felt were securely my mom's domain. But she didn't want this problem either. My mom just kept repeating: "I don't know why you told us you were dating this boy."

Because I'd thought we were dating! And even when he'd made it clear we weren't, I wasn't ready to let go. My mom had been thrilled I had a boyfriend. At last I was doing something that she understood. We'd gone shopping and she'd even taken me to Planned Parenthood so I could get on the pill. Now this was turning into something else I'd done that made no sense to her. I couldn't even date normally. Whereas if Connor had really broken my heart, she would have loved that.

"Your mom said you were quite hurt."

I nodded. She knew I was hurt, but she didn't understand it. She would have tackled me being dumped like a regular person by buying ice cream and sitting on the edge of my bed, rubbing my back while I cried it out. She'd tell me how I'd find someone better, and she'd squeeze out at least two or three blog posts about the pain of watching your kid go through heartache and how to be supportive. *Picking Up the Pieces: Top Ten Ways to Help Your Kids Put Their Heart Back Together After a Breakup.* Or *Five Activities You Can Do with Your Kids to Raise Them Up When They're Down.*

But she had no idea what to do with a relationship that had been one-sided. Mom had been okay with imaginary friends when I was a kid, but imaginary relationships as a teenager struck her as pathetic, maybe pathological.

"But you still decided to come on this trip," Detective Sharma said, her voice hinting at her confusion as to my motives.

"My mom wanted me to. She thought it was the best way for me to get over him. To move on."

"And have you moved on?"

My brain scrambled to think of the answer the detective wanted from me. "I'm trying," I managed to finally say. It was the truth, too. Time had made a difference. I realized that what I'd felt for Connor had been all about insecurity. Alex had shown me relationships could be different. That someone who really matters makes you feel better about yourself, not worse.

But then I heard the bell above the door chime as Alex rushed out of the coffee shop. Detective Sharma and I both watched him as he disappeared into the crowds on the sidewalk. I felt my heart drag after him, the connection to him growing thinner and threatening to snap.

TWENTY

I promised Detective Sharma I would notify her before leaving the city and caught up to Alex. He was walking quickly back toward Metford. His shoulders were hunched up around his ears. I tugged on the back of his shirt.

"Wait up."

He stopped and I heard him sigh before he turned around.

"I can explain," I said, not certain that I could.

"Why did you tell me you *dated* Connor? I don't get it. First you don't say anything, then you confess he was your ex, and now I hear you weren't ever dating. I don't understand."

"Things were . . . complicated." I couldn't come up with anything better.

Alex crossed his arms over his chest. "But things with *me* aren't supposed to be complicated. Why not tell me the truth?"

"Because *I* can't handle the truth!" I burst out. "The truth is, I slept with him. I thought we were dating, I thought he was my boyfriend, but it was never that. It was just sex and I was too stupid to know it."

A woman walking along the sidewalk paused as if she wanted to hear more.

Alex took my elbow and led me down the block, away from the people around us who were now staring. "You're not stupid," he said at last.

The fight bled out of me. No matter how much I tried to run away from the situation, it kept catching up to me. What did you call someone who slept with a guy an hour after he kissed her for the first time and then didn't even realize that the only reason he kept seeing her was more sex? I didn't always like myself, but I'd always seen myself as smart, and this made me face the fact that I wasn't. At least not smart about people. "I wanted to believe he liked me."

"Look, I don't know what happened between you and Connor, and it's none of my business. You don't owe me some kind of list of every guy you've ever been with."

"He's the only guy," I said quietly. Connor had been the only guy I'd ever even kissed, unless you counted Dex, who had shoved his tongue into my mouth at the spring dance in ninth grade.

Alex pulled me toward him. "I'm really sorry he hurt you."

I closed my eyes and let myself melt into him. Alex was the first person to say that. Connor hadn't cared how his actions made me feel. My best friend had been out of town and felt guilty about not being there. My dad hadn't known what to say, and my mom had been annoyed the entire situation had blown out of control and embarrassed her. But Alex's words were like cool water on a burn, making the sting evaporate.

We stood that way, Alex's arms around me and my eyes closed, while people moved past us on the sidewalk.

"Yo, you two, touching moment, but I want the cash machine." A bear of a man with hairy arms jutting out of his tank top stood there, his biceps looking as though someone had shoved frozen chickens under the skin. He jerked his head in our direction and I realized we were embracing inches from the ATM.

"Sorry," I mumbled, and we moved away. I glanced over my shoulder. The guy was covered in a thick pelt of dark hair. He looked as if he were half werewolf, grabbing some cash before finishing his transformation.

I felt for the werewolf guy. To have someone trapped inside you, a not-nice person, one who came out when you least expected it.

"I lied to you about something else," I said.

Alex braced himself. "Okay."

"Remember when I told you my cousin did the travel for that band?" I said.

"Yeah, the Ravens."

I stared down at my shoes. "He doesn't."

Alex shook his head. "Why do you feel like you have to lie to me?"

"Because I want you to like me."

Alex kicked a loose stone down the street. "Jesus, Kim, why do you think I won't like you otherwise? Don't you get it? I *like* you."

"It's not that easy. That first day, you talked to me because we had the band in common. You said how you wanted to be my buddy on the trip *after* I told you. It's what made you notice me."

He took a step back. "You're clueless. I liked you since the information session, before we even came here. Shit, I counted down the days until the trip and freaking made lists of stuff to talk about with you."

I shook my head, startled. "That's . . . not true."

"Yeah, it is. I can tell you what you were wearing the first time I saw you. You had on those jean shorts, the same ones you brought on this trip, and a baby blue shirt that had these, like, circles on it. You were asking if we were going to go to the Science Museum as part of the schedule, and when you laughed, you did that thing you do, where you cover your face and snort."

I blinked, trying to make sense of what Alex was saying. I didn't even remember him at the information session. But I vaguely recalled wearing that shirt. It was one of my favorites. He'd noticed things I didn't think anyone noticed. He hadn't seen the image I was usually trying to project, but the real me. Snorts and all.

"I found you interesting because you were cute *and* smart.

You told a joke about Charles Darwin, for crying out loud. When I quoted Star Wars, you got the reference and didn't think I was a total dork. You even knew it was *The Empire Strikes Back* instead of *Return of the Jedi*. You're basically my dream girl. Our first day here I told Jamal to ask Sophie to be his buddy so that the numbers would work out and you'd be stuck with me. Hell, I don't even like the Ravens that much — I just wanted an excuse to talk to you."

I stared at him blankly. "I had no idea."

He liked me. I'd known something had been growing between us, but this was different. He liked the sum of my parts, the whole — he wasn't picking and choosing. And I'd blown it.

Hot tears filled my eyes. "I understand if you don't want anything to do with me anymore."

Alex threw his hands up into the air. "Argh, you are the most frustrating woman ever. That's not what I'm saying. I can be mad at you without wanting to break up with you."

Air froze in my lungs. "You said you don't want to break up . . . Does that mean you feel like we're going out?"

Alex buried his head in his hands. "It's like you're trying to drive me crazy right now."

"I'm sorry," I whispered.

"Listen, I need some time alone, okay? I can't figure out what to say and I feel like I keep making it worse," Alex said.

I nodded. I pressed my lips together to keep from crying.

He stepped toward me and held me by the shoulders. "I'm mad at you and I don't want you to lie to me anymore, but I like you. I want to be with you. I want you to want to be with me."

"I do," I said.

He leaned forward and kissed my cheek softly. "I'll see you later."

I watched him walk away.

I wanted to believe him — I just wasn't sure I did.

TWENTY-ONE

This might have been a huge mistake, but knowledge is power. It had been hours since I'd talked to Alex, and I knew I needed to learn whatever I could if I wanted to gain control of the situation. I'd waited until everyone was busy before slipping out of Metford. I spent a couple hours in a remote coffee shop before heading here. I glanced over my shoulder, but no one seemed to be paying me any attention. I paused, backing up against a building and pretended to check my phone, thus giving a chance for everyone who'd exited the Tube station at the same time to disperse.

A slight Indian man stopped to stare into the darkened bookshop window across the street and I focused in on him. Was he following me? I guessed him to be midthirties, but he walked as if he were a hundred and ten. He had three large reusable blue plastic carrier bags with him. One of them was bursting at the seams with a box of diapers. He seemed more likely to be a sleep-deprived new dad.

The Indian man trudged down the street without even glancing over. If he was following me, he was doing a pretty lousy job. I checked the map on my phone even though I had it committed to memory. I slipped down Baker Street toward Regent's Park.

The pedestrian gates were closed for the night. The thick trees surrounding the sidewalk made the park look eerie, as if I went inside, there would be a candy house staffed by a witch just waiting for innocent people to stumble past. I followed the path along the park until I saw the side street I was looking for.

For a second I contemplated turning around and going back, but I had come this far. I had to check it out. I crossed the street and examined the house numbers out of the side of my eye, doing my best to appear as though I knew where I was going.

There it was. Assuming Google Maps wasn't wrong, I was looking at the address Nicki had given me. The house next to it was for sale the way she had described, so that confirmed it. They were linked together—a row of town homes, most with a single green box hedge in a planter on the stoop and black wrought-iron gates across the front. You couldn't tell them apart except for the house numbers and the different colors people had used to paint the front doors.

The downstairs was dark, but there was a light on upstairs,

filtered through the curtains in a big bay window that arched out over the front of the house. I could just make out the gate that would lead to the garden in the back. I couldn't tell if the light was out back there like Nicki had promised, but I was willing to guess it was.

It was a nice night to commit a crime. Maybe that was why Nicki wanted me to kill her mom tonight. The moon was almost nonexistent, just a tiny sliver of a crescent, like a water ring on a wooden table. The cloud cover kept any stars hidden. I'd worn the fleece Nicki had suggested, the hood pulled down low, hiding my face.

Someone moved in front of the window. It had to be Nicki's mom, but she hadn't passed out as Nicki had said she would. In fact, she looked pretty damn sprightly for an alcoholic who had been drinking all day, not at all like someone who wouldn't even notice an intruder sneaking into her bedroom with pills or a pillow.

Not that I had any intention of going inside. I just wanted to see the place. I wasn't sure what I'd been expecting, but it was just a house, like every other house on the street. I walked to the end of the block and then turned to retrace my steps. The next day must have been garbage pickup, because everyone had bins out. I bent down, pretending to tie my shoes, and peered into the recycling box in front of Nicki's place. Inside there was one empty bottle of Chardonnay along with stacks of papers and empty cans.

Nicki said the house had been her grandparents'. She and her mom had moved in with them after the divorce. When her grandparents had still been alive, her mom had held it together. Once they died, Nicki's mom no longer bothered and slid from drinking too much to being a flat-out drunk.

At least that's what Nicki said.

I had no way of knowing if she was lying. If anyone knew that the truth was sometimes elastic, it was me. She'd fed me a story of an alcoholic mom who wouldn't let her have her own life, but that might not have been the truth.

I saw a woman across the street walking her tiny corgi dog in my direction. I couldn't let the opportunity go by. "Hi," I called out, and then crossed over to her. I plastered a smile onto my face and hoped she couldn't tell how nervous I was. "Do you live in the area?"

"Yes . . ." She pulled her pink sweater tighter around her.

"My parents are looking at maybe buying that house." I waved to the FOR SALE sign over my shoulder. "They're out at the pub tonight trying to get a feel for the area."

"At the Hound and Whistle? A block over?" The woman's dog snuffled my feet. "That's the best one, or there's the wine bar, Sour Grapes, down the lane just a bit, but it gets more tourists."

"I was just curious what you thought of this neighborhood. It seems pretty quiet."

She looked at me. "Yes, and we like it that way. No wild parties around here — most people are a bit older."

I nodded seriously. "Do you know much about the people who live in the house next door?" I motioned to Nicki's place.

The woman shifted and then fished a dog treat out of her sweater pocket and fed it to the corgi. "There you go, Winston." She wiped her fingers on her pants. "The owner's all right. She's had her share of trouble, keeps to herself, mostly."

"The thing is, another person I talked to said she was a bit of a drinker," I said. I couldn't believe how easily the lies were slipping out of my mouth. "My parents don't want a neighbor who's loud or trouble."

She arched an eyebrow that had been tweezed almost to nonexistence and then drawn back in with a reddish-brown crayon. "Who told you that? This is that stupid neighborhood scandal again, as if it's anyone's business. What with her no-good husband gone off to Canada, who's to fault her for having a glass or two in her own garden? Was it those nosy people on the corner?" Her dog lay down and seemed to fall asleep.

"I think so," I hedged. "What about her daughter? Do you know anything about her?"

She yanked on the dog's leash, pulling him up. "I'm not saying a word about that girl."

Her reaction startled me. She seemed angry. *What had Nicki done that made her neighbor so leery to talk?*

"I'm so sorry. I just wondered—"

The woman jammed her sleeves back as if ready to wade into a fistfight. "How dare you ask questions about that wee girl? What business is that of yours?"

I took a step back. "I guess I just wondered if she and I might be friends," I said.

"What are you playing at?" Her nose wrinkled up. "What did you say your name was?"

I started walking away. "I need to get going. I'm supposed to meet my parents."

"Now, wait a minute—" She took a step toward me, but her dog held her in place like a fat furry anchor.

I walked quickly back to the Tube stop, my feet feeling light for the first time in days. The trip had been worth it. I'd learned a few things. As I suspected, this was an expensive neighborhood. I'd also learned that for a supposedly sloppy drunk, Nicki's mom didn't have a lot of bottles in her recycling box. Maybe she was ashamed and threw them away someplace else, but people who went to that kind of trouble usually weren't yet to the full-blown alcoholic stage that Nicki had described. But the neighbor had made it sound as though there were problems of some sort. Nicki's issue with her mother might not be that she was a drinker.

Her issue could be that her mom was alive. In Nicki's way. Without her mom, Nicki would inherit the house and any money left over. It would be a pretty nice setup. And it struck me that that might have been Nicki's plan for a long time. Long enough that she'd been on the lookout for someone like me. Someone she thought she could manipulate. She'd lucked out when she bumped into me at the airport.

But she was going to learn that it wasn't that easy.

"Where do you think you're going?"

My foot froze a few inches above the step. *Shit.*

Metford House had a curfew, but no one paid any attention to it. There was only the one ancient security guard, who could be counted on to never leave his office near the front desk. He would sit with his feet propped up on an open drawer, his head back, snoring.

Except for this time.

I turned around slowly. "Oh, hey," I said. I pressed my mouth into a smile as if I were thrilled to see him.

The guard tapped his foot on the floor. The rubber soles made a dull *thwak, thwak, thwak* sound. "Go on, what were you up to?"

"I was just outside . . ." I motioned behind me with my thumb as if maybe he was confused about where I had come from. Telling him I had been casing a house for a possible murder wasn't going to reassure him. I scrambled to come up with an excuse for being out past curfew. My ability to lie on demand seemed to be drying up. The last thing I needed was to be in more trouble. I had the feeling he wasn't going to buy the story that I was volunteering with the homeless.

"Did you find my lighter?" Alex came down the stairs in a thundering rush as if he were half walking and half falling.

I stared at him with my mouth open. I didn't have a clue what he was talking about.

Alex turned to the guard. "I went out for a smoke and must have dropped it out there." Then he smiled at me. "So, did you? Find it?"

I glanced behind me as if I half expected to see a lighter lying in the foyer. I held up my empty hands. "Um. Nope."

Alex sighed. "Can we borrow your flashlight?" He pointed to the giant utility belt around the guard's waist. "I want to check one more time."

The guard's eyes narrowed and his giant bushy eyebrows came together over his nose like mating caterpillars.

"It's my lucky lighter," Alex added with a wide innocent smile on his face.

I had to hand it to him. He lied brilliantly. He had the face for it: lots of freckles. Anyone with freckles automatically looks sincere. I believed him and I knew for a fact he didn't smoke. His asthma was bad if it was even a slightly smoggy day.

The guard unclipped his flashlight and handed it over. "Don't you kids be out there too long. And get that torch back to me." He hitched his pants up over his thin hips, under his swaying gut.

Alex pushed me toward the back door, practically saluting. "No sir. I'll bring this right back."

We stepped onto the back patio. Alex swept the light beam across the ground in case the guard was watching us from a window. Discarded cigarette butts were sprinkled around. An empty gin and tonic can slid across the pavement with a screech. I followed it with my eyes—I'd never seen a cocktail in a can until I'd been on the trains here. Thumping sounds from the dryers came through the narrow casement window to the laundry room in the basement. I shivered, wondering if Nicki could be in there now, waiting for me.

We stood silently for a beat. "Thanks," I said at last. "You didn't have to do that."

Alex plopped down onto a rickety bench. "I like to do things for you. Did you have an okay night?"

I nodded. "Yeah. I just didn't feel like hanging around here."

"I get that. You didn't miss much. A few of us went out for Indian food and a movie."

"Seriously, I really appreciate you covering for me with Deputy Grumpy in there. For a minute, I thought he might handcuff me and do some waterboarding."

He laughed. "It's okay. I considered saying I was going out for a 'fag,' since that's what they call cigarettes here, but

I couldn't do it. My friend Jordan's gay, so it just feels gross to use that word, but honestly, I swear the British have the best slang. You heard of *bollocks*?"

I smiled. "Yeah."

"I mean, could there be a better term for balls? *Gormless* is another one of my favorites. I'm totally using that in casual conversation when I get back home — it's about a million times better than calling someone clueless. Anyway, I'm making a list." He swept the flashlight around for emphasis.

I felt the corners of my mouth pulling up into a smile. "You going to write some kind of paper?"

"You know we homeschooled kids can't get enough independent learning," Alex said. "You laugh now, but this may turn into a thesis someday. I could be, like, a professor of Briticisms."

"You going to take up an English accent, too?"

"Hell yeah, if I could pull one off. Who knew you could learn another language all while still speaking English?" Alex started talking with a thick British accent, although it sounded like a bit of a mash-up with some Irish and Australian, too. "I say, good sir, tallyho, what-what."

I couldn't stop giggling. I sat down, leaned back on the bench, and stared up at the sky. There were so many lights in London that it was hard to make out any stars. It was as if night never fully arrived. But it seemed bizarre to be sitting there, joking with Alex as if everything were normal, while both of us tried to ignore the awkwardness between us.

Nicki was out in the city somewhere, waiting for me to kill her mom. Making sure her alibi was airtight, toasting pint glasses with friends or splitting an order of chicken tikka masala, making sure a security camera caught her on film. I wondered if she felt even the slightest regret, or if she'd already determined that her mom wasn't worthy enough to occupy space on the planet. It must have been nice for her to be so certain of herself and her place in the world. I wished for the one millionth time that I could call Emily. She wouldn't know what to do either, but I still wanted her advice.

"You're a natural," I said to Alex. "With that accent, I would have thought you walked right out of Buckingham Palace."

"Tell me about it. Lots of people say I am a dead ringer, voice wise, for Prince William."

I was suddenly exhausted. I pushed off from the bench. "We should go in before he starts looking for us or wants to share a cigarette with you." I held out my hand to help pull Alex to his feet. I shuffled behind him as he returned the flashlight to the guard and asked courteously to be told if anyone turned in a silver lighter. We paused on the worn carpeted steps. I could see the individual threads breaking free, like tiny whiskers.

"Tomorrow should be good," Alex said, his foot kicking aimlessly at the balustrade.

"I forget what's on the schedule," I admitted.

"The war rooms museum thingy. The underground one."

"Oh yeah." The idea of rummaging around in a World War II bunker didn't set me on fire, but everyone's got his own thing. "Should be fun. See you tomorrow," I said, trying to sound plucky and upbeat.

"Sounds good."

Neither of us moved. My hand rested on the waxed wooden banister. "If you want, we could grab a cup of coffee or something after," I finally suggested. "We didn't really get to go out today." I held my breath, waiting for his response. I hated that my lies had made things between us strained.

"I might have plans," Alex said, not looking up from his shoes.

My gut ached as if he'd punched me.

He poked me in the ribs. "I'm joking."

"Not funny," I said.

He shrugged. "Social skills aren't my strongest asset."

"I suppose your accent is what you've got going for you."

"That and my good looks and charm." He smirked, then leaned over to kiss me softly. "I'd love to go out with you. Sleep well."

"You too."

TWENTY-TWO

The Churchill War Rooms museum was more interesting than I had imagined, but not so interesting that my ass didn't drag the entire time. I could find history only so fascinating when current affairs were keeping me up nights. Being in the tight bunkers with the low ceilings made me feel claustrophobic, but it wasn't Winston Churchill that I felt breathing down my neck—it was Nicki.

My poor sleep was catching up to me. I was exhausted, but at night I would toss and turn, trying to figure out what to do next, unable to drift off. My eyes felt constantly gritty and my nerves raw.

Now that I had an address for Nicki, I'd decided—at one a.m. when I'd been unable to sleep—to talk to Detective Sharma. She was the kind of person who didn't like loose ends. She might not believe anything I said, but she'd check Nicki out just to make sure she'd done her due diligence. My real stroke of genius came an hour later, around two, when I realized I didn't need to tell her the *whole* story. This was a case when the truth was way too weird to be believed.

Instead I'd talk about how Nicki and I had met on the plane and that she had been really interested in Connor. And how I'd seen her around town—almost as if she were following me—so when I got the clipping, it seemed as though it must have come from her. It wouldn't be enough to get Nicki in any trouble, and she could easily come up with an excuse to explain everything, including why she had given me a fake name, but having the cops show up to ask questions would give her pause.

What I was really proud of was the fact that *my* plan stopped *her* plan in its tracks. There would be no way her mom could be murdered once this happened. The police wouldn't think Nicki had done anything to Connor. There was no reason to suspect her. But if her name came up connected to Connor's death *and then* her mom ended up at the bottom of a staircase with a broken neck? Well, that was going to raise some serious questions.

Nicki wouldn't be able to go through with her plan to kill her mom, or at the very least she would have to leave me out of it. Once I was safely back home, I'd mail a letter to Nicki's mom warning her. She might not believe me either, but she'd be more careful. If she had any suspicions about her daughter, it might be enough for her to take the step to kick her out. I was absurdly proud of having outmaneuvered

Nicki. And after I'd thought that far, I'd finally been able to fall asleep.

When we left the museum, Alex went with Jamal to a game store. We had plans to meet up for dinner, but I told him I had something I needed to do first. I didn't tell him that I'd made a call that morning and I knew the police would be waiting for me at the dorm. I was nervous, but also excited. I didn't want this hanging over me anymore. When Alex got back, I'd tell him that I talked to the cops. It would be out of my hands. I could move on. We could move on. There wouldn't be anything standing between us anymore.

Detectives Fogg and Sharma were in the lobby of Metford. Detective Sharma pushed herself up off the sofa, tucking away her phone as soon as she saw me.

I took a step toward her. The front desk clerk called out, "Kim? You've got a phone call." She held out the receiver. I opened my mouth to tell her to take a message. "They say it's important," she said before I could speak.

I waved at Detective Sharma to let her know I saw her and jogged over to the desk. My stomach felt as if it were full of lead. I could think of only one person who would call me.

I took the receiver as though it were a poisonous snake. It was still warm from the clerk's hand. "Hello, this is Kim."

"You let me down," Nicki chastised.

"I told you I wasn't going to do it," I said.

Nicki sighed as if I were a difficult toddler having a

meltdown in the candy aisle. "You can't just *decide* that you don't want to. We had a deal. What kind of person would I be if I let you walk away from that agreement?"

"I'm not going to debate this with you."

"I had a hunch you might do something stupid and I was right. Why in the world would you call the police? You must realize that won't go well for you."

"How do you know —"

"Look toward the library." I spun and peered down the hall. Nicki was leaning against the door, holding her cell phone to her ear. She waggled her fingers at me in greeting. "I saw the police as soon as I walked in. Trust me, that's the luckiest thing that could have happened. I'm guessing you haven't told them about me yet?"

I swallowed hard. "I wouldn't do that."

She cocked her head with one eyebrow raised. "Liar, liar, pants on fire."

"Leave me alone," I whispered.

"I thought we could be friends, but if that's not what you want, that's fine. However, it seems to me you could use a few people in your corner."

Now it was my turn to raise an eyebrow in disbelief. "You're not my friend."

"Of course I am. Otherwise I would have given it to the police right away."

Frost crept over my heart. "Given *what* to them?"

"Ask the clerk. I left something for you." Nicki paused, watching me from down the hall. "Go on, ask her."

I turned around slowly. I cleared my throat. "Excuse me, did anyone drop anything off for me?"

The clerk looked up from her desk as if surprised to still see me there. "Let me look." She checked the cubbyholes where they slotted our mail. The clerk pulled out a plain white envelope with my name on it and passed it over. "Here you go."

The thick envelope felt almost oily to the touch. I tucked the receiver under my chin and tore open the letter. There was a single sheet of paper inside. I unfolded it carefully, as if it were a ticking bomb. It was a photocopy, slightly crooked and a bit blurry, but there was no mistaking my handwriting.

WHY I HATE CONNOR O'REILLY AND WHY HE DESERVES TO DIE

The long list I'd made on the plane stared up at me. I remembered writing it, but it felt like something that had happened a lifetime ago. The saliva in my mouth dried up and I wanted to drop the toxic paper. I vaguely recalled her placing it, along with the list she'd written about her mom, into her bag on the plane. Thanks to the vodka haze, I hadn't thought about it since. I shoved it into my pocket.

"Now, if the police were to get a copy of that, I have to think it wouldn't look good. I'm sure they've wondered about your interactions with Connor, but I doubt they think you *murdered* him. You've got no history of violence. And even if you were going to kill him, you wouldn't strike anyone as the type to do it that way. Too messy. Heavens, they're not even certain that it wasn't just a tragic accident. No point in giving them a reason to rethink that theory."

"You kept this on purpose," I said.

"Of course I did."

"You planned it."

She pursed her lips as if considering. "No. I wouldn't say that. I tucked it away, just as a spot of insurance. I certainly didn't plan to *use* it. I still don't. I don't want you to get into trouble. You're acting like I'm the bad guy, when I'm simply asking for you to keep your promise. You're not doing what you said you would and then you're trying to get me into trouble." Nicki shook her head. "Honestly, you're the one making things difficult. How do you think I felt when I got home this morning and there was my mum puttering about in her dressing gown in the kitchen? Then I come here and see a couple of detectives in the lobby. You're the one not leaving me a lot of options."

I tried to imagine explaining to the police that I hadn't meant anything by the list, that I'd just been blowing off steam, and that she'd been the one to trick me into writing the part about how he deserved to die. The cops hadn't decided it was murder, but they also hadn't declared it an accident, either. If the police got this note, that could sway the investigation. Sure, there was no proof that I did it, but I'd been on the platform. If they put pressure on Alex, he might not be willing to lie for me anymore—not after all the other lies I'd told. Not if he saw this. I'd basically stalked Connor at work and followed him here to England, and there were plenty of people who would testify I wasn't happy about what he'd done to me. Then I'd lied, saying I didn't know him, then saying we dated, then admitting we hadn't. This sheet of paper basically tied up the investigation with a nice, tidy bow. CRAZY GIRL KILLS HER EX.

I clutched the phone. "Please don't tell," I whispered into the receiver, as if talking into her ear.

Nicki smiled. "I keep trying to get you to believe me: I don't want any trouble. Now, first things first. I'm going to hang up. Then you're going to give those nice detectives some story about why you called them, but it's not going to involve me. If it does, I'll hand this list right over."

I squeezed my eyes shut. "I can't do it."

"Can't do what? Talk to the police? Of course you can. Just spin them a little tale."

"No, I mean I can't—" I glanced over my shoulder at the front desk clerk, who was busy tapping away on her laptop. "I can't do the other thing."

"Murder my mum?"

I flinched as her words seemed to scream through the phone. "Yeah."

"We'll worry about that later. First, get rid of the detectives. Then we'll talk." She clicked her phone off and then motioned for me to hang up.

I slowly passed the receiver back to the clerk. "Thanks," I said.

Detectives Fogg and Sharma were both standing, waiting for me. I trudged over and shook their hands. "Thanks for coming," I said.

"We were glad to get your call." Detective Fogg smiled. There was a sliver of something black wedged between two of his teeth. I focused on that instead of his eyes. "You said you had something to tell us?"

Could Nicki hear our conversation from the hall? I shoved my hand into my jean pocket and felt the wadded-up paper. That list would bury me. "Yeah. I did," I said, playing for time.

They both waited for me to speak.

"Did you want to go somewhere else to talk?" Detective Sharma eventually asked, breaking the uncomfortable silence.

"No. I, um . . . it's just that it seemed more important earlier and now it seems silly." I hitched my bag up higher on my shoulder.

"We never know what might be useful in an investigation," DI Sharma said. She motioned for me to sit on the sofa, and she and DI Fogg took the two wingback chairs across from me.

"So, I was just thinking about Connor. He was really worried about his college applications. His grades weren't as high as he needed for some of the schools he was wanting to get into."

The detectives looked at each other in confusion. "Okay. And . . ."

"And you'd asked if there was any reason he might be depressed. I didn't think of it at the time."

"Mm-hmm."

"Yeah." I picked at a crack in the leather sofa cushion. "I thought I should mention it. You know, just in case." I crossed my fingers that they wouldn't ask me, *In case of what?* "Maybe he really had decided to kill himself, because he was so stressed, or maybe he hired someone to push him in front of the train because he was worried he wouldn't get into McGill, his top choice." I paused and sighed in real embarrassment. "I know. It seemed important this morning when I thought of it, but I guess I wanted to help so badly, I let my imagination get away from me."

The lipstick around Detective Sharma's mouth was a bright red, like an angry slash across her face. She slapped her thighs and stood. "Okay, then. If you think of anything else, you let us know. We want to hear from you if you get any more ideas."

Detective Fogg looked less convinced that he wanted to ever hear from me again.

"I'm so sorry I dragged you down here." I meant it, too. I wished now I'd never called them. I'd thought I was so clever, coming up with a way to get rid of her. It was beginning to dawn on me that that would never happen. "I didn't mean to waste your time."

"Getting clarity for Connor's family is our number one priority. There's nothing that we won't do to further that aim."

I couldn't tell if Detective Sharma was reminding herself or if she was warning me.

TWENTY-THREE

AUGUST 25
6 DAYS REMAINING

You're going to love it!" Nicki gripped the rail of the Thames Clipper as it cruised down the river. She bounced on her tiptoes with excitement. "The observatory is one of my favorite places in the city. You can stand right on the prime meridian." She glanced over at me. "Do you know what that is?"

"It divides the earth into Eastern and Western hemispheres," I said, my voice flat. She raised her hand for a high-five, but I refused to slap it back.

"Got it in one. Nicely done. The observatory was built in 1670."

I couldn't stand her nonstop tour guide patter. She'd called and insisted we meet at the wharf. I agreed because I was fresh out of ideas. I'd had to skip our official activity, too, pleading a fake migraine headache. Kendra had made a snide comment about how it was turning out that I was quite the delicate flower with all my health issues. So not only was I missing a chance to see Stonehenge and ticking off the other people in my group, but I was also stuck with a psycho.

"I went here the first time as a kid with my grandfather," Nicki said. "He was an amateur astronomer. He had his own telescope, and when I would stay with them at their cabin up on the Orkney Islands, he would wake me up late at night and take me out to look at the stars."

"Sounds nice," I mumbled.

"It felt so naughty, being up past bedtime, when of course my grandma *knew* the whole time. She was the one who would make sure we had a big thick quilt and a thermos of hot chocolate and ginger biscuits, but I liked thinking it was something special, just for Grandpa and me. As if we were getting away with something. We'd sit in the garden, me in my pajamas, and he'd tell me all about the various constellations and Newton and Herschel and Halley." Nicki's voice trailed off as if she were still listening to the far-off voice of her grandfather. "I think that's when I got interested in science. His excitement was infectious. How about you? Who got you into robotics?"

I watched the brown water slip past the boat, turning into a frothy cream in our wake. The Thames had an interesting odor, briny like the ocean, but with a thick, murky smell of mud. "My dad, I guess." I shrugged. "I was always good at it. It made sense to me. I like things that can be measured. Data. Stats."

"Was that hard with your mum? She seems a bit more . . . woo-woo. All that *trust in your destiny, find your passion, know your moon cycle* blah blah, she seems like the kind who'd believe in crystals."

My hands tightened around the rail, the knuckles turning white. "What do you know about my mom?" I refused to even think about the line of "healing" crystals that Mom had lined up in the kitchen, reflecting light across the walls.

Nicki tossed her head to get her hair out of her eyes. "I checked you out online. I found her blog and started reading. Fascinating stuff."

My heart clenched into a hot fist in the center of my chest. I hated the idea of Nicki crawling all over stories of me as a kid. Picking apart my history by reading between the lines. It was also a reminder that she didn't leave any stone unturned. She thought of everything. She knew too much.

"Mothers, huh? Can't live with them, hard to get away with killing them." Nicki barked out a laugh just as the Clipper bumped against the Greenwich dock. Nicki squealed and grabbed my hand. "We're here! Come with me."

She pulled me through the crowd, weaving our way up to the observatory, calling out the sights as we went. I tried to pull my hand out of hers, but it was as if we were handcuffed together.

Nicki stopped short at the top of the hill. "Ugh, there's a line to get in." She glared at the people waiting to get inside the observatory. "Let's wait a bit to see if it clears. It's no fun to look around if a bunch of insipid tourists are milling about." She poked me in the ribs. "No offense. I feel like you're an honorary local. Here, check out the view."

I walked over to stand next to her. There was a field of green below us leading to a cluster of old buildings, then the river and the glass high-rises just beyond. "Nice." There was no way I was going to admit it was impressive, as though we were in the past looking toward the future. London was always overlapping the present onto the past, blurring the two together.

"We can talk here," Nicki said.

Hot acid rose up in my throat. I'd known that's why she wanted to get together, but now that she was going to speak, I wanted to bolt before I heard what she had to say. "Okay," I said. I made sure I was ready.

"Now, this might seem rude, but I'm going to need your phone"—Nicki shrugged—"and I'm going to pat you down." She smiled. "No bad touch, I promise."

I stepped back. "What?"

"I want to make sure you're not recording what I say. I want to trust you, but with recent events . . ." Nicki let her voice trail off.

I handed over my phone, feeling my hopes shrinking down, collapsing in on themselves. She smirked when she saw the record function open, but she didn't seem angry. If anything, she seemed proud of me for making the attempt. She erased the track, then clicked the phone off, jamming it into her bag. I stood stiffly while she quickly patted down my pockets and ran her fingers through my hair, making sure I wasn't wearing any kind of wire. "You done?" I asked coldly.

"Don't be a cranky pants. I'm just making sure that we go into this discussion as equals. No more trying to outmaneuver the other—we'll start fresh, okay?"

"Clean slate?"

"Exactly." She linked arms with me. "Let's walk and talk. We started off well, but we got onto a bad track."

I blinked rapidly, trying to clear the fog of anger. "A bad track? You murdered Connor. That's not bad. That's a fucking disaster." I glanced around belatedly to make sure no one was close enough to overhear our conversation.

She rolled her eyes. "A disaster would have been getting caught. We went over this last time. Connor isn't worth being this upset."

"He didn't deserve what happened to him." I flashed to the image of his shoe lying on the train platform.

"You want the world to be this place where things happen because people deserve them, but you know it's not that way. Does someone who gets cancer deserve it?"

"No, of course not," I said furiously.

"And someone who's born into a family with a lot of money, did they do something to deserve their privilege?"

I pulled my arm back from hers. "No, I'm not saying that . . ."

I wanted to shake her words out of my ears. They had this tendency to burrow in, as though they wanted to take root. She repulsed me, but she was also fascinating.

"But you are. You're trying to insist that there is some ultimate sense of justice in the world. My point is that Connor wasn't a great guy. Because he's dead, you're focusing on the good stuff instead of remembering his real character."

"I'm not saying Connor was perfect, but he wasn't evil." My mind darted against my will to what Miriam had told me about him manipulating girls to get photos and then sharing those pictures with the world. I shoved away the uncomfortable truth that Nicki might be right, that he wasn't worth it.

Nicki giggled. "Evil? Jesus, you do have a bit of your mum's woo-woo genes. Next thing I know, you'll be reading his aura. Of course he wasn't *evil*—this isn't some BBC drama with angels and demons. He was in your way and now he's not. It's that simple. If it had been an accident, you wouldn't admit it, but part of you would have felt he got what he deserved."

I refused to even let myself think about how I might have felt. It didn't matter. It hadn't been an accident. "And your mom is in your way," I said.

Nicki nodded enthusiastically as if she were my tutor and I'd finally figured out a tricky geometry problem on my own. "Exactly."

"I can't just *kill* someone." I cracked my knuckles in the hope that that would release the tension building up in my body.

"Do you know how the military trains people to kill?" Nicki asked. "They studied it—an American, I think. He called it *killology*." She noticed my expression. "I'm not making it up. I can't recall the guy's name, but he wrote a book about it after studying World War Two. It's complicated, of course, but it's all about training. If you want to make people who are generally not killers into a military unit capable of shooting and bombing others, you have to change how they think."

"And that's what you've done?"

"You're making it sound like I've got loads of people buried in the cellar or something." She rolled her eyes. "Do you think a soldier in the army is looking at the guy across the field from him and pondering how that guy might have a family, or own a dog who likes him, or be a great painter? No, of course not. He thinks, *That guy is in my way. That guy's my enemy.* He doesn't even really see him as human, but an obstacle. That's how you win wars."

"At least that's how you get what you want."

"If that's your best option, then yes." Nicki pointed to a small food cart ahead of us on the path. "Do you want something to drink?"

She didn't wait for me to answer. She walked up, considered her choices, and fished through her pockets for some money.

"A Perrier and . . ." She looked back at me. I shook my head. I was certain if I swallowed anything it would come right back up. Once she had her drink, we kept circling the observatory building.

"Why is your mother in your way?"

Nicki unscrewed the top of her Perrier with a crackle of the metal cap and took a drink before answering. "Did you know that you have to be really careful if you're trying to rescue someone who's drowning?"

"No." The headache I'd faked to get out of going with my group was developing for real. Trying to keep up with Nicki's conversational train was like navigating a carnival fun house. You'd turn one way and it would be a dead end. You'd go in a new direction and think you were going the right way and then run smack into a mirror. Up was down, right was left, and nothing made sense.

"I worked for a summer as a lifeguard. Lousy job, by the way, sounds way better than it really is," Nicki said as an aside. "One of the things we were warned about in our training is that if someone is going down, they'll do anything. They're in survival mode. They'll try to crawl up your body to get out of the water. All that matters to them is getting their head clear so they can breathe."

"Okay."

Nicki took another long sip of her water. "That's my mum. It's bad enough that she's going down, but she's trying to take me with her. She's drowning in regret for her horrid decisions. She drinks too much. Then she falls for these guys who are total wankers and is surprised every time when they show their true colors. And then that makes her want to drink more, and that takes us full circle back to more bad decisions. She got a decent settlement from my dad when they split, and my grandparents left her money. She doesn't have to work, but she's spending cash like she's trying to punish someone. Except she's the only one who's going to get hurt."

"Why don't you move out?"

Nicki rocked back and forth on her heels. "It's not that easy."

I wanted to pull my hair out in frustration. "It's a hell of a lot easier than murdering her." I realized my voice was getting louder and forced myself to quiet down.

"God, you have a flair for drama." Nicki tossed her empty bottle into a recycling bin with a loud clank. "I chose you because I thought you were more of a scientist, but now you're acting like you're trying out for the Globe Theatre summer series.

"My mum is spending every last pound she has in the bank. Money that my grandparents meant to be for *my* university education. Maybe even to buy a small flat in the city. If I move out, I'll get none of that. My mum will cut me off to punish me for leaving. What I *will* get is an earful. How I've abandoned her just like my dad." Nicki's eyes narrowed and her normally calm demeanor broke as she spat out her last words. "She's used to getting her way. She thinks she's entitled to what she has, but I intend to teach her she's wrong."

I seized on what Nicki had said. "So, this is about money."

She sighed dramatically, her shoulders dropping. "It's partly about money. It's also about my freedom, which doesn't come without a cost after all. It's about doing what's right. And I know you don't believe it, but it's also about helping my mum."

I choked on the spit in my mouth. "Are you kidding? Getting me to kill her is doing her a favor?"

"Yes." Nicki paused. "Do you think things are going to get better for her? Because I don't. She's going to keep drinking. She's going to end up broke with a liver that gives out. If she goes now, it's ending all of that before it gets worse, before she ends up in some shitty bed-sit that she can barely afford while being on the dole. My mum's going to keep spiraling down. She's going to be miserable. And she's going to try to take me with her. Just like a drowning victim."

"She could turn her life around."

"Please. Let's not bother talking about things that are never going to happen. Let's keep the focus on finding a way you can do it that doesn't freak you out too much. I don't want you running off with things unfinished."

"It doesn't matter what you say. I'm never going to think the solution is killing your mom." I could hear the quaver in my own voice.

Nicki stopped walking and turned to me so we were face-to-face. "You don't have to think it's the best solution for me, or my mum. But you better realize it's the only solution to the problem you've got." Nicki tossed me my phone and it bounced off my chest. I caught it just before it hit the ground. She waved and then melted into the crowd of tourists.

I backed away from her. I refused to believe that homicide was my only solution, but I was scared. I couldn't go to the police or she would make it look as though I had murdered Connor. I couldn't tell my parents about her; with my past, they'd never believe me. I couldn't bear to tell Alex — the last thing I wanted to do was enmesh him in this black hole. Emily was too far away to give advice, and this wasn't the kind of thing I could put in a letter. Every direction I turned mentally, a door slammed shut, closing me in tighter and tighter until I felt ready to scream.

TWENTY-FOUR

I've knowingly killed only one thing in my life. I still have nightmares about it. It happened the summer between sophomore and junior years. My mom had gotten me a job helping a woman that she knew through church. Betty was old. Not like parent old, but seriously ancient — great-great-grandparent old. She'd shrunk down into a question mark and her skin was thin, as if she were disappearing one layer at a time. I worried that if I touched her, her flesh would tear away from the bone like wet tissue paper.

Betty was nice, and despite looking like an innocent old lady, she swore like a sailor. My summer job was being her "companion," which was a much nicer term than *babysitter*. I enjoyed hanging out with her; it didn't feel like work. I drove her to appointments and to the grocery store. I did a bit of cleaning, but not even that much because she had a maid service come once a week. Mostly I sat around with her and let her tell me stories about when she was younger, and we watched a lot of *Judge Judy*. The only downside to the job was that she lived way out in Deep Cove. I had to turn off the main parkway and follow a bunch of back roads that twisted into the hills to get to her place.

I'd been driving home one day after work thinking about what I was going to do that night when I saw a blur at the side of the road and then there was a sickening *thunk bump*. I hit the brakes and looked in the rearview mirror, but I didn't see anything.

The car door squeaked as I opened it and I stepped out carefully. It was like a scene from a horror film: a deserted road lined with tall pine trees, dark, complete with stupid teen girl wandering around. That's when I saw the bunny.

It lay on its side. It wasn't dead, but it was clear it was never going to be okay. The bunny's light gray fur was soaked with blood, and parts of its insides — pink twisty things — lay out-side, ripped from the stomach. One back leg was thumping madly as if the bunny wanted to run away, but the other back leg had a jut of bone poking up like a spear.

It was looking at me with a frantic, panicked eye.

I ran back to the car and then back to the bunny. I was crying, big fat tears and snot smeared together under my nose. Hot dread was in my stomach. I'd been going too fast. It was my fault. But I was also mad at the bunny. Why did it have to run out into my lane just as I was going past?

I looked up and down the road, hoping someone else would come by. Someone who would know how to handle this situation. I didn't have a box in the car, and I wasn't sure I'd even be able to scoop up the bunny. Its insides were on the outside, and I was certain there wasn't anything a vet would be able to do, even if I drove like a madwoman to the emergency veterinary clinic in Burnaby.

I considered driving away, but I hated the idea of just leaving the bunny there. It was clearly in agony. It was panting, and the eye that faced up kept darting around. And the leg. God, the leg didn't stop. It kept running and running in place. I closed my eyes so I didn't have to see it. Then opened them again because I had to look — this was all my fault.

"Please die," I whispered.

The bunny kept staring at me as though it wanted me to take some kind of action. I crouched next to it. I wondered if it would bite me if I tried to pet it. I didn't even know if petting it would make the bunny feel better. It wasn't someone's dog — it was a wild animal. Being stroked by a human wasn't going to make its final moments any easier.

Then I knew what I had to do. I got back into the car and turned around on the narrow road, being careful not to get too far over and drop a tire into one of the ditches. I could see the bunny in my headlights. I prayed that it would be still, but I could see the leg moving. I lined up the car and then I ran over the bunny again. There was another *thunk bump* as the car passed over the bunny's body. I might have been screaming. I can't really remember.

I got out, shaking. If that hadn't killed it, I was certain I would lose my mind. I didn't think I had it in me to drive over it again.

The bunny was dead.

I threw up, heaving repeatedly until the only thing I could bring up was a foamy yellow bile. I went to the side of the road and found a large stick. I used it to sort of push and poke the bunny off to the side. I didn't want anyone else to hit the body. I found some large rocks and piled them on top. I almost felt as if I should say something, like a eulogy, but my brain was blank. My mom was always the one who was better at finding the right words for things.

"Sorry," I said eventually, and then got back into the car. I told my parents about it when I got home, but I couldn't express just how awful it had been.

If that had upset me so much, how would I ever manage to kill a person? There would be no way I could run over a person. I didn't have a car here, for starters, and hadn't a clue how to drive on the other side of the road. Not to mention I'd also have to find a deserted road, and I hadn't seen any place in London that wasn't crawling with people, double-decker buses, or cars. There would be no way for me to escape. I wouldn't make it a block before someone would catch me.

I flopped onto my other side in my dorm bed, punching

my pillow to fluff it up. Not that I was considering doing it. What Nicki wanted. I wasn't a *murderer*. I didn't have it in me. I would never be able to go through with it . . . but at the same time, ever since I'd met with Nicki, my brain couldn't stop turning over my options.

I blew my hair off my face. Maybe, and it was a big stretch, *maybe* I could shoot someone. Especially if I could do it from a distance, like a sniper. But first off, there was no way for me to get a gun. England wasn't like the United States, where you could pick up a rifle at Walmart while also grabbing nail polish and a family-size bag of Cheetos. Even if, and it was a big *if*, I figured out a way to get a weapon illegally, I didn't know the first thing about how to fire a gun. Watching the occasional war movie with my dad on Sunday afternoons didn't make me a crack shot.

Fire wasn't an option. Their house was part of a row of town homes. There would be no way to control the flames. The fire would quickly spread; those buildings were old. All that ancient plaster, wallpaper, and oversize wood furniture — it would go up with a *whoosh*. If I felt horrible about the idea of killing Nicki's mom, the idea of taking out a bunch of her neighbors made it worse. Besides, whenever I played that "would you rather" game, I always chose being frozen to death instead of dying in a fire. *Hmm.* No, there wasn't exactly a way I could lure Nicki's mom onto a passing ice floe.

I squeezed my eyes shut. My thoughts were making me

nauseated. I tried to think of something else, anything else, to stop my train of thought. *Trains.* Nicki knew the underground stations. She'd been aware of where the cameras were located and where she could stand to push Connor without being seen. I didn't have a clue. Not to mention her mom struck me as the kind to stick to the oversize black cabs and not venture onto public transit. I didn't have the time to follow her around for weeks and wait for her to be standing at the top of a staircase all alone, just slightly off balance.

I got up and cranked the window open wider, seeking cool air. Stabbing was out. The way the knife would hesitate for just a second before the skin gave way and the knife slid in made me shiver. And I'd have to do it more than once. The odds that the first go would sever an artery weren't good.

I crawled back into bed. My best option would be poison. It wouldn't hurt. She'd just fall asleep and stay that way. Done right, the police might think it was an accident. It was an old house—it wouldn't seem weird if they owned rat poison. The whole city was filthy with rodents. You saw them in the Tube tunnels all the time and scurrying around openly in the streets at night. If Nicki's mom had seen a rat in their garden, she might have bought stuff to deal with it, and if she kept the poison in her kitchen, *and* she had been drinking . . . well, accidents happen.

Not that I was going to do it.

I rolled over onto my stomach, punching my pillow again,

trying to make the flat dense foam into something comfortable. The window was open as far as it would go. I was trying to lure a breeze, but the only thing that drifted in was traffic noise. I felt sick to my stomach. Nicki had gotten into my head. The sheets were twisted around my legs and I had to kick to get them free. An image of the bunny kicking on the road flashed into my head.

The bunny had thought it was getting away too.

TWENTY-FIVE

AUGUST 26
5 DAYS REMAINING

I sat there, intending to read, but I kept staring out into space. Metford's library had floor to ceiling bookcases and two long tables that ran the length of the room, looking as if they belonged in a castle's dining room. There were a couple of shelves of reference books, but the bulk of what made up the library was abandoned paperbacks. Residents left behind whatever they had brought to read, so there were ample copies of Stephen King novels, battered Agatha Christie and P. D. James mysteries, romance novels, and every sci-fi story you could imagine.

I was curled into a corner of the green velvet sofa by the window. The cushions were rock hard, and every time I shifted, ancient clouds of dust belched up. Yet I still felt as though I could have fallen asleep right there. I was exhausted. All night I'd tossed and turned, unable to shut off my racing brain. If I didn't get sleep soon, I was going to fall apart.

I had finally broken down and tried to call Emily. She's known me forever and she was the master at seeing through tricky problems. Granted, the worst moral quandary we'd faced so far was deciding if we should tell her parents about her brother planning a party for when they would be out of town. But when I reached the camp and begged the secretary to let me talk to Em, the woman had refused. I'd stared at the phone in shock. I repeated that it was an emergency and she'd *laughed*. She said that if she had to call camp counselors to the phone every time one of their friends had an emergency, they'd never get a thing done. Then she softened her voice and said they put through calls to counselors only from their parents. Camp policy. Right then, I hated Em for going to camp. Millions of summer jobs, and she had to choose one that might as well have put her on the moon.

I couldn't stand being in my room any longer, and I also didn't want to join everyone else in the cafeteria. So I'd headed to the library and grabbed a book, but it sat unopened on my lap. I was still staring into space.

Hands covered my eyes, plunging the room into darkness. I screamed and jammed my elbow back hard, connecting with someone who let out a loud *ooph*.

I leaped to my feet, ready to hurl the book at Nicki, but it was Alex standing there, rubbing his side.

"Note to self: never sneak up on you," Alex said. "You've got a nasty hook."

My heart vibrated at a thousand beats per second. "I didn't know it was you," I said, stating the obvious. Why did I have to constantly screw everything up? "I'm so sorry." My eyes flooded with hot tears.

Alex came around the sofa, stuffing his hands into his pockets. "Hey, it's okay. I know I look soft, but I'm tougher than I appear. I can take a blow and keep ticking. It's no big deal."

The smell of him — clean laundry mixed with sunshine and something spicy — made my heart slow. He was like human Xanax in a sweatshirt. "Sorry, I'm being a freak."

"You know mentioning your freak tendencies just turns me on, right?" I punched him lightly in the stomach. He backed up, laughing. "Just because I said you could hit me once doesn't mean you can make a habit out of it."

"Look, I feel —"

"I hate that th —"

We'd both started talking at the same time and then laughed. Alex held up a hand. "I was going to say that I hate that things are weird between us."

"Me too," I replied.

"Let's just forget that all that stuff happened."

I nodded. *All that stuff* were my lies and his need to run to Tasha and tell on me. I wondered how he'd respond if he saw the list I'd made of why I wanted to kill Connor. We both looked away from each other. Clearly neither of us was great at the whole talking-about-our-feelings thing.

"So, I had an idea and I made a plan for something for us to do. That is, if you're game." His mouth curled up at the corner and I felt a flutter in my chest.

"What kind of plan?"

"A surprise." He bounced on his feet like a toddler. "Grab your phone. We're going out."

I narrowed my eyes, trying to guess what he was up to. "Out where?"

"You do understand the concept of a surprise, right?" When I opened my mouth to protest, he turned me by my waist and pointed me toward the stairs. The heat of his hands felt as if they were burning through my thin shirt, marking my skin. "No more debating — get your phone, unless you don't want to go?"

I liked the feeling of his hands on my hips. "I want to go."

"Of course you do. Who doesn't like an adventure?"

"Is everybody going?"

He shook his head. "Nope. This is just the two of us."

I wanted to tell him I couldn't care less about any adventure. We could sit on this stupid dusty sofa all night and he could give me a blow-by-blow description of some stupid role-playing game he liked and I'd be thrilled. It was his company that I loved.

"Count me in," I said.

Alex pulled me down the street. I liked the feel of my hand in his, as though it belonged there. "C'mon, we don't want to be late," he said.

Alex weaved between people on the sidewalk and then stopped short. "Ta-da!"

We were at the base of the London Eye, the huge glassed-in Ferris wheel attraction right on the river. It spun slowly, impossibly high in the sky, its glass pods full of people.

"Are you serious?" My voice went up. My inner afraid-of-heights voice was already screaming, *Hell no!* "I heard this sells out a lot." My guts were turning to water. *Please let him not have tickets.*

"Would I drag you all the way here and not make sure we were ready to go?" Alex pulled two tickets out of his pocket, fanning them out. "I even splurged for the VIP option. We get a glass of sparkling cider and chocolates when we're at the top because we are very important people."

"Wow, it's really tall," I said, shading my eyes to look up even though the sun was no longer in the sky.

"It goes up something like five hundred feet! It's Europe's tallest Ferris wheel."

"Huh, how about that."

There was no way I could do this. I would throw up or pass out. Or throw up and then pass out.

Alex bowed and pointed me in the direction of the entrance. Clammy sweat broke out all over my body. I forced my legs forward, marching like a stiff toy soldier. Alex passed over our tickets and we were moved to the next area to wait for our car.

"Are you okay?" Alex asked.

So much for thinking I was playing it cool. "Heights freak me out a little." I managed a watery smile.

His expression crumpled. "Oh. I had no idea." He stepped to the side. "We can do something else."

I felt a wave of relief. And then tension swept back in. The tickets weren't cheap. He'd planned this whole thing to do something nice for me, something special. I stiffened my spine. "No, I want to go."

"Are you sure? I don't mind if you don't want to do it."

I sucked in a deep breath. It wasn't just about the price of the tickets. Being scared was illogical. This thing had passed a million and one safety checks. The only thing in my way was my own fear. I had to stop being afraid of everything. And it wasn't about doing it because he'd planned something special. I believed him that it didn't matter to him. What mattered is that I wanted to do it. "No, I'm going."

Our car coasted to the base, and the guide started to direct everyone in. The pod moved slowly enough that it didn't have to come to a complete stop. Alex hesitated, but when he saw the determination in my eyes, he reached for my hand.

"You can do this," he said, then squeezed.

I paused as I stepped over the threshold. There would be no getting off once I was on. They weren't going to stop the whole thing just because I was freaking out. Once we were inside, my knees felt as though they were going to give out. I had a death grip on Alex's hand.

"Do you want to sit down?" Alex motioned to the curved bench in the center of the pod.

"No. I want to see." I clutched the railing as we — very slowly — started to rise. This was going to be the longest thirty minutes of my life.

Alex kept up a nonstop chatter as we went, talking about what we were seeing and random bits of related trivia. His words trickled into one ear and then disappeared in a fog, but they were still comforting. He didn't pause for me to say anything. He seemed to know that I needed him to keep talking.

When we reached the top, I closed my eyes briefly. I was doing this. Then a zap of joy ran through me. *I was doing this!* I turned and noticed that Alex was watching me.

"Okay?" he asked.

I smiled. "Yeah. I am."

At least I would be, as long as I kept my eyes on the horizon and not down on the ground.

He squeezed my hand. "You're more than okay."

"What is it Yoda says? 'Do, not try'?" I said, getting the expression wrong on purpose to make Alex smile.

He shook his head in fake annoyance. "Close enough. I'm proud of you."

I flushed. "Proud of me for basically doing a jazzed-up carnival ride?" I tried to wave off his compliment.

"No, for doing what scares you."

I smiled back and stood up straighter.

After the ride, we walked across the river and ducked into a pub. We lucked out — there was an empty table just inside the door. Alex tossed his jacket onto the back of one of the chairs.

"Is this okay? You sit on the far side so you don't get cold with people going in and out. I'll go get us something to drink. Coke okay?"

I nodded and sat, wiping off the damp table with my sleeve. I felt almost high from the experience on the London Eye — no pun intended. I'd done it.

Alex was back a minute later, putting down two glasses. "I ordered some fries, too."

"Chips," I corrected him, grinning. "They call them chips here. If you're going to collect slang, you've got to get that right."

The pub was loud. A crowd of rowdy guys at the bar were cheering on a soccer — oops, *football* — game on the TV. Every few seconds they would scream out advice or heap scorn onto the players. Alex and I sat side by side at the tiny table, holding hands underneath it.

The waitress dropped a basket in front of us. The fries were molten lava hot, burning the top of my mouth right behind my front teeth when I bit into one. I sucked in a breath, trying to cool down my mouth.

"That's what you get for being greedy," Alex said.

I picked up two more fries, held them up in front of his face, and then stuffed them into my mouth, knowing it would make him laugh. Alex snorted, his shoulders shaking. I felt my heart surge.

Then something caught his eye and he waved madly at the far end of the bar, trying to get someone's attention. "Do you know Erin?"

I shook my head. "Erin who?"

"She's at Metford too. I've met her a couple of times. I want to thank her—she gave me the idea for tonight. I saw her in the laundry room and she mentioned how there was the VIP option."

I turned, scanning the crowd for a familiar face from the cafeteria. "Is she from the U.S.?"

"No, she's Scottish. Down here for a term doing something with art history before she starts university up there next year. You'll like her." He waved again.

I wasn't really interested in having to make nice with a stranger. I wanted Alex to myself.

"Hey-ho, you came," drawled a Scottish brogue. "Did you love the views?"

"It was gr—" My tongue locked into place. It was Nicki. I felt off balance, as if I were back on top of the Eye, spinning slowly over the city.

She held out her hand. "I'm Erin." She squeezed into a chair. She smiled at me across the table.

"I owe you—it was a fantastic idea," Alex said.

"Did you like it too?" she asked me. "Some people find it a bit too tall."

I just sat there. What the hell was she doing?

"They overthink things, imagining risk where there isn't any. You're more likely to be hit by a train than fall off that thing." Nicki smirked.

I'd told her at the airport I feared heights. She found ways to use everything I'd ever said. It was as if she could see into my brain.

Nicki shook her glass, the ice rattling at the bottom. Then she slowly wrapped her mouth around the straw, drawing in her cheeks as she drank the last of the liquid from the bottom. "I think I've sucked this dry," she said, with a wink at Alex. And then she licked her lips.

My hands underneath the table clenched into tight fists.

Alex flushed. "I'll get you another." He took a few steps away and then came back to my side. "Sorry—did you want anything, Kim?" He motioned to my half-empty glass.

I managed to shake my head and waited until he was gone. Then I grabbed Nicki by the arm, yanking her close. "So now your name is Erin?"

She shrugged and then picked my fingers off her sleeve. "He's adorable, by the way. Geek chic. I kept seeing you together, out and about, and I said to myself, *Now, that right there might be what has Kim all aflutter.* I made a point to meet him."

"Leave him alone," I hissed.

"Are you afraid I'm going to steal him away?" She let her mouth curl up and then patted my hand. "Don't worry, he's crazy about you. He makes moon eyes when your name comes up—I swear. It's the cutest thing ever. Is this why you haven't had your eye on the ball?"

"I don't know what you're talking about." The crowd at the bar let out an anguished groan. Someone had missed the chance to score a goal.

Nicki shook her head. "No playing like you're an idjit. It's not that I don't understand how intoxicating a new bloke can be, but you need to get your priorities straight."

"You made him take me on the Eye."

She sat back with a sigh. "I didn't make him do anything. I simply talked about how this was such a once-in-a-lifetime experience. The kind of thing you should share with someone special."

"I told you I was afraid of heights the first time we met."

One perfectly tweezed eyebrow twitched. "Did you?" She tapped her lips with a finger. "You know, now that you mention it, you may have said something. But look at it this way: you confronted a fear and did it. I had a hunch you wouldn't back down when he was around and I was right. It was like a little experiment and you passed."

"You let him think you're an art history student?"

Nicki picked at her nail polish. "What? I love art history. I might study it someday." She looked up at me pointedly. "It depends on if I have any money to go to university."

"I don't know how to do it," I said. My voice was tight, like an archer's bowstring. "I'll get caught."

Nicki paused, letting a group of women teeter past our table in impossibly short skirts and incredibly tall heels. "I like that we're discussing *how* instead of *what*. That's progress, at least. Looks like facing down a fear might be moving you forward in general."

"I keep trying to tell you—I'm not the person to do this. If I get caught"—I leaned forward—"which I will, it isn't going to go well for you, either. The cops are going to want to know why I did it. The truth is going to come out. You'll end up in jail right next to me. You need to hire a professional." I lowered my voice even though there was no chance anyone could hear me in the loud bar. "You need a hit man."

She laughed. "A hit man? You sound like you're in a bad gangster movie. I must hand it to you: At least you're no longer talking about how people don't deserve it. And how it's wrong. Blah blah blah. Honestly, all that morality was getting dull."

"Being a decent person isn't dull," I said.

"Says the person who made a list of reasons why Connor deserved to die. Guess your morality was less exacting back then." She tapped her fingernails on the table.

"That doesn't mean I wanted him pushed in front of a train," I fired back.

"No, that is exactly what you wanted; it's just that you were too scared to do it. Or maybe you thought you couldn't get away with it. But here's the thing." She tapped me on the shoulder, like a queen anointing a knight. "I believe in you. I know you're smart. You can figure this out. But you're running out of time."

"I can't—"

"I don't want to hear any more excuses." Her voice was tight and clipped. Her teeth looked sharp in the dim pub lights. "I'll be out tomorrow night. This time I don't want to be disappointed when I get back home."

Alex approached the table with a glass in hand. Nicki jerked her head up, her lips peeling back into a jack-o'-lantern-size smile. "Oy! That's my man." She took the drink from Alex's hand and took a long sip, then stood. "Now, I'm not going to stick my nose into your date any longer. I'll let you lovebirds have some time alone. I've got to run."

"Do you want to go back with us? It's getting late," Alex offered. I tried not to react.

Nicki smiled. "Aw, love a gallant man. He's right—it is a dangerous city . . ." She let her voice trail off.

"I'm sure you'll be fine," I said.

"Oh, you know it." Nicki tossed back the rest of her drink and walked out of the bar.

TWENTY-SIX

AUGUST 27
4 DAYS REMAINING

Every second of the next day I could sense a huge clock running above my head: the countdown to when Nicki would be expecting me to do something. Not *something* — murder.

As the day crawled by, I kept checking my phone on the off chance that the camp secretary had broken down and told Emily I needed to reach her, but there was nothing. Just the ticking of the clock, lurching toward the point of no return. Nicki's expectations grew heavier and tighter, suffocating me until I couldn't breathe.

There was a quiet tap on my door just before midnight. My throat seized shut as if someone were choking me. It had to be her. She seemed to have no trouble sneaking in and out of the building and now she was wondering why I wasn't at her house pushing her mom down a flight of stairs. I closed my eyes and prayed she would go away, but there was another soft knock.

Metford didn't have peepholes, so I had to settle for cracking the door and peering out. It was Alex. The tension in my muscles vanished.

I opened the door. "What are you doing here?" I glanced up and down the hall to see if anyone had spotted him on a girls' floor after hours.

"I was worried about you."

I motioned him in. The room was so small that his body touched mine as he slid past. There wasn't much space, so we both sat on the bed. I was wearing a sweatshirt, which needed a wash, and a pair of old boxers that I slept in. I hoped he hadn't been expecting me to be busting out the Victoria's Secret.

"You don't need to worry about me," I said.

"All day you seemed off. And then tonight you hardly talked to me." Alex shifted. "Did I do something?"

"What? No."

Alex swallowed hard. "I wondered if it was about Erin from last night. We were having a good time before I said hi to her, but then you got quiet at the pub and stayed that way all day today. You know she's just a friend, right? I mean, not even really a friend, just someone I talked to a couple times. I know she can be a bit . . . sorta . . . over-the-top." He shrugged embarrassedly. "But I don't, like, like her or anything."

I winced. The last thing I wanted was for him to feel bad. Alex was the one good thing I had in my life.

"I'm sorry." I picked at the blanket on the bed. I wanted to tell him that Erin was more than an "over-the-top" flirt — she was dangerous — but he'd never believe me. "It's not you. I don't know what's wrong with me. I'm just distracted. I'm not sleeping well lately." I motioned around the small room. "Although with this kind of posh sleeping quarters, I don't know what my problem is."

I did know the problem. Nicki expected me to kill her mom at some point tonight and that wasn't going to happen. Nicki was running out of patience and that wasn't going to go well for me.

"Why can't you sleep?" Alex said.

We were sitting side by side, our legs touching. I was suddenly aware that we were on my bed. The space between us seemed charged.

"I don't know. Nothing," I said.

He sighed. "You know, everything is going to be okay." He turned my chin so we were looking at each other.

I nodded, but I didn't believe him. My heart picked up at his touch, but not just at that; I was terrified about what would happen when I didn't kill Nicki's mom, or, worse, if she finally ground me down and I did something unforgivable just to make her go away. I'd worked the problem every way I could think of, but I couldn't come up with a solution. My lower lip started to shake.

"Hey, come here." Alex pulled me close, pulling the tension out of me. He was warm, and the pressure of his arms around me wrapped me in security. My flesh lit up wherever his touched mine.

Alex rested his chin on the top of my head. "Tell me what you're afraid of."

I closed my eyes. "Feels like everything."

"Not me, I hope."

I pulled his arms tighter around me, liking the heat of him. "Not you. I'm sorry I keep screwing everything up. I'm supposed to be smart, but I don't feel like I'm acting like it." My voice was tight, strangled by tears that wanted to come out.

"You didn't screw everything up. Some things just *are* screwed up." The pad of his thumb rubbed along my shoulder.

My arm was at an uncomfortable angle, but I didn't want to shift because I was afraid if I did he would move away.

Alex's chest rose and fell, lifting me with it like a wave. "What you have to remember is that things usually work themselves out. Life has a plan. Just think about it. What were the odds that we would have both taken this program? Then take it bigger: What were the odds that both of us would have been born around the same time? Think how awkward this would be if I finally found you and you were ninety years old. Everyone would call you a cougar for hanging out with me."

I giggled. "Or you could have been born in another country and we might not even speak the same language," I offered.

"With luck I'd speak French, the language of love." His

hands ran down my arms. Goose bumps popped up in their wake. "My point is, we don't know what will happen."

"I know," I said.

His mouth was near my ear, and the touch of his breath made me shiver. "I really like you. I won't hurt you. I promise."

"I like you too," I whispered. In the silence, I felt as though he must have been able to hear my heart.

"We'll just figure it out as we go. Things are partly weird because we're here and because of everything that's happened. We go home in just a few days. It will be different there."

"I'd like to meet your family," I admitted. "Your kid brother sounds pretty amazing."

"Clearly you haven't been listening. My brother is an escapee from one of the levels of hell. He's half demon. And he smells bad. Did I mention that? It's like he's allergic to soap. But you *should* meet my dog. My dog is awesome."

"I suppose he smells better?"

"Mmmm, that might be debatable. Chewbacca has a tendency to roll in dead shit on the beach. Drives my mom insane. But I love him."

"Then I'll love him." I nestled deeper into Alex's chest.

"Better now?" he asked.

"Yeah," I mumbled, letting myself finally relax.

"You going to be able to sleep?"

I doubted it. "You know how it is sometimes? Like you can't turn off your brain? It just seems easier when you're here."

"Then I'll stay."

I pulled out of his embrace. "You can't."

"Sure I can. It's not like they have random bed checks." Then he flushed. "I mean, if you want me to go, that's fine. I didn't mean, like, we'd do anything. I just meant I could stay until you're asleep."

I grabbed his hand. "Would you do that? Keep the monsters away?"

He placed his hand over his heart. "I happen to be the master monster slayer."

"My dad used to do that," I said. "When I was little."

"Kill monsters?"

"He'd go around the room with a flashlight, calling for all the monsters to get out from under my bed or the closet. Then he would use the monster spray." I rolled my eyes, feeling absurd. "Obviously, it wasn't really monster spray; it was some kind of air freshener."

"You don't know—the man could have a patent pending on that shit." Alex kicked his shoes off and pulled his sweatshirt over his head so he had on just a thin white T-shirt. "Now, nothing against your dad, but I like to take monsters out in hand-to-hand combat. Way more manly." He flexed his arm.

I stood so Alex could slide under the covers. I turned off the lights and then slipped into bed next to him. "Are you sure about this?" I asked softly. I didn't want to push him, but I wanted him to stay so badly I ached.

"About you, I'm sure." He pulled me to him so that we were spooned together, his body running the length of mine. Creating a wall behind me, keeping me safe.

"What are people going to say?"

"I'll leave early before anyone's up." We lay silently in the dark. After a few moments, our breathing synchronized. I'd never slept with anyone before. Connor and I had always been scrambling for some place to be alone. His friend's house, once in his car. His bedroom when his parents were at work. It was always rushed. Lying next to Alex felt more intimate than being with Connor. This was vulnerable in a different way. Alex's arm was around me, his palm on my waist. His thumb traced the length of my hipbone through the boxer shorts. I wanted to turn and kiss him, to let go of the tension inside me, lose myself in him, in how he made me feel. I knew if I did, I wouldn't be able to stop. As it was, I felt the core of myself melting at his touch. But I didn't want us to be together in that way yet, not when Nicki was still between us.

His breath was warm and I could feel the weight of him against me. My eyes drifted shut and I counted our breathing. Then what I thought would never happen did — I slept.

TWENTY-SEVEN

AUGUST 28
3 DAYS REMAINING

The next day I woke up feeling clearheaded for the first time in more than a week. Sunshine was streaming in through the crack in my curtains. I heard the *slap-whack* of the flip-flops everyone wore to the showers on the wood floors outside in the hallway. We'd overslept.

We were still wrapped together in a warm cocoon in the center of my bed. It was like a blanket fort. Alex was sound asleep, his breath warm on the back of my neck and his hand resting on my thigh.

I shifted slightly and Alex rolled over, his arm flopping above his head. He looked younger sleeping, with his mouth slightly open. I traced his jawbone with my finger, feeling the bristles of his beard coming in, and his eyes fluttered.

"Morning," I said softly.

"Hey," he mumbled. He ran his hand through his dark hair.

"Everybody's up," I warned him. "People are going to see you leave."

He sat up. "I can wait in here until everyone goes down for breakfast. Then I'll sneak back to my room."

"That will make you late. Do you really want to face the wrath of Tasha?"

He rubbed his chin, his spotty whiskers rasping against his hands. "It's okay."

I realized I didn't really care what anyone else thought. I touched Alex's face again. "No. Don't worry about it."

He stood up and stretched. With his arms above his head, his T-shirt rode up, exposing his stomach. The quick peek of his brown skin against his white shirt made my heart skip.

"Thanks for staying," I said. "I got some decent sleep for a change."

He smiled. "That's me — I'm a giver. Boring women to sleep is a skill." He hugged me, holding me for a beat. "I'm glad you slept." He pulled away, both of us slow and groggy as if hungover from the intoxication of being together. "I should get going. I'll meet you downstairs. I don't even remember what we've got on the schedule. You?"

"No — maybe another museum?" Then reality snapped back into place.

Nicki.

All day long I'd be waiting for her to pop up, demanding answers for what hadn't happened. But maybe now that my head was clear, I could come up with a better plan to deal with her, could finally think of a solution.

Alex's shirt was rumpled and his hair stuck up, the soft curls spiking off in different directions.

"I need to talk to you," I said. Once the words were out, I realized they were true. *That* had to be my plan. I'd finally tell Alex everything. Not just because I needed the help, which I desperately did, but also because I realized that he mattered to me. I wanted things between us to work out, and they couldn't if this secret was between us like some kind of bloated, ugly thing. With him I could figure out the best next step. I'd been afraid to involve him, but I needed him. I wasn't going to sit back and let her control things.

I'd tell him everything. About talking to Nicki on the airplane, about wanting Connor to die, even though I hadn't meant it. I didn't want to lose Alex, but there was no way I'd keep him if I continued to lie. I couldn't be afraid. I had to believe he'd have my back. We'd find a solution together. We'd beat her.

"Sure. What's up?" Alex pulled on his shoes.

I glanced at the clock by the bed. Now wasn't the time. Not when we had to be downstairs in half an hour. If I was going to do this, I needed to do it right. "It's a long story. Can we go out later? Just us."

"Sure—maybe we can grab lunch at our Thai place?"

I inhaled deeply, letting my lungs fill. "That would be

great." My phone rang and I fished through a pile of laundry for it, hoping it was Emily.

I clicked on the call.

"I'll see you downstairs," Alex said.

"I guess that explains where you were last night." Nicki's voice was clipped. "Don't make an excuse. I can hear him in the background. You two were messing around instead of doing what you promised. I don't mind you getting a bit on the side, but not when you've got a job to do."

Alex paused at the door, waiting for me to acknowledge him. My mouth was totally dry. I nodded and forced my lips into what I hoped looked like a smile. He blew me a kiss, then opened the door.

"Well, well, well, what do we have here?" someone called out.

"Damn! Things on the third floor are getting hot!" another voice yelled.

Before the door shut, I could make out the sounds of Alex mumbling and people teasing him as he headed for the stairs.

"You're going to wish we'd never met," Nicki said, her voice sliding through the phone like ice shards into my ear.

"I already do," I said, but she'd hung up.

With any luck, by the end of today I'd have figured out a way to make *her* regret meeting *me* even more. I was pretty sure what I would have to do. Alex would want me to go to the cops. But he'd come with me. It was risky, but it wouldn't be so scary with him.

A few hours later I squeezed into a tiny booth at the back of the restaurant. I wanted to sit against the wall so I could make sure that Nicki didn't sneak up on me. All morning long I'd practiced how to tell Alex.

The waitress didn't even bother with handing us one of the battered laminated menus. She knew our regular order. "Two Thai tea, one order veggie spring rolls, one pad thai, no shrimps?" she asked as she poured two cups of water from a scratched plastic pitcher. We nodded and she bustled off.

"I'm going on the record: I don't think I get modern art," Alex said, referring to what we'd seen earlier at the Tate museum. He picked up his untouched fork and knife and wiped them with his napkin.

"I liked some of it."

"I wasn't sure what most of it was supposed to be." The waitress put down our drinks and Alex smiled in thanks. He mixed the thick condensed milk into the tea, the colors swirling together.

"I'm not sure the art is supposed to *be* anything. I think it's meant to make you feel something." I rubbed my hands on my pants. "Thanks for coming."

"So what's going on?"

I swallowed hard. I could do this. "I need your help. I have to tell you something and it might change how you feel about me."

Alex put down the fork he'd been messing with again. "Okay."

"Promise me that you'll hear the whole story before you walk out or anything."

"I'm not going—"

"Just promise." I waited for him to nod. "I told you about Connor." He nodded again. I could see in his eyes that he was wondering where this was going. "I was really mad at him for what he did. For how he treated me."

"I get that."

"I didn't kill him," I said, just in case Alex was unsure.

"I didn't think that," he rushed to say, looking really worried now.

I paused, waiting for a large group of businessmen dividing up a check at the register to finish their argument over who had the beef satay with extra peanut sauce before I continued. "Have you ever gotten yourself into a situation and not known exactly how things got so bad?"

"Um, sure." Alex had his palms down on the plastic tablecloth as if he were bracing for a blow.

The waitress dropped our plates onto the table. "I met someone—" Alex pulled back and I rushed to explain. "No, nothing like that. I'm talking about Nicki, the girl from the plane. I told you that I told her about breaking up with Connor. She had a story to tell me too, about her mom."

"I don't understand—"

"I need you to just listen."

"Sorry." Alex held up his hands in surrender and then started to eat. "I'll keep my mouth full so I'll shut up." He spun his fork through the rice noodles and popped them into his mouth.

"So, Nicki seemed to get how I felt. I told her how angry I was, how I could just kill him."

Alex paused with his fork halfway to his mouth. "Seriously?"

"It was just a thing to say." I touched my chest. "I didn't mean it."

"But then—"

"Then Connor ended up dead."

Alex froze and I wondered if he was starting to put it all together, but then he dived under the table, fishing through his bag.

"Alex?"

"Do you see my Epi?" He wheezed, struggling back upright, dumping the contents of his backpack onto the table in front of him.

"Wait, what?"

"There must have been some shrimp—" He sucked in air, the cords on his neck standing out.

I jumped up, searching for the bright orange and blue capped pen in the pile of items, tossing things onto the floor. The EpiPen wasn't there. "You always have it with you!" I cried.

Alex's eyes were wide as he struggled to breathe. His fingers kept picking through the remaining items on the table.

"Is there problem?" the waitress said, coming over.

"Call nine-one-one!" I yelled.

"Nine what?"

Shit! What was the emergency number here? Alex was no longer digging through his stuff. Instead he was bent over, sucking in air with tiny squeaks.

"Call an ambulance," I begged. I knelt at his side and did a quick sweep of the ground beneath us in case we'd somehow missed the pen, but it wasn't there. I grabbed his sleeve. "Do you have a spare one in your room?"

Alex nodded. He didn't have air left to say anything.

I was already standing. "I'm going to go get it. They're getting help. Hang on."

The cook came out of the kitchen and the waitress brought Alex a glass of water, her hand shaking. "I call for help," she said.

"Stay with him. I'm going to get his medicine." I didn't wait for an answer and instead hit the push bar on the door, ripping free the tiny brass bell that had been suspended above it, before flying out onto the street. I heard the bell bounce down on the ground with a clang. I ran as fast as I could. My ears were on high alert listening for the sound of a siren, but all I could see was traffic filling the streets. How would an ambulance even get through? It was only half a block to the residence, but it felt like a mile.

I took the steps to Metford House two at a time and

slammed into the lobby. "I need the key to room four-fifty!" I shouted at the clerk. "I need to find his medicine *now!*"

The guy working the desk locked up for a split second, but then jumped up and grabbed a set of master keys off the giant board behind him and tossed them to me.

"Get Tasha!" I yelled behind me as I bounded up the steps. My heart slammed into my ribs and I was also having a hard time breathing. How the hell had the restaurant screwed up? He'd told them! They knew!

My hands were shaking so badly it took me three tries to get the key into the lock. I swung the door open. His room was laid out the same as mine. I was never so glad for a small space. I leaped over to the desk first, fishing through the stuff on top. A couple paperbacks, an iPad, a few candy bars, but no EpiPen.

I picked up the plastic bucket we all used for our bathroom supplies and dumped it onto the bed. Shampoo, deodorant, a razor, soap, but no pen. The smell of his after-shave filled my head.

I swept his clothes off the shelf above the hooks on the wall, boxer shorts and T-shirts and jeans raining down. I kicked through the clothes, but the Epi wasn't there, either.

"What's going on?" Jamal said from the door, looking at me and the destruction I'd made in such a short period of time.

I spun around in circles, trying to think where else Alex could keep his medicine in such a small room. I was panting.

I dropped to my knees and looked under the bed. His luggage was there. I yanked on the handle but the suitcase was wedged tight.

"C'mon!" I yelled, pulling on it. How much time had gone by? I hadn't heard an ambulance siren yet, but it was possible I'd missed it. The suitcase came out with a pop and I stumbled back. I unzipped the main compartment, but it was empty.

"Are you supposed to be in Alex's room?" Jamal asked.

I ignored him and went through the suitcase's pockets. In the zippered section on the side I felt something. I pulled it out and started crying. I held the EpiPen aloft as if it were an Olympic torch and then ran back out, pushing past the knot of people who had gathered by the door.

The clerk called out something as I bolted through the lobby, but I didn't bother to pause to ask him to repeat it. My foot slid on the top outside step and I landed hard on my ass, bumping down two steps and slamming my elbow into the railing before coming to a stop. I yelped in pain, but I didn't let go of the pen — it felt as if it were welded to my flesh. I pushed myself up and pelted back to the restaurant. My tailbone was screaming and I could feel blood dripping from my elbow and skinned hands. I must have looked crazed, because people skittered out of my way.

There was an ambulance parked in front. *Oh, thank god.* I yanked open the door to the restaurant. "I got, I got—" I wheezed, holding up the pen.

The two paramedics were already standing, lifting the gurney with Alex on it. The wheels underneath clicked into place and they started to roll toward me. I could see he'd thrown up on the floor. My entire body started shaking. The tables had been pushed to the side and a cluster of customers stood by the fish tank in the corner.

The paramedics noticed me standing there. "We've already given him a shot," one said to me. Alex's lips were blue and his eyes weren't open. His face looked swollen and the paramedics had snaked a tube into his mouth. His backpack and its scattered contents were on the gurney next to his feet. I held the door open as the other paramedic spoke into a walkie-talkie attached to his shirt. "We've got an anaphylactic," he said.

"Is he going to be okay?" I croaked.

"Do you know what he's allergic to?"

"Shellfish," I said.

"How about latex?" I shook my head. "Any medications?"

"No. I mean, I don't think so. He's allergic to lots of stuff—cats, mold, grass, strawberries—but shellfish is the only thing that, you know, that . . ." I looked at Alex lying there, unresponsive.

"We're taking him to Cromwell Hospital," the guy told me over his shoulder as both paramedics heaved the gurney into the back of the ambulance. He stayed with Alex while the other guy jumped into the front. I had so many more questions, but the guy in the back was already shutting the door, and the WHOOP WHOOP of the siren drowned out my thoughts.

It felt as if my bones had melted, and I dropped into the closest chair.

"Here, here, take this." The waitress handed me a glass of water. I tried to drink it but my hand was shaking so badly I spilled more than I drank. "He stop breathing, but they do CPR. He breathing again."

He'd stopped breathing? Oh god.

The cook stood in front of me. "No shrimps in the dish." His hands twisted the stained towel that was tucked into the strings of his apron.

"There had to be—he's allergic," I pointed out.

"No shrimps," the cook insisted, although he looked ready to cry. "Look!" He picked up the plate of pad thai and dumped it onto the plastic tablecloth. He separated out the noodles, squares of tofu, and bean sprouts. Tears ran down his cheeks. "No shrimps."

I touched the pile of noodles. The food was still warm. I pressed my fingers to my lips and tasted the sour spicy mix.

That bitch.

I pushed the thought out of my head. I wasn't going to think about her now. I was going to stay focused on Alex.

Tasha burst through the door, looking around wildly before spotting me. "What happened?"

"Alex had an allergic reaction."

"No shrimps!" the cook insisted again.

"Why didn't he have his pen on him?" Tasha asked, burying her hands in her thick Afro as if she were going to pull it from the roots. "He knows he's supposed to have it." She pounded a fist on the table, making the glasses jump.

"I don't know," I said. "I ran to his room to get the spare." I held it out limply.

"Why would he leave it in his room?" Tasha took the pen from me.

"He thought he had one in his bag, but it wasn't there. It must have fallen out at some point. I don't know."

"Jesus wept." Tasha sat next to me and drank my glass of water in one long gulp. "I can't call another parent. I can't." Her voice was flat. She stared forward as if she didn't see me anymore. As if she didn't even see the restaurant.

"He's going to be okay, isn't he?" I knew Tasha had no more idea than I did what was happening, but I needed her to tell me everything would be fine.

My words seemed to shake her back to herself. "Of course he'll be okay," Tasha said. "He'll be fine," she said, louder and more certain. "Did they say what hospital they were taking him to?"

My mind went blank.

"Cromwell," the waitress offered.

Tasha pulled up from the table. "Okay, I'm going there to check on him. I'll call you as soon as I know something."

"I'm going with you." I scrambled to pick up my bag. I pulled out some money to pay for the meal but the waitress backed up quickly, shaking her head as if I were offering her a viper.

"You should go back to Metford."

I stared at Tasha. "I'm going to the hospital. If you don't take me, then I'll figure out where it is on my own. You can't stop me."

She must have seen something in my eyes, because she backed down. "All right. Let's go."

TWENTY-EIGHT

AUGUST 28
3 DAYS REMAINING

It was just before midnight by the time I got back to Metford. Tasha had paid for a cab, which was good because if I'd had to take the Tube, I don't think I would have been able to manage it. As it was, the cab driver had had to clear his throat before I realized that he'd stopped in front of the building and was waiting for me to get out.

The rest of our group was waiting up, sitting in the lobby. Sophie looked as though she'd been crying. They stood when I came in.

"He's okay," I said.

"What happened?" Jamal looked angry, as if he wanted someone to do some explaining.

I told them about Alex's allergic reaction, how serious it had been.

Kendra mumbled something to Jazmin, Kendra's eyes

darting over to me. Jazmin waved her off. My hands balled into fists. Kendra thought I was to blame.

"Someone should sue that Thai place—they basically tried to kill Alex!" Jazmin said.

I shrugged. "The cook was positive he didn't put any shrimp into the dish. The doctor thought it was likely cross contamination. If the chef used the same knife to cut up shrimp and then cut up Alex's tofu, that might have been enough to cause the problem." Again, I shoved away an image of Nicki.

"But he's going to be okay?" Sophie hugged herself.

"He stopped breathing, but the doctors don't think it was for long. The paramedics were there pretty quickly. They're keeping him overnight for observation because he had to be revived, but he was conscious when I left." I'd wanted to speak to him but neither the doctors nor Tasha would let me. Instead I'd had to make do with peeking into his room to get a glimpse. I needed to ask him if he'd seen "Erin" around before it happened. "They said he wasn't up for talking yet."

"It's like this trip is cursed," Kendra said.

Jazmin punched her in the shoulder. "Cut it out with that crap. No one needs your voodoo hex on this shit."

"I'm just saying it's weird. Connor ends up dead and then this."

A ripple of unease ran through my chest. Hours in the

sterile waiting room with outdated magazines, bad coffee, and hushed conversations had given me a lot of time to think.

What were the odds that Alex would have been exposed to shrimp hours after I'd failed to do what Nicki wanted?

My math teacher was always on me to understand that correlation doesn't mean causation. Just because your dog barked when you ate a banana doesn't mean that the banana caused your dog to bark. They just happened at the same time. It's sloppy science to confuse the two. But this nightmare had Nicki's name all over it.

"So, what happens now?" Sophie asked.

"Tasha talked to Alex's parents. They're flying over. They were hoping to get a flight as soon as possible." I didn't share how Tasha had looked when she'd made the call, as if she'd rather peel her own skin from her bones than tell them. "The hospital will keep Alex until tomorrow to make sure his blood-work and everything comes back looking like it should."

"And the rest of us?" Jazmin asked.

"There're only a couple days left," Jamal said. "I suspect they'll just have us finish. It would take us almost that long to make other arrangements."

"I guess. It just seems weird to be doing touristy stuff with . . ." Jazmin looked over at me. "You know."

"I'm going to bed," I said.

Sophie touched my arm lightly. "You need anything?"

I shook my head and trudged up the stairs, each of my legs feeling as if it weighed a thousand pounds. I'd go back to the hospital in the morning and I wouldn't take no for an answer about seeing Alex.

I shut my door behind me and leaned against it. I was debating if I should bother washing my face. All I wanted to do was strip off my clothes. They smelled like the hospital, a mix of pine cleanser and rot. I glanced around. It seemed impossible that we had woken up here together just this morning.

That's when I noticed my bed was made. And not just *made* —arranged with military precision. The covers were pulled up tight, the corners folded, the pillow vertical against the wall. I didn't make my bed like that. I rarely made my bed at all, and if I did, I settled for yanking the blankets up rather haphazardly.

There was something tucked in, half of it under the covers and half on the pillow. I jerked the covers back with a *swoosh* as though doing a magic trick. A small jar, like one for baby food, tumbled down the mattress. I picked it up.

Most of the writing was in Japanese, but there was some English, too. Just enough.

SHRIMP POWDER

TWENTY-NINE

AUGUST 29
2 DAYS REMAINING

I sat on one of the Kensington Gardens park benches that lined the walkways. I'd taken a photo of the statue of Peter Pan and posted it to Instagram so Nicki would know where to find me. I didn't bother with any kind of message. She was clever. She would know where I was and why I wanted to see her. Then I waited.

There weren't many people out this early. A few joggers and moms pushing baby carriages. I clenched my hands into fists and released them, my fingernails leaving dark red crescent moons in my palms.

"There you are!" Nicki called out. She was already swinging her leg off her bike as she coasted up. The bike wheels crunched through the gravel like the sound of cereal in milk. She wore a flowery dress with a full skirt. She looked as if she belonged on the cover of a romance novel.

I hurled the tiny jar at her and it hit her chest with a *thump* before falling to the base of the statue and shattering in a firework burst of glass and powder.

Nicki dropped her bike and rubbed her breastbone. "Hey, that hurt—"

She didn't finish because I'd flown through the distance between us and punched her in the face, my knuckles connecting with her jaw with a meaty *whack*. Her head jerked back.

She stumbled over her bike, going down on one knee before quickly popping up and scrambling three steps back.

"Hey, you girls, what are you up to?" an elderly man yelled over, his accent thick and almost unintelligible.

I backed up. I panted with rage. The bones in my fist felt as if they'd exploded on impact. I shook my hand, trying to get the stinging to stop. I'd never hit anyone before in my life. Adrenaline pumped through my body; it felt as though every muscle was throbbing with energy. I wanted to hit her again. If that guy hadn't been around, I might have done it.

"We're fine," Nicki said. The man walked away but kept shooting glances at us over his shoulder, hitching up his baggy sweatpants, until he was out of sight. "Let me see your phone."

I fished it out, showed her that the record function wasn't on, and then dropped it into my bag. She pointed at my chest and I lifted my shirt so she could see I wasn't wearing a wire. Nicki looked me up and down and then lightly touched the side of her mouth. She pulled her fingers back. They were smeared red. The tip of her pink tongue darted out and licked away the blood. Then she smiled.

"I didn't think you had that in you."

"You stay away from him," I whispered. All the anger that had built up since finding that small jar on my bed was gone, burned up in the one punch. I clenched my fist and pain shot into my wrist and to my elbow and then to my shoulder. I might have broken a finger. I didn't care. "He could have died." My voice cracked on the last word.

Nicki bent down and righted her bike, nudging the kickstand into place so the bicycle was propped up at the side of the walkway. "You say it like I should be surprised. That was the entire point." She brushed her skirt, ridding it of nonexistent dirt. "I had to make you understand that I mean business. I realized that all the time I'd been threatening to tell the police that you were the one who killed Connor, I'd been going about it the wrong way. You don't much care what people think at this point. And clearly the concept that you might go to jail wasn't enough." She held up a finger as if making a point. "But ah, threaten the boy genius and that was a game changer."

"His *name* is *Alex*."

She stepped past me, brushing my shoulder. Her perfume smelled like oranges and baby powder. I wanted to rub the sweet smell out of my nose. Nicki sat on the park bench. "Is this some kind of thing where you try to personalize him so that I'll feel bad? It's like when vegans call a pig Wilbur. It's supposed to make you turn to broccoli over bacon if the creature has a name."

Is that how she sees all of us? Like livestock? "Leave him out of this."

She tucked her hair behind her ears. It had grown longer since we'd first met; it no longer popped right back out. "I wasn't the one who dragged him into this — that was you. You're the one playing Romeo and Juliet with the nerd king . . ." She smirked at my expression. "My apologies — you're the one playing Romeo and Juliet with *Alex,* instead of doing what you need to do."

"I'm going to the police."

"And telling them what, exactly? First off, right now everyone thinks it was an accident. I mean really, what kind of food handling can you expect from a restaurant like that?"

"Shut up," I snarled.

"I'm not trying to offend your merry band of Thai friends; I'm merely pointing out that right now it's just one of those things that can happen. If you go to the police with a wild conspiracy theory, it opens up other options for them to consider."

"Like what?"

"Like that maybe you did it."

I wanted to rip my hair out in frustration. "Why would I do it?"

"You're a troubled girl. Perhaps you made him sick because you wanted to save him. Then he'd be in love with you. There's even some kind of name for that — I've read about it in those insipid women's magazines my mother loves so much. The articles all have titles like 'The Girl Who Loved Him to Death,' with a lot of color photos and exclamation marks." Nicki paused to smile at a young mom pushing a toddler in a stroller. She waved at the little girl, who waved back, her tiny pink starfish hand opening and closing.

I waited until the mother was out of view. "I would never hurt Alex. I'm in love with him." As soon as the words were out of my mouth, I realized they were true. That was another thing Nicki had ruined. The first time I acknowledged that feeling should have been to Alex, not to her.

"I know that, and you know that, but given everything else, plus the evidence . . ."

I clenched my jaw. The wind rustled through the trees. "What evidence," I got out.

She motioned to my tote bag. I pulled it open. Lying on top was an EpiPen.

I dropped the bag to the ground as if it were on fire. When she'd brushed past me, touching my shoulder, she must have slipped it in.

"Now, that's not actually his. It's a spare I picked up. But it could be his, and think how that would look?" She tsked.

"How?" I asked. "How did you get the shrimp powder into his food?"

Nicki rocked back and forth on the bench as if excited. "How do you think?"

"Did you bribe the kitchen staff?"

She looked disappointed. "Of course not. Never involve other people — it just causes trouble. Look at all the headaches you've caused me, for example. Makes me wish I could handle my mother on my own. It would be far easier."

"Did you slip into the kitchen somehow? But that meant you knew we would be there. And you knew about his allergy."

"He told me that eons ago." She looked down at her nails. "Or I should say, he told Erin. It's remarkable what people will tell you if you pretend to be interested in them. And you never know how the information will be useful. It almost makes listening to people blather worthwhile."

Nicki patted the seat next to her. "C'mon, sit with me."

I crossed my arms over my chest. "No."

She sighed as if I were being difficult. "I know what you're doing, by the way."

"What do you mean?"

"You're avoiding the problem. You're hoping it will all go away, that you can get on a plane in another two days, fly home, and all of this will be some kind of horrid bad dream." She waved her hands in front of her face. "Like you're some kind of magician that can make all of this disappear by simply stalling."

"You can't make me do anything. You can't make me be like you."

She stood up. "Oh, please. You're already like me. That's why I picked you. You've never fit in with other people. They've never made sense to you. You told me that yourself. You've always been manipulating things to try to blend in with all of *them* . . ." Her hand gestured to include the people walking in the distance. "What I'm trying to make you understand is that there's no point in blending in. Those people are pointless. You're the one who's worth something. The only reason you don't act is because you've been afraid."

Nicki stepped closer to me. We were just inches apart, close enough that I could smell the mint on her breath from her toothpaste and see the red mark by her mouth where I'd hit her. She reached up and tenderly brushed the hair off my face. "You're smarter than them. They're the ones who will need you at some point, not the other way around, so why not use them to get what you want?"

"This is about what *you* want," I spat back, but I didn't move away. If I moved, she would likely strike, like a snake.

"Perhaps. But I got you what you wanted first, so this is just a payback. I believe in keeping the ledger even. When I do something for someone, I expect them to return the favor. And when someone crosses me, then I'm sure to make them pay. You're right, though — I can't make you do it."

"But?"

"But I can make you wish you had."

I stepped back as if pulling away from a spell she was weaving. "What does that even mean?"

Nicki walked over to her bike and kicked up the stand. "It means you owe me. You can go to the police, but you have no evidence. You can run home, back to Vancouver if you want, but you'll eventually pay. It will almost be worse if you insist on putting this off, because you never know when I'll come to collect. Maybe something else happens to Alex. He can't avoid food forever. And your dad, doesn't he cycle to work? I think I saw that on your mom's blog. How very environmentally responsible. People have accidents on bikes all the time."

All the blood in my body slid down toward my feet, leaving me pale and ice cold as she talked.

"Or I still have the list you wrote about Connor. Maybe I save it up for later to send to the police. When you're about to graduate, for example. There's no statute of limitations on murder. But you know what you can be one hundred percent certain of?"

I opened my mouth but at first nothing came out and I had to swallow. "No — what?"

"I won't forget the debt. And I *will* collect it. In fact, it would be more fun to wait, letting you fret and wonder when everything in your life finally will blow up. I can be very patient." She climbed onto the bike, one foot still on the ground, the other on a pedal. "Or you take this final opportunity and kill my mother tonight. It's your last chance. You do that and I promise you I go away."

"How do I know that you will?"

"You have to trust me," she said.

I snorted. "That's just perfect."

She scrunched up her face. "Now, that's not fair. I've kept every one of my promises to you. You do this and we're done. Consider it my gift to you."

"A gift?"

"Then you'll know what you're really capable of. After that, nothing will hold you back." Nicki pushed off and started to cycle away. "Just imagine what you might accomplish!"

THIRTY

I had no idea if British hospitals had set visiting hours, but I didn't intend to ask, in case someone told me I had to leave.

I wrinkled my nose against the strong smell of cleanser mixed with something sour and musky that I didn't want to identify. I paused outside the third-floor elevator to stare down the hall at his closed door. I stiffened my spine before I could lose my courage.

I moved around a nurse pushing an older guy in a wheelchair and cautiously nudged the door open. Alex pulled himself up when he saw me. A middle-aged man in the bed next to him snored away.

"Hey!" Alex waved. A tube that led from his elbow to the IV pole knocked against the metal rail of the bed.

I slid inside the room and drew a chair up next to him. "Hey to you too." I touched his arm, almost as if I had to convince myself he was really there and okay. "You look better than when I saw you last."

Alex rubbed his chin, his whiskers rasping. "Sorry."

I pulled back, shocked. "Why are you sorry?"

"I imagine it was freaky, seeing me like that. Thrashing around, throwing up, passing out," Alex said, not meeting my eyes. "Not exactly the kind of thing they advise when you want to impress a girl."

"I don't know," I hedged, picking my words carefully. "Remember our waitress? She looked like she thought you were pretty hot." His lip twitched and I could see he was trying not to laugh. "After all, some people are into weird shit."

"Nothing against her, but she isn't the girl I was trying to impress."

My heart cracked like brittle ice. "I'm glad you're okay."

"Me too. I could kick myself for losing that stupid EpiPen. My mom is going to have a goat when she gets here."

I held his hand through the metal railing on the side of the bed. There was no point in telling him he hadn't lost the pen. I didn't know exactly how Nicki had taken it, although it didn't surprise me that she knew how to pickpocket. She might have bumped him on the sidewalk or sat next to him on the Tube and picked it out of his backpack as though she were a character from a Dickens novel.

"Your mom won't be mad — she'll just be glad you're okay."

"You might think that, but you haven't met my mom. She

didn't want me to come on this trip because of my allergies. We almost never go out to eat because she doesn't trust restaurants. When we travel anywhere, including to my grandma's, she brings our own food in a cooler. This is going to convince her that her paranoia is justified. She's going to take me home and seal me in a bubble."

"I'm so sorry this happened," I said. My heart gave way and broke into a thousand pieces. This was my fault.

Alex reached over and wiped a single tear off my cheek. "Hey, it was just some stupid cross-contamination thing."

I nodded to please him, but it *was* my fault. He wouldn't have been hurt if it hadn't been for me. Nicki had gone after him to get to me. "You almost died," I said quietly.

"But I didn't. And who knows, maybe the exposure to the shrimp will end up giving me superpowers."

"Like Batman," I said.

Alex closed his eyes. "We soooo need to take you to a comic con at some point. For a woman who knows sci-fi, your superhero references are shit. Batman wasn't bit by a bat. I was going for Spider-Man. I'm thinking I'll be known as Crustacean Man. Shrimp Man sounds wimpy."

"You can't have that—then the bad guys won't be afraid of you." I liked Alex's cartoon view of the world, where a bad guy was easy to identify. Not like real life, where she looked like a nice person to pass a plane delay with.

"I've got to figure out something for an outfit. I look pretty good in pink, so I've got that going for me." He rubbed my knuckles and I flinched — they were still sore from hitting Nicki — but I didn't pull my hand away. I deserved the pain.

"They're supposed to discharge me later today once my parents get here," Alex said. "Staying overnight at a hospital is a first for me and I'm not keen to repeat it."

"Are you going home tomorrow?"

He nodded. "I tried to tell my parents I wanted to stay, but there's no way. My mom is already preparing my hypoallergenic bubble."

My throat grew tight. "I'm going to miss you." I hated the idea of him leaving, but it was better. Safer.

He made an exaggerated dismissive wave. "Woman, you're going to have to do your best to live without me for a couple days."

"Yeah, about that . . ."

I hated to do this, but I had to. I had to put him first. Being close to me put Alex in danger. The best thing I could do for him was to get as much space between the two of us as possible. As long as Nicki thought he was important to me, the greater his risk, if I didn't do what she wanted.

And if I did murder her mom, then I'd never be able to look at Alex again. How could I kill an innocent person and then go back to living my life as though nothing had happened? Alex was a good person. He deserved someone who was the same. I had no choice.

Alex pulled himself farther up on the pillows. "Wait, what's going on?"

"I think it might be good if we took a break," I said, pushing the words out.

He blinked. "Are you joking?"

"I mean, it's been great, but when we get back, we're both going to be really busy with school and stuff," I said. I couldn't look at him.

"You're dumping me?" Alex's voice was so loud, the guy in the next bed jolted awake with a juicy snort, as if his tongue had slipped down his throat. He looked surprised to see me there.

I lowered my voice. "We've both got a lot going on and—"

"Stop saying 'we' when this is clearly about you," Alex said.

"Um, do you want me to leave?" the man in the next bed said, holding the blanket to the side, exposing his scrawny legs, as if he were ready to make a run for it. Alex waved him off without even acknowledging what he'd said.

"Okay, *I've* got a lot going on. I'm not sure I can be in a relationship right now. I don't have the emotional resources."

Alex crossed his arms over his chest. "Do you hear yourself? 'Emotional resources'? You sound like a bad episode of *Dr. Phil.* Is this because I got sick? They're *allergies*—I don't have some kind of plague."

"It's not that."

"Seriously, I could just pop down for a cup of tea . . ." the man offered.

"You just happen to be dumping me while I'm in the hospital. You expect me to believe that's just a coincidence?"

"I could make a couple calls or something." The guy had his feet on the floor at this point. His pajama pants were a washed-out gray and the elastic at the waist was loose, the pants threatening to fall down. I wished he would just go instead of waiting for permission. Alex was right. The allergic reaction *was* why I was breaking up with him, but not because it had grossed me out. I had to hurt him now to keep him safe, even if every word out of his mouth was a punch to my heart.

"Your allergic reaction has nothing to do with it," I said. "The whole reason I wanted to talk to you yesterday was about this."

"So, your plan was to break up over pad thai so that I wouldn't make a scene? You were *managing* me." He shook his head. "That's just great. You couldn't say anything when I stayed the night at your place?"

I winced. The man in the next bed was no longer asking to leave. Now he looked ready to munch on some popcorn and watch the show.

"It's not that I don't care about you, but—"

"You know, please spare me the 'I care about you, but' speech. If you don't want to be with me, then that's fine, just go."

"Alex—" I touched his elbow, but he yanked his arm back, making the IV pole shake.

"You should go. You said what you came to say. Thanks for the good times. It's been fun. We'll always have London, blah blah blah."

"I'm really sorry." I stood, my legs shaking.

"Just leave."

"I wish things were different," I said.

"Just get the hell out!" Alex yelled, and I bolted from the room, his hurt and anger chasing me into the hall. I bumped into a squat nurse right outside the door.

"Is everything all right?" She peered into Alex's room.

"Uh-huh." I dodged past her and down the hall. I stumbled down the stairs and spilled out onto the first floor. Every direction I turned, there were more people. Then I saw the sign for the nondenominational chapel. I pushed open the door, praying for quiet.

The room was blissfully empty. I shut the door behind me and slid to the floor onto the industrial carpet. It was a good thing I was already in a hospital, because my heart was failing. I could feel it shredding inside my chest, tearing free. I squeezed my temples, trying to hold in a scream.

I hated that I'd hurt Alex. I could see in his eyes that he didn't understand. He thought it was him, that I found his love for comic books too geeky, or his encyclopedic knowledge of video-game strategy too useless, or that I looked down on the fact that he'd actually taught himself Elvish by reading *The*

Lord of the Rings. But I loved all those things. I loved how different he was from everyone else and how he saw adventure and magic in everything. I loved how there was a tiny chip in his front tooth and how his body was always so warm, as if he were his own nuclear device sending out heat waves.

I wiped my face with the back of my hand, trying to pull myself together. My breath came in shuddering gasps and I focused on taking slow, deep inhales through my nose and then exhaling through my mouth. I couldn't afford to lose my senses now. I had no doubt Nicki was serious. If I didn't kill her mom, she would hunt me down. Worse than that, she would hunt down the people who mattered to me.

Going to the police was no longer an option. They weren't going to believe me. I'd cried wolf too often. Not to mention I could just imagine how Nicki would perform under questioning. Smooth. Like a duck, perfectly calm on the surface but paddling like mad underneath the water. She'd bury me and get away. And then who knew what she would do in revenge. I'd risk myself, but not everyone else. I had to handle this on my own.

Nicki said that she'd picked me because she thought I was smart and analytical. That I could divorce myself from emotion and do what needed to be done. Clinical. If I was going to survive this, I needed to be that person. I had to focus on what I was going to do. What would give me the outcome I wanted. The tears on my face started to dry and I could see options in my mind as if I were writing them down on the whiteboard in Mr. Donald's class. The squeak of the dry-erase marker as I flew over the calculations. My breathing evened out.

I needed to work the freaking problem, and that wasn't how to kill Nicki's mom. My problem was Nicki.

THIRTY-ONE

AUGUST 29
2 DAYS REMAINING

Tasha was looking for me. She'd sent multiple text messages commanding me to call her, and when I slunk into my room at Metford, there was a note from her waiting under my door. I understood why she was worried. She'd already had one kid die on her watch and another end up in the hospital. The last thing she needed was for me to go missing. I'd taken off without telling her or anyone where I was going, and after seeing Alex, I'd walked the city for hours, coming up with a plan.

I checked the clock. If Tasha was sticking with our schedule, she would be with our group touring the Parliament buildings. That would give me the time I needed, even if they didn't wind up going to the restaurant scheduled for afterward. I fired off a text to her saying that I just needed some time by myself given everything that had happened, but that I was okay. I hoped that would pacify her for the time being.

I went through my room quickly, pulling out all my things. I wasn't sure what would happen after tonight, but I didn't want to risk that other people would go through my stuff later. I ripped pages out of the travel journal I'd brought with me. There wasn't much in there — I hadn't written down all the details about Nicki; most of it was about Alex — but I wasn't taking chances. I dropped the sheets into the metal trash can and set them on fire with a match, blowing the smoke out the window. I also burned the newspaper article about Connor and the photocopy of the list Nicki had sent. I watched them until they had charred to unsalvageable ash.

I refolded my clothes and lined them up on the shelf after shaking out each item, making sure I'd left nothing behind and that Nicki hadn't sneaked anything into a pocket. It was something she'd do.

The communal bathroom was just a few doors down, but instead I went two flights up to the other girls' floor to make sure I didn't run into anyone I knew. I stripped down and took a quick shower. London was a dirty city, but the reason I felt as if I needed to scrub my skin raw didn't have anything to do with the smog that could settle on your hair and skin.

I checked my phone when I got back to my room. It was still way too early to do anything, barely four in the afternoon. I needed to wait until it was dark. That meant I had hours to kill. There was no way I could eat anything; my stomach was rock hard. I lay down on the bed and stared up at the ceiling.

My brain raced, cycling around the idea that I was really going to do this.

I jolted awake. My room was dark. I didn't know what had woken me, and then I realized my phone was chiming to let me know I had a new text. I fumbled for the device in the dark and clicked it on. Tasha.

Want to see you. Meet me in lobby?

I rolled out of bed onto my feet. *Shit.* I had planned to be gone before they got back. It had never occurred to me I might fall asleep. I checked the time — it was after nine. I'd slept for five hours. I shook my head to clear it. My heart went from a slow speed to a full gallop. If I didn't text her back, she'd come looking for me. I yanked on my gray fleece and tossed my messenger bag over my shoulder. I had to get out of here. Now.

I crept down the stairs and peered around the corner. Tasha and our group were in the lobby. Sophie was leaning against Jamal. There was something brewing there. Kendra and Jazmin were hotly debating something, but Tasha was barely paying attention to them. There was no way to walk out the front door without someone spotting me.

I had another option that didn't require me to go right past them — following the stairs into the basement — but there was still a chance the group would see me. I stood like a flamingo, one foot on the step and the other waiting to make a move. I closed my eyes and took a slow, deep breath in and out. I had to at least try. Being scared didn't mean you didn't do it. I hefted my bag back up on my shoulder and took the last few steps quickly, wrapping around the balustrade so that I was headed down to the basement. No one seemed to look my way.

I crossed my fingers, but luck was on my side: the laundry room was empty. A high and narrow window was above the folding table. I jumped up onto the table and twisted the window's rusty lock. The casement was stuck. I hunched over and used my shoulder to shove open the window.

Mentally I calculated the space. It was going to be tight. It was a good thing I hadn't eaten dinner. I pulled off my fleece to give myself a bit of extra wiggle room and tossed the jacket and my bag outside. Then I hefted myself up, swinging one leg through until I was lying flat on the sill, one leg still hanging down inside. My hand scrambled to find something to grab so I could pull myself out, but there was nothing in reach. I sucked in my breath and squeezed through. My arm scraped on the cement and then suddenly I was free.

I lay on the asphalt for a second gazing up. I could see the lights on in various dorm rooms, but thankfully no one seemed to be looking down at me. I pulled myself into a crouch, yanking my fleece back on and grabbing my bag.

It was time. I walked to the Tube station and did my best

to glance around casually as I rode the escalator down to see if anyone was following me. I waited on the platform, feigning an interest in the posters that lined the walls advertising theater shows, museum exhibits, and sales at H&M. When the train pulled in, I got in a car, and when the doors pinged that they were closing, I jammed my arm out, making the doors bounce back open. I quickly got off. No one else exited the train. If anyone had been following me, no one would have been expecting that move. Two minutes later the next train pulled in and I got on that one instead.

I changed at Edgware, taking the stairs as if I intended to leave the station and then doubling back so I could get on the Circle line. Near as I could tell, no one was behind me. I sat on the train and it took off with a lurch. The carriage smelled vaguely like motor oil mixed with lemons. I picked up the abandoned newspaper on the seat next to me and stared down at a Marks & Spencer ad so I didn't have to look around. The guy standing in front of me had his music on so loud I could make out the song leaking from his ear buds. The train lurched and squealed as it went around corners.

I stared out the window in the dark tunnel. Alex's parents must have been here by now. The hospital had probably already discharged him. I could picture his mom fussing over him, and Alex dodging away from her touch. I wished I could make him understand. I pinched my thigh. I couldn't afford to think about him now. Even conjuring up his face in my mind caused a dull ache in my chest, like someone pushing on a bruise. I had to stay focused.

I exited the train at Baker Street and let people stream past me to the stairs. By the time the train pulled out, I was alone on the platform. The only sounds were the buzz of the overhead fluorescent lights and the scuttle of trash blowing around the tracks. I walked to the edge of the platform and leaned over, feeling the stale breeze from the tunnel like hot breath on my face. I wondered if Connor had known what was going to happen before the train hit him. It must have happened fast. He might not have even known he'd been pushed.

Or maybe time had slowed down in that moment. If he'd glanced up, he would have seen the light of the train bearing down, felt himself tilting forward, off balance and falling. Connor had gotten an A in Physics. He would have known there was no surviving what was about to happen, how the velocity of the train would have exploded flesh and bone. His death would have been fast, over in a second.

One Mississippi, I counted in my head. It felt long. Not fast at all.

There was a squeal of a train in the distance and a rush of air down the tunnel that lifted my hair away from my face and rustled the trash on the ground. The tracks below were laid on a bed of loose rocks, all a uniform dark charcoal gray. I stared down and then the trash rustled again, but this time because of the rats. They were the unofficial maintenance men of the Tube, cleaning up anything edible. I'd seen them before, scurrying up and down the tracks. I'd heard that in London you were never more than six feet away from a rat, but that sounded like the kind of thing people said on Facebook without ever bothering to check if it was accurate.

In grade six our science teacher had kept pet rats in the classroom. Their names were Mickey and Minnie — so original. Minnie was nice, but Mickey wasn't a particularly affectionate rat. I didn't recall him ever biting anyone, but he wasn't snuggly, either. When they died, I'd suggested we do an autopsy to figure out what had happened. My classmates freaked out over the idea. It was science class, for crying out loud. They made me feel like a weirdo for even having had the thought. But scientists do what they have to do — and that was what I was going to do now. Unpleasant, but required.

One Mississippi.

The roar in the tunnel increased as the train approached.

Two Mississippi.

The sour rush of air flew down the tunnel, making my nose twitch.

Three Mississippi.

The rats on the tracks fled.

Four Mississippi.

I took a deep breath and a step.

Five.

THIRTY-TWO

AUGUST 29
2 DAYS REMAINING

I took another step back as the train raced into the station. I knew I wouldn't kill myself. As scared as I was to do what had to be done, I had to see the situation through. The doors whooshed open and the platform flooded again with people. I drew in a deep breath. I couldn't procrastinate any longer.

I didn't have to use my phone to find the house this time. My brain had memorized the route and my feet led me there without hesitating. The click of the side gate seemed noisy and I flinched, but there was no one on the street to hear. The TV was on so loud in the house next door, I doubted the neighbors could even hear themselves think, let alone any sound I made. I heard the beeping chimes counting down to the BBC news.

I stepped lightly along the path. The air smelled like the lavender plants that lined both sides of the paver stones. I paused when I reached the end of the house. The garden beyond was overgrown; an ivy plant had gone crazy and taken over huge swaths of the yard. A teak wooden table with four chairs was tucked off to the side, and I could make out a large striped umbrella leaning against the far fence. At the very back I could just see in the moonlight where a vegetable garden had been laid out. Perhaps Nicki's great-grandparents had planted it as a victory garden, doing their part for the war effort. Carrots and potatoes to crush Hitler. If so, they'd be shocked to see the garden now. Tall weeds had taken over, lacy plants that reached for the sky.

The light above the back door was out, the way Nicki had promised. I crept up to the house, half expecting someone inside to fling the door open, demanding to know what I was doing. But nothing happened. If Nicki or her mom had fixed the lock, I wouldn't be able to get in and everything might be over before it even began. The brass knob was cool and I twisted it, holding my breath. The door clicked open, swinging in with a faint squeak.

I stood in a small mudroom leading to the kitchen. It was just large enough to fit a tiny bench where you could slip off your shoes. I took mine off, but instead of lining them up next to the pairs of Nikes and black rubber Hunter boots, I put my shoes into my messenger bag. If I needed to leave in a hurry, I didn't want to go searching for them, but I also wanted to be as quiet as possible. I picked up an envelope and noted the name it was addressed to before putting it back down next to discarded real estate flyers. The name didn't mean much to me, though, since Nicki's name was fake and I didn't know her last name.

I pulled out the knife from the bottom of my bag. Its weight surprised me. It looked as if it should have been heavy, but it was light. I'd snatched it that afternoon from the kitchen at Metford. I'd wanted to find something bigger, like a giant carving knife, but the only one that had been sitting out on the counter was this one. It was small, meant for deboning fish, but it would work for my purposes.

I passed through the kitchen, sliding along the floor in my socks. The counter was piled with dishes and there was a sour smell in the air. Something in the garbage was off. At the base of the stairs I peeked into the living room. I wasn't sure what I expected, but it looked ordinary. There was a book on the sofa —a Ruth Ware mystery—and a nearly empty glass on the side table with a sticky clot of red wine left at the bottom.

I counted to five hundred while I listened to the house. I wanted to make sure I was alone. Nicki shouldn't have been home—there was no point to any of this if she hadn't arranged an alibi—but I didn't trust her, either. Maybe she wanted to stick around to make sure I would go through with it. Or maybe she was the kind of person who wanted to watch.

I didn't hear anything. The place seemed empty. A giggle started to burble up and I had to bite down hard on my lip to stop myself. The irony if I'd finally gotten up the guts to do this and Nicki's mom wasn't even home was almost too absurd not to consider.

As I crept up the stairs, I remembered to avoid the creaky third step. At the top, I counted two doors to the right. Part of me was tempted to try to find Nicki's room first. If I rummaged through her belongings, perhaps I could find a clue as to how her brain worked. Was her bedroom still stuck in childhood, with a stuffed teddy named Oliver on the bed, a dancing ballerina jewelry box on the dresser, a pink floral duvet? Or had she redone the décor: dark colors, muted throw pillows, stripped of anything personal? Maybe instead of posters of a cute boy band, there would be photos of famous serial killers. That would certainly be a giveaway. I hesitated, but if I wasn't careful with the sounds I made, Nicki's mom would wake up. I could imagine kneeling next to Nicki's bed to look underneath and having her mom stumble in, her bathrobe open and flapping behind her. There was no amount of explaining that would make my presence okay.

I caught myself a split second before I tapped on her mom's bedroom door to ask if I could come in. Habits die hard. My mom hated it when I barged in without knocking. This door wasn't latched shut, just pulled most of the way closed. I gave it a light shove and it swung open silently.

The room wasn't huge. The large bay window I'd seen from the street was directly across from me with long white curtains pulled shut. They moved in and out, as if they were breathing in tandem with the breeze. The walls were painted white, and the bit of moonlight creeping through the cracks in the curtains lit things up enough that I wouldn't stumble around. Nicki's mom lay in the center of the bed, her mouth open, her breathing heavy. A thin blanket was tangled up around her legs, as if she'd been cycling through it.

I reached out for her. My hand wasn't shaking the way I'd expected. Now that I was here, I was calm. Focused, every sense on high alert. I could hear everything: the tick of the clock from downstairs, the faint hum of the fridge in the kitchen, and the very muffled sound of the TV from next door through the wall. Even in the weak light I could make out everything. The tiny print of pink forget-me-nots on her cotton pajama gown, the loose change on her dresser, and the pattern on the floor made by the light from a passing car. I'd never felt more alive in my entire life.

I leaned forward again and tapped her on the shoulder with one hand. Her eyes opened and then widened when she realized she wasn't alone. I was ready. I slapped my hand down over her mouth, her lips feeling dry and hot on my palm, like snakeskin. She tried to pull back when she saw the knife, but there was nowhere to go; she was pressed against the mattress.

"Shhh," I whispered. "I'm not going to hurt you, but you have to be quiet." A tear slipped from her eye and ran down her face. "Do you understand?"

She nodded frantically. I hesitated before pulling my hand away. I was counting on the sight of the knife to make her comply, but if she started screaming, I didn't have a plan B. Once my hand was gone, she sucked in a shallow breath that turned into a strangled sob.

"You have to listen to me. What I'm going to tell you is important." My voice was low but steady and calm. I felt a rush of pride, a tingling that ran down my spine and then into my arms and legs.

"I have a bit of money in the top drawer," Nicki's mom said. "There's maybe some more in my purse downstairs, and my credit cards." Her words tumbled over one another, racing out of her mouth. "I don't have much jewelry. I don't—"

"I'm not here to steal from you," I cut her off. I sniffed the air, trying to tell if she'd been drinking. She didn't sound confused or drunk, just terrified.

She swallowed. "Okay." Her eyes darted around the room as if she thought there might be someone else here. "What do you want?"

"I've been sent here. To kill you."

Her eyes shot back to mine. She whimpered, seemingly trying to pull herself deeper into the mattress. "Please . . ."

I shook my head. "I'm not going to do it. But you have to listen to me. We need to call the police together." I fumbled for my phone, not taking my eyes off her in case she lunged at me. I dropped it onto the blanket.

Her eyebrows shot up. "You want *me* to call the police?"

I could tell she didn't believe what I was saying. "Yes. We're going to talk to them together."

She didn't pick up the phone—maybe she thought I was messing with her, that I would stab her if she reached for it. "I don't understand."

Nicki's mom glanced behind me and I was suddenly certain that Nicki was standing there with a weapon. Out of the corner of my eye I caught a flicker of movement. My heart shot into overdrive.

I whirled around, the knife in front of me, while at the same time throwing myself to the left, but there was no one there. The curtains billowed with the breeze. Nicki's mom scrambled for the far end of the bed, like an insect scurrying for safety. I poked the knife in her direction and she froze.

"Don't move," I said. If she ran away, then this was all going to fall apart. She'd seen my face. She could identify me. "Find the phone."

Her hands rummaged through the covers and then she held up the device. "Here it is."

"We're going to call the police. I'm doing this to help you. I'm here because of Nicki. She wants you dead. She's blackmailing me, telling me I should murder you. If I go to the cops on my own, they're not going to believe me, but they will if we go together." I wanted to explain how brilliant this plan was — it completely backed Nicki into a corner. If I went to the police *with* her mom, it changed everything.

Nicki's mom looked confused. I was counting on the fact that in her heart she would know there was something off about her daughter. How could she live with that creature and not know? I had to convince her. "I know Nicki isn't her real name, but I haven't found out what it is. It's your daughter. She hates your drinking. She blames you for not letting her live with her dad."

"Her dad?"

"Yes. But I think it's really about the money. She wants this house. Nicki thinks you're blowing through the money her grandparents left. She feels it belongs to her. You may not want to believe me, but you have to. Think about it. How else would I know all of this? I'm telling you: She wants you dead so she can move to Vancouver to live with her dad. Or maybe she just wants the money — I don't know."

Nicki's mom shook her head. She didn't want to believe me. I couldn't blame her. Who would want to acknowledge they'd given birth to something like Nicki? That your own daughter would hate you enough to want you dead? I had to drill through the mom's defenses, make her realize this wasn't a horrible joke.

"I'm not making this up. Nicki told me everything. How your husband left and moved to Vancouver."

"How do you know—"

"I know he's started a new family. She told me all about her grandfather, your dad. How they had a place in Scotland and how he had a telescope."

Nicki's mom held up a hand to stop me. "You have this all wrong—"

"I don't," I insisted. "You have to believe me. I've tried to think of every single option. If I don't kill you, she's going to hurt my family. Nicki already tried to kill someone I care about. She's capable of it—she murdered my ex-boyfriend just to make sure I had no way out of this. I can't kill you and I can't not kill you. That's when I realized this was my only option. We have to go to the police together."

"No, you don't understand," Nicki's mom said. "I don't have a daughter."

THIRTY-THREE

AUGUST 29
2 DAYS REMAINING

My stomach turned to thick churning acid. What the hell was she talking about? She didn't look intoxicated. Her eyes were wide but clear. Her words weren't slurred or confused.

"What do you mean?" I asked.

She held up both hands as if trying to make sure I stayed calm. "I don't know who you're talking about, who this Nicki is."

My hands, which had been rock steady, started to shake, a faint tremor. "She's your daughter. I know that's not her name, but how many daughters do you have? You won't let her move out because you're still upset about the divorce. You were crushed that your husband left and you're afraid you'll be abandoned again." I kept trying to supply more details, as if that would convince her.

"I've been divorced for more than a year. Good riddance."

She tried to smile as if she were making a joke. The smile fell off her face when I didn't return it. "I don't have any children."

"Yes, you do," I insisted.

She shook her head. "I swear to god, I live here alone."

The blood was rushing out of my head. Then I remembered the woman I'd met on the street outside the house six days ago. I seized on the memory as if it were a life jacket and I was on a ship going down. I jabbed at Nicki's mom with a finger. "You're a liar! You do too have a daughter. I talked to one of your neighbors and she knew who I was talking about."

The woman held up both hands, shaking her head again. "I have no idea who you talked to or why she would tell you I knew this Nicki person."

"Stop lying!" My voice cracked. I realized I was holding out the knife.

"Yes, okay, I *had* a daughter!" she cried out, covering her face. "I had a baby girl. She died of crib death nearly two years ago. It's partly why my marriage broke down, that and the fact that he'd been shagging the sitter. When I lost my baby girl, I couldn't stand the sight of him anymore. It was like he'd brought all the bad luck into our house, but I swear to god, she was just a little girl." She started crying, giant hiccupping sobs. "My daughter's name was Sarah. She wasn't even a year old. I don't know who this Nicki is. I don't know why any neighbor would tell you I had an older daughter. I swear to god, none of this makes sense. I have no idea why this is happening to me."

I watched her cry. If she was faking it, she was good. My brain scrambled to remember the conversation I'd had with the woman with the dog. She'd hinted something bad had happened, some kind of scandal. *But did she ever use Nicki's name?* She'd never said she was talking about a teenager. It could have been crib death followed by a divorce.

"Did you inherit this house from your parents?"

The woman shook her head rapidly, her hair whipping back and forth. "I bought it with my husband. I had some family money, but my parents are still alive. They live in Cornwall." She pointed to the dresser. "There's a picture of me with them over there."

I crossed over and picked up one of the silver frames. It was a photograph of the woman between a smiling elderly couple, posed in front of a giant hydrangea bush, its big blue flower balls sprinkled behind them like polka dots. I searched the other frames. There were other people, but none of them were Nicki. This woman would have had a picture of her daughter, wouldn't she? If she had all these other pictures, there would have been at least one of her and her own kid. I mentally went through the house as I'd come in. Had I seen anything that belonged to Nicki? A coat hanging in the mudroom, books, or her leather messenger bag? Any sign at all that she lived here? There was a loud buzzing growing in my ears.

I motioned to the woman, flicking the knife up and down. "Get up. I want to see the other bedrooms." My mouth was dry.

She lay there crying, her breath coming in hitches. There was a smear of shiny snot under her nose like a snail trail. "Get up," I repeated, this time pointing the knife at her. "And give me my phone back."

She clambered out of bed. She tried to pass me the phone, but her hand was shaking so badly that the phone dropped back onto the blanket. I snatched it up and shoved it deep into my pocket. I motioned to the door and she walked in front, leading the way, her bare feet sticking on the floor. We went out into the hall and she pushed open the door of the room to the left. It made a perfect horror-movie creak.

"Turn on the light," I demanded.

She flipped a switch and I blinked from the sudden brightness. It was a sterile spare bedroom. Nothing personal at all: no shoes on the floor, no photos on the wall, just a small painting of a rolling landscape in the corner. Nothing on the bedside table: no bottles of nail polish, eyeglasses, half-read magazines, stuffed animals, discarded earrings—nothing. No one lived in here.

I slapped off the switch. "Let's keep going." I followed her down the hall and she flung open the other door. It was an office. A cluttered desk and bookcase stuffed with various worn hardcovers and clusters of paperback novels. There was a wingback chair and ottoman by the window, but no place where anyone could sleep. The walls were a soft pink and I suspected this used to be the nursery. "Are there other bed-rooms?" I asked, hating the tremor in my voice.

"No. That's the bath there." She pointed. "Downstairs there's a dining room, the kitchen, and the parlor, but that's all. I can show you if you want."

"And the basement?" Even as the words left my mouth, I knew that idea didn't make sense. Nicki wasn't going to live in some windowless space.

The woman crossed her arms over her chest, hugging her-self for comfort. "I use it for storage. There aren't any bedrooms down there." She looked thin and vulnerable standing there in her pajama gown. Her arms were like twigs jutting from the short sleeves. She didn't look like Nicki. I hadn't noticed that at first, but now I couldn't identify a single feature they had in common. Then I noticed her nose. Thin and straight. It wasn't broken or bruised. Nicki had told me her mom had broken her nose while drunk, that she'd walked into a doorjamb, but this woman's nose was perfect. "Maybe you have the wrong place," she suggested timidly.

My stomach went into a free fall. Was Nicki's mom sleep-ing off a bottle of vodka a few doors down or a block over? I bit my lip, trying to focus. That didn't make any sense either. Nicki had written down the address. She would know where she lived — that wasn't the kind of thing that a person got wrong. And even if she had, if she had transposed numbers like some kind of numeric dyslexic, how was it possible that the floor plan was exactly the way she'd told me it would be? The light was out above the back door. The lock was broken. All of it was the way Nicki had said it would be.

Except this wasn't Nicki's mom.

"Are you okay?" the woman whispered.

I wondered how long I'd been standing there just staring off into space. The sound in my ears was turning to a roar and there was a layer of clammy sweat down my back. This wasn't Nicki's mom. I'd broken into a stranger's house. I'd brought a knife. I stared down at my hand. *Jesus, I brought a knife.* The roar turned to screaming static.

". . . help?"

I hadn't heard what she'd said. There were black dots popping up in the corners of my vision. I was going to pass out. Right here in the hallway. And when I woke up, this woman would be long gone and the cops would be on their way to pick me up. I forced myself to suck in a deep breath and poked myself in the thigh with the tip of the knife — not hard, just enough to hurt — bringing the world back into focus.

"I have to go," I said. My mouth opened and closed. I felt as if I should apologize, but this went way beyond the kind of thing you could make go away with a simple sorry. I hadn't put a dent in her car or accidentally spilled coffee on her white blouse.

I backed away from her slowly. "Don't tell anyone about this," I said.

"I won't," she said. "I promise." She held up her right hand as if taking a vow.

I felt the top stair under my foot behind me. I made it down three or four steps before I heard her bolt for her bedroom and slam the door shut behind her.

"Help!" she screamed. I heard a screech as she yanked her window wide open. "Someone help me," she yelled into the street.

I flew down the last of the steps, skidding on the wood floor. I bolted for the back door. The woman wasn't screaming anymore. If I had to guess, she'd gone for the phone to call 9-1-1 or whatever the hell they called it here. I shoved my feet into my shoes and ran alongside the house. I peeked my head over the gate. The houses all around had flipped on their lights and there was a guy in his bathrobe standing outside the home next door, looking up and down the street. He was holding a cricket bat. If I went out that way, he'd see me and force me to stay until the cops came.

I was shaking. Maybe I should just wait for the police. Give myself up.

No.

My feet slid on the wet ground as I ran for the back of the garden. I heard the distant sound of a siren. The fence was covered in blackberry bushes. The thorns and branches snagged at my fleece, scratching my arms and face as I ran straight into them. My hands reached through, finding the chainlink fence hidden behind the plant. I vaulted up and over, using strength I didn't even know I had.

Mud squished up around my shoes as I landed with a plop on the other side, making me feel cemented in place. This garden wasn't overgrown but instead tidy and perfect, as though the homeowner trimmed it with nail clippers. The entire back of the house was a huge glass conservatory, which thankfully was still black.

I was picking my way through the yard when a bright light clicked on, blinding me. I flung my hand over my face and stopped dead. If it was the cops, I didn't want to give them a reason to shoot. It was silent except for the sound of the sirens getting closer. That's when I realized it must have been a motion-sensor light. I opened my eyes, but I was still alone and the house was still completely dark. They were either sleeping through all of this or weren't home. The sound of tires squealing one street over jump-started my heart. The police were almost here.

I had to get moving. I had to run.

THIRTY-FOUR

I ran and then walked for miles. I was afraid to get on the Tube. I couldn't handle the idea of being in such a well-lit place surrounded by crowds of people. For now, I preferred the shadows. I ducked into a doorway and pulled off my fleece. I shivered in my T-shirt in the cool summer night air, but on the off chance the police were looking for someone with a dark jacket, I didn't want to wear it. I shoved it into my bag and kept walking.

For a while I didn't know where I was. One street led to another. Stores, banks, and pubs lined the roads. I would start to think about what had happened and then my brain would go completely blank as if it had shorted out from too much information. The loud buzzing in my ears that had started at the house was still a nonstop background noise.

A group of drunk people stumbled out of a cab in front of me. A guy in a Manchester United jersey swayed in place, staring at me, and then started laughing. "You talking to your-self, crazy girl? Having yourself a nice conversation?"

I jerked back. I'd been mumbling to myself. *How long have I been doing that? What the hell was I saying?* I shook my head and crossed the empty street.

"Nothing wrong with being crazy," the guy called out after me. "All the best people are!"

I turned down another street. It looked like every other one I'd been on. My legs were heavy and I fought the urge to start running again. It seemed by now I should have walked the entire length of London. I couldn't shake the feeling that I was hopelessly lost, not just in the city, but altogether, as if I'd fallen through a portal that had taken me to an alternate real-ity, one that was anything but Wonderland.

A police car passed me, then slowed. When it reached the end of the block, it turned around and came back. *Shit.* I glanced to either side, trying to figure out if the car could fol-low me if I ran.

The window rolled down. "Everything okay?" The officer smiled.

I nodded. "Mm-hmm."

The car kept pace with me as I walked. "It's awfully late to be out walking on your own."

"Broke up with my boyfriend. Just wanted to get some air."

"Do you need a ride?"

I wanted to scream for him to get the hell away from me,

but that wasn't going to make this situation go well. "Nope. I'm fine." There was no way I was admitting I was lost.

The cop stared at me. I could feel him taking in my description, mentally memorizing me. "All right then, you take care."

I smiled and raised my hand as he pulled away. I managed to hold myself together until he turned the corner and then my entire body broke into tremors. I ached to be home. Not at Metford, but *home* home. In my own room, my own bed. The pink afghan my grandmother had crocheted pulled up around me. My favorite books on the shelf above my desk, and the faint outlines on the ceiling of where glow-in-the-dark star stickers used to be. I peered up into the sky. Our forebears navigated by stars, after all. But it was too bright in the city to spot a single one.

Then the street opened into a large green space. I followed the metal fence that ran along the sidewalk until I saw the sign. HYDE PARK. I grabbed the wrought-iron gate, practically hugging it in relief. It was okay—I knew where I was now. I could walk back to Metford from here. I wasn't lost anymore. I glanced down at my phone. It was almost two in the morning.

The rushing in my ears increased. How the hell had I lost so much time? I was left with a bigger question. I'd been so exhausted, walking around in a fog. What did I not remember?

Down the block was the hum and swish of a street sweeper as it grew closer, like a giant swaying elephant lumbering along. A couple of guys in orange safety vests kept pace with

311

the truck. They unlocked the trash cans on either side of the street and then hefted bags of garbage into the back of the truck. I glanced up and down until I saw the closest can and jogged over. I reached into my bag and, using my body as a shield from any security cameras, pulled out the knife, wiping it off before shoving it deep under a layer of fast-food cups and trash. Now at least if the cop came back, the knife wouldn't be on my person.

I walked away but stayed close by until I saw the can get picked up. I watched it carefully to make sure nothing fell out. The trash was tossed in with everything else. No one was going to find that knife. I felt a bit better, but I still didn't know what to do next. My brain was spinning, jerking from one thought to another like an out-of-control carnival ride. I couldn't focus. Nothing made sense, but as soon as I tried to break down the problem, my brain would fly off in another direction. I was tired and shaking. I had to sleep before I collapsed. I stumbled back to Metford.

I couldn't run the risk of meeting up with the security guard. Thankfully, the window to the laundry room was still unlatched. I lay down on the cold cement and swung my legs in, dropping down to the table with a *thunk*. It was completely dark inside, and for the first time in hours I felt safe.

I couldn't go back to my room. I suspected Tasha would be waiting for me. Even if she wasn't, the idea of climbing the stairs seemed impossible. I couldn't escape the feeling that I was missing something, that some uncomfortable truth was hiding in the back of my brain. Someone's laundry had been dumped on top of the table, so I wadded it up to make a pillow and lay down. All I wanted to do was sleep and forget any of this had happened. I closed my eyes and was gone.

Sounds in the hall woke me up with a start. I sat up, instantly awake with my heart racing. I held my bag clutched to my chest, but whoever it was walked past the laundry room without coming in.

I turned on my phone. I had turned it to airplane mode at some point the night before. I blinked when I saw the time. It was still early, just before seven. My notifications went ballistic, tons of missed calls and texts. Most were from Tasha, but the real shocker was one that came through from Alex.

You okay? Your parents called, said you're AWOL. Text me.

I read it over and over as if there might have been a secret message contained within. The text showed he cared, right? He was worried. There were no protestations of love, or regret that things had ended the way they had, but he hadn't had to send a message at all.

Unless my parents had made him.

They'd called. Seven messages.

beep *Kim, it's your mother. Please give me a call.*

beep *I don't care what time it is there — please call as soon as you get this message.*

beep *We trusted you to behave on this trip. If you don't call back, you can consider yourself grounded the instant you get home.*

beep *Honey, I'm worried about you. Please call.*

beep *Kimberly, Tasha is considering calling the police. I know you don't want that, so you need to call.*

beep *Kim, I'm not mad. Forget what I said about being grounded. I just want to know you're okay.*

beep *Kimber-bear? This is your dad. Give us a call, sweetie. You can come home tomorrow and then we can figure out together what's going on.*

I stared down at the phone. My dad had called. Shit must be serious. He usually left all these parenting things up to my mom, who, if not an expert, played one online. She'd get plenty of blog posts out of this one. *What to Do When Your Daughter Cracks Up.* Or *Mental Health Problems: It's Not All in Her Head.*

My stomach rumbled. I was hungry. It seemed that with everything going on, my appetite should have shut down, but it was still there, reminding me that at least the biological part of my life was continuing as normal. I mentally did the math. It was unlikely anyone in our group would be in the cafeteria this early.

I crept up the stairs. The lobby was empty. The kitchen

staff had just opened the doors, so I ducked in, grabbing an apple, a couple slices of bread, and an individual packet of peanut butter before slipping back out.

"Hey, Kim!" I froze, the apple in my mouth. I turned around slowly. One of the desk clerks stood there smiling. "You know Tasha's looking for you."

I nodded. "Oh, yeah. I found her," I lied.

"You got some mail." She leaned over the desk, waving a white envelope in my direction like a surrender flag.

Bile rushed up my throat. I forced myself to reach for the envelope. As soon as I touched it, I relaxed. The paper wasn't like what Nicki had sent before, not thick or fancy; it was a plain business envelope from an office supply store. It was pretty battered and adorned with Emily's handwriting across the front, along with the goofy cartoon characters she always scribbled on things.

"Thanks. I better go put my stuff in the dryer." I paused as if waiting for the clerk to call me on my lie, but she'd already started reading her book. I took my haul back down to the laundry room and plopped myself back onto the table. I spread a thick layer of peanut butter on the cold bread and inhaled it in three bites. Once the demon in my stomach was slightly mollified, I opened the letter from Emily.

Her light tone threw me until I checked the postmark. She'd sent it the day that Connor had died. She'd had no idea what had happened when she'd written it. It had passed the bad news somewhere over the Atlantic. I stroked the paper. I wished I could go back in time with the letter—a time before all of this had happened. Where her discussion of getting sick of eating hot dogs, how she had to pull a kid out of the water who went down during swim class, and how she'd kissed one of the other counselors behind the canoe shed seemed like idealized perfection. A tear trickled down my face as I read the final lines.

> *Anyhoo, I have to go if I'm going to get this out in today's mail. I can't wait to see you in a few weeks and hear all the deets of your trip. I know you didn't want to go—but I hope it's going well. Everything happens for a reason. Maybe you've met a prince! You don't need a science award—you're one of the smartest people I know. Here's to doing great things.*
> *Love, Em*

I didn't feel like the smartest person. Nicki had been one step ahead of me every step of the way. I chewed on the apple and started to break down the problem. I had to face what I'd been running from all night.

Was it possible that Nicki was just a figment of my imagination?

I'd blown the relationship with Connor into more than it had been, but this was a totally different level of delusion.

If Nicki had never even existed, that was seriously messed up. That made *me* messed up. She seemed real to me — not like a voice in my head, but three-dimensional. As real as anyone else. Imagining a relationship is one thing; imagining an entire person is something else entirely. But it could be done. Didn't people who had multiple personality disorder black out and then operate as someone else? Had *I* been wandering around thinking I was Nicki? The realization of all the missing time I'd had — time I couldn't account for — boiled over in my mind.

I mentally went through every encounter I'd ever had with Nicki and tried to pinpoint any occasion where she'd inter-acted with other people. I was a hundred percent certain she had been there at the duty-free store. She was the one who'd tripped on the bags. She argued with the clerk about if she'd have to pay for the perfume. That wasn't all in my head. I repeated that thought over and over, finding it comforting.

But what about since the airport?

Talking to her on the plane had been a bit surreal. There had been a lot of vodka. Was it possible I drank it by myself and just pretended she was there? Taken a girl I'd hung out with for a couple of hours and then spun her into a friend? I'd convinced myself Connor really liked me. It was possible I had made up a friend so I wouldn't feel so alone.

There had been so many times on this trip where I'd been distracted. I'd chalked it up to stress and lack of sleep, but it might have been more than that. I quickly went through every meeting Nicki and I had had since I'd been in England and came up blank.

Wait! Yes! My fist jammed into the air. Alex had met her. She'd talked to us at the bar after we'd gone on the Eye. Except she hadn't called herself Nicki that night, but Erin. Alex seemed certain she was another student living at Metford. I pinched the bridge of my nose. What if there was an Erin here and I'd superimposed my idea of Nicki onto her? How would I know if Alex had met the real Nicki or simply someone who looked a bit like her in my mind? She hadn't said anything about Connor in front of him.

But if Nicki wasn't real, then what had happened to Connor?

I closed my eyes, trying to put myself back onto the Tube platform. I evoked the smells of metal, mildew, and old coffee that filled the space. The stale breeze coming through the tunnel like a ghost. It had been so crowded. With the canceled train it had been a sea of people all packed together. Connor had been near me.

Was it possible I had pushed him? He'd threatened to tell Alex about our history. I squeezed my eyes together even harder, as if I could teleport through time. Maybe. I had hated him. Perhaps it had been an instinct, a momentary chance to lash out, and then the instant it was over, my brain fabricated Nicki to cover what I'd done.

My imaginary friend had killed my imaginary boyfriend. A hysterical giggle escaped from me and I slapped my hand over my mouth. I had to keep it together. I had to stay logical. Approach this like a scientist.

I sucked in a deep breath, trying to clear my head. If Nicki was real, why would she tell me she wanted me to kill her mom if it wasn't really her mom? That didn't make any sense at all. My eyes skimmed over Em's letter. *Everything happens for a reason.* Action, reaction. Having me kill a stranger didn't make sense, which seemed to lean toward Nicki being all in my head, perhaps a way to deal with the guilt of what I had done to Connor.

An idea struck me. How had I known the door would be unlocked and the light would be out? I had a vivid imagination, but I wasn't psychic. That was a point for Nicki being real, unless . . . *Oh god.* What if I had gone door to door trying knobs, looking for a place that was unlocked, and then forgotten I'd even done it? What if, during the times everything had seemed fuzzy because I was overtired, I'd been wandering the city, breaking into people's homes until I found one that fit the delusion my brain had built?

Shit, I really should have taken that psychology elective in junior year. I'd always made fun of psychology and sociology as pseudosciences. Too wishy-washy, no right or wrong answers. Now I'd kill to know a bit more about how the mind worked.

Kill to know. Another giggle burbled up from my chest. That was me. Killer. I bit hard on my lip and the coppery taste of blood was in my mouth. I paced back and forth in the tiny space of the laundry room.

I stopped short. What about what had happened to Alex? If Nicki wasn't real, then how had I ended up with a jar of shrimp powder in my room? If I was blacking out, then I would have to be the one who had taken his EpiPen and essentially poisoned him. On purpose.

I wouldn't have done that to Alex. I could accept that it might have been possible that I'd blocked out what I'd done to Connor, and that I'd even gone door to door looking for a place to break in and then blocked that out too, but I loved Alex. I wouldn't have hurt him. Even if I had some kind of multiple personality, I couldn't fathom that any part of me would have done that. I might have been messed up, but that was going too far. It meant I was willing to hurt someone I cared about to keep the delusion going.

But if Nicki was real, why would she want me to kill some random stranger?

My phone buzzed. Another text from Tasha.

Text or call me NOW.

I imagined she'd already called the police to report me missing. I glanced down at the phone in my hand. Could they track me? I'd had it on airplane mode most of the night before, but now that I'd turned it on, was it pinging off cell towers, narrowing down the search grid? Detective Sharma could be hunched over a computer right now, making a note as to my location.

I didn't want to be caught, but it was becoming clear I needed help. I could potentially outrun the cops, my parents, Tasha, and even Alex—but there was no running away from reality. Connor was dead and Alex had almost died. I might be a danger to other people.

Unless Nicki was real.

Only one way to find out and I had to know. I opened Instagram and took a quick picture of my shoes. *Running out of time. Meet me where we met last. Now.* I then cross-posted the message on every social media account I had. It wouldn't mean anything to anyone else, but Nicki would remember the conversation we'd had at the Peter Pan statue.

I clicked off my phone. I needed to get the SIM card out. That was how the phone connected to the cell towers. With that gone, the phone couldn't be used to track me. I searched around the room for something the right size. I found a pencil, but the tip was just a smidge too big to fit into the slot. The lead broke the second time I tried it, and I chucked the pencil down onto the floor, frustrated. Then I saw something buried in a pile of dust and lint at the baseboard: a paper clip.

I bent the end of the paper clip and said a quick prayer that it would work. It slid into the slot and the hinge opened, popping the tiny plastic SIM card into my hand.

I felt strangely calm. What I had to do was clear. I needed to confirm Nicki was real. If she wasn't, and I was responsible for everything that had happened, then I'd turn myself in. Get help. Spend the rest of my life trying to make up for my actions in some way. But if Nicki had done all this, then I needed to be one step ahead of her for a change.

I glanced down at Em's letter. I *had* met a prince, and while I was still sure I'd done the right thing by breaking up with him to make sure he was safe, that didn't mean I didn't regret it. I texted him back quickly.

I'm really sorry. You've been my Samwise and I've been Frodo off on my own mission. I'm not okay yet, but I will be.

The message wouldn't be sent until I popped the SIM card back in, but I still felt better for having written it. It was time to get going. I jumped back onto the table and peered through the narrow window to make sure the courtyard was empty. It was raining. Not drizzling, either — it was a full-fledged down-pour. I tried to see the positive. People would be less inclined to hang out in a park.

I hefted myself up, chucked my bag outside, and started to crawl back through the window. Then the door to the laundry room swung open. I went completely rigid.

"Kim?" Sophie stood there. "The front desk clerk said she saw you." She looked confused, which, given that I was half hanging out a window, wasn't an unreasonable reaction.

Shit. It was bad that anyone had seen me, but Sophie

especially would want to do the right thing. It was her nature. She'd tell Tasha where I was, not because Sophie wanted to get me in trouble, but because she'd think she was helping. I scrambled the rest of the way out, letting the window bang shut. I scooped up my bag and hustled for the street. I needed to disappear. I heard the window being pushed back open.

"Kim! Come back!"

I didn't even bother to turn around. I had a date with someone more important.

Unless she was a figment of my imagination.

THIRTY-FIVE

I ducked into a Waitrose grocery and bought one of the prepared ham and cheese sandwiches in the deli. My makeshift breakfast hadn't been enough. I was ravenous.

The rain plinked down onto my head. I chewed the sandwich. The bread was dry and sucked all the moisture out of my mouth. I circled the streets around the park, taking in my surroundings and debating my options.

Everything happens for a reason.

I turned over one option in my mind, considering the angles. Was that my solution? Would it even work? I thought I'd had her before and I had been wrong. I went through everything I knew, looking at the facts fresh. Science is about looking at the data. Truth hides in details. As I sifted through the information, I realized I'd missed something. I'd accepted things as true without question. But now that I had different information, it threw everything into a different light.

Things happen for a reason. Nicki would have had a reason and I was pretty sure I knew what it was. If I was right, I had a possible solution. I grunted in satisfaction.

I pushed away the worry that no one would come to the park. I refused to believe that all of this had been in my head. I'd deal with it if I had to, but I wasn't ready to admit defeat.

I walked to the park and wove my way to the Peter Pan statue, but Nicki wasn't there. I chucked the rest of my food into the bin. I glanced up and down the pathway, but no one was coming. I didn't want to sit on the bench; it seemed too suspicious to wait there as the rain fell. Instead, I walked in circles, never straying too far, my stomach a tight, sour knot.

No sign of Nicki. I pictured the solution (if she did show up) over and over in my mind. It might seem like my mom's usual woo-woo, but visualization made a difference. It had been proved in studies. I slowed the steps down, playing them in slow motion in my head, imagining how she would react and how I would respond. My feet traced calculations in the gravel. Doing the math relaxed me.

The rain slowed to a light drizzle. With my phone turned off, I wasn't sure how much time had passed since I'd posted the message. I realized I was picking at my fingers and shoved my hands deep into my pockets to keep myself from peeling the flesh down to the bone.

I reminded myself of Emily's letter. I was smart. Things happen for a reason. This trip had taught me at least one thing:

I needed to rely on myself. I was the only one who could find the answers. I could do this.

I nibbled on a sliver of fingernail. At least an hour must have passed by now, maybe as much as two. If Nicki was real, then she would have seen the message. She'd be looking to reach out to me because of the night before. She knew everything. Which meant that if she didn't show up, I was going to have to face the idea that it had all been in my head.

I didn't have to tell anyone about Nicki. The police hadn't been able to prove anything in Connor's death. They hadn't even officially said it was a murder. They didn't have proof. And if Nicki was in my imagination, I didn't have to worry about her accusing me. Figments of my imagination weren't going to chase me down, threatening to blackmail me if I didn't kill their mother. I would be free and clear.

Except for the fact that I knew what had happened. I was thinking clearly *now*, but who was to say I would stay that way? It was possible in an hour from now I could decide that Nicki wanted someone else to die, someone else in "her" way. Who knew — maybe I'd get a dark wig and start running around, thinking I was Nicki while lost in some kind of fog.

If she didn't show up soon, I would record everything I could remember into my phone, then call Detective Sharma. I'd let her take me to jail, or to a mental hospital, or wherever she thought I needed to be. It wasn't about doing the right thing for my parents, or Em, or Alex, or even Connor. It was about doing the right thing because it mattered to me. I'd spent too much of my life trying to be what other people wanted, trying to make them happy. Being here, being stripped of everything, made me realize that what mattered most was my own opinion of myself.

"There you are!" I spun around. Nicki was here. "I thought we were going to meet by the statue?"

"I was walking around. Waiting for you." My breath was slow and shallow.

Nicki spun in a circle with her umbrella as if she were Mary Poppins doing a dance number. "Well, here I am."

I took a step closer. "I wasn't sure if you would come."

Another step.

"Of course I came. We have a lot to talk about."

One more step. "We do." I tried to calculate the distance. I lunged forward before she could dart away and seized Nicki's arm. She tried to wrench it back, but I hung on, pulling her toward me until we were inches apart. Her eyes were wide, shocked. I could feel her breath on my face. I was close enough to count her individual eyelashes and stare into her eyes. I'd never really noticed the color before. I'd thought they were a light brown, but they were actually almost yellow. Lizard-eye yellow. I smelled the sticky sweet scent of her shampoo, like overripe strawberries. My nose twitched as I tried to suck in every detail. I felt the heat of her skin where I held her wrist and even the buried ripple of her pulse. There was a faint bruise by her mouth, covered with a thin layer of concealer.

"What are you doing?" Nicki hissed, still trying to pull back.

I leaned forward as if to kiss her cheek and lightly touched my tongue to her skin. Salty. "You're real," I said, the certainty of it spreading through me like fire.

Nicki yanked herself free and wiped her face. "What the hell? Of course I'm real."

I felt lightheaded. I hadn't invented her.

Nicki backed up a few steps and inspected me. Then she burst out laughing so hard she bent in half. "Oh my god, you thought you *imagined* me?"

"It's not funny," I said.

"That is so perfect," Nicki crowed. "It never even occurred to me that you would think I was some kind of psychotic voice in your head. You must have thought you were going insane." She trailed off in giggles. "I wish I could have known what you were thinking for the past few days. Wandering around all Lady Macbeth–like: 'Out, damned Nicki.'" Her eyes popped and her mouth made a perfect doll O. "Wait, so did you think you were the one who killed Connor?"

I hated her. "It's *not* funny." I reminded myself to stay calm and logical.

Her shoulders shook with laughter. "That would be where you are wrong."

"I went to your mother's house last night."

"I know. I was watching." She smirked.

"I want nothing to do with you." I turned and began walking away. I was counting on the fact that she'd follow me. She wouldn't want this moment to end. Like a cat who had cornered a mouse, she wanted to play with me first.

But what she didn't realize was that I'd been paying attention too. After her comment about there being cameras everywhere in the city, I'd realized she was right and now I knew a place where we could truly be alone. And this discussion required privacy.

She trailed after me on the path, catching up in a few short steps . . . just the way I'd visualized it. She linked arms with me. "Okay, we'll walk. It's chilly just standing here." She rubbed her hand up and down her arm. There was a red imprint where I had held on to her wrist.

"I didn't see you leave the house," she said. "But then that woman started screaming out the window like her hair was on fire, so I knew something happened." She glanced over. "Even if the something wasn't what was supposed to happen."

"That woman wasn't your mother."

"Nope." Nicki hopped over a puddle. It reminded me of that nursery rhyme: *Step on a crack, break your mother's back.*

"I don't get it."

"I was just curious if I could make you do it." She leaped lightly over another large, muddy puddle, like a gazelle.

I stopped walking and stared at her. "What are you talking about?"

"I wanted to know if I could make you do it," she repeated. "How far you'd have to be pushed to take that action. What would it take to make someone like you"—she paused to inspect me up and down—"do something so totally out of character. You're smart, but you've got no spine. I wanted to know what would happen if I pushed the right buttons." She rubbed her hands from the chill and waited for me to respond.

I crossed the bike lane and headed out of the park. If she was being honest, then I'd gotten it all wrong again. I refused to believe that.

She chased after me. "Now, don't be mad. It's not your fault that you're not as smart as me."

"You can't be serious. This was some kind of a sick game?"

Nicki snorted. "Not a game. Research."

"You're what? Some kind of fucked-up moral Dr. Frankenstein?"

She laughed. "I guess that makes you my monster." She threw her arms up in the air. "It's alive! It's alive!"

I shook my head and crossed the street. "What about what you did to Alex?"

"I didn't do a thing to him. He had an allergic reaction." She stared at me as if she was trying to figure out how to explain it using smaller words. "I followed you and saw what happened. Bingo. Opportunity. I went out and bought the shrimp powder and sneaked it into your room so you'd think I did it. It was just lucky."

"Lucky," I repeated, my voice flat.

"Pretty much."

"What about his EpiPen? How do you explain that it was missing?"

The traffic noise faded as we left the main streets behind. "I don't know anything about his EpiPen. I guess he lost it."

I searched her face, looking for a tell — a twitch of the eyelid, or the licking of her lips — trying to ferret out if she was telling the truth. "Alex always made sure he had that with him. Always."

Nicki rolled her eyes. "I don't know what to tell you. I didn't touch lover-boy's medication. All I did was let you think I did, to see if that would be enough to nudge you forward."

"You're lying," I said. I was certain now. She'd done it on purpose and was trying to dance out of it.

She giggled. "Maybe. Guess you're getting a bit smarter all the time, or at least more skeptical. Does it really matter if it was an accident or on purpose? The whole point is that it was the pressure point you needed."

A train whistle blew in the distance and the sound broke through my thoughts like a bullet. "But you killed Connor," I said. "That wasn't just a lucky accident." I made finger quotes in the air around the word *lucky*.

Nicki paused to look over the side of the bridge we were on

and watch the tracks below. "It might have been." She glanced over her shoulder and smiled. "Or maybe it wasn't. When doing research, some test subjects have to be sacrificed. Scientific progress can be messy. Look at any of it — you don't move forward without having to step on some people to get there. I mean, they blind little bunnies to test mascara." She shook her head. "I feel worse for the bunnies than I do for someone like Connor."

What she was saying felt like a punch in the gut. "You killed Connor to see what I would do."

"Pretty much." She sighed, sounding like my mother when she was disappointed. "Why are you looking at me like that? I told you the first time I met you what fascinated me: why people do what they do. How they can be influenced. You're acting like all of this is coming as some big surprise. I would think it would make you feel better to know that Connor died for a greater purpose."

I barked a bitter laugh. "Your research is some great purpose. Now you're like a twisted Dr. Freud."

Nicki screwed her mouth to the side. "I picture myself more like B. F. Skinner. Operant conditioning, behaviorism, that kind of thing. I was never into Freud. I don't really care about penis envy or how your childhood impacted you, although I have to say, for the record, you have some major mother issues."

"You're fucked up," I said.

Nicki tucked her hair behind her ears. "That's rich. An hour ago, you thought I was just a voice in your head. I'm not sure you should be chucking rocks from inside your glass house about other people's mental health status, if you know what I mean."

"I'll go to the police. Even if you didn't try to kill Alex, you murdered Connor."

"Maybe. I haven't admitted to anything." She waved off what I was about to say. "It might have been an accident. Maybe he died and I decided to see how I could use his death." She glanced up. "Or maybe not. Let's say, for the purposes of the argument, that I did kill him. What makes you think the cops would believe you?"

"They will."

She shrugged and I felt the tension in my chest tighten another notch. "Maybe. But I still have this." Nicki reached into her pocket and dangled the list I'd written about Connor in my face and then pulled the paper back. "Keep in mind that even *you* thought you might be responsible. And given how good I am at shaping people's reality, imagine what I might do with the authorities." She winked.

"You don't shape people; you manipulate them," I spat out.

"Call it what you like, but even you won't argue with the facts." She leaned against the wall. "I'm simply giving you the advice that you might want to think about it before you go to the police."

"What if I taped all of this?" I opened my arms wide. "You forgot to search me this time."

Her eyes narrowed and her mouth pinched in. She wasn't

used to being caught out. Her eyelid twitched and then a smile broke across her face. "You're lying. You didn't record this." She tapped me on the nose. "I know you. Don't be mad. You can't think of everything all the time. I'm not even going to hold it against you that you lied."

"How kind of you," I said, my voice flat.

"Don't be snotty. I'm just pointing out that I could be angry. Technically, in addition to the lie, you still owe me a body."

I closed my eyes, trying to shut her out. I opened them again. "You still want me to kill someone?"

"Perhaps. That will be the fun of it, won't it? Wondering what type of favor I'll call in, and when." She smiled, her expression softening. "I'm going to miss you when you leave tomorrow."

"The feeling isn't mutual," I said.

She laughed. "Fair enough. Hopefully over time our relationship will at least include respect." Nicki held out her hand. "Despite the hard feelings, I owe you sincere thanks. You're my first *real* research subject, and the past few weeks have been fascinating. I haven't had this much fun in years. I know you're mad at me, but honestly, I adore you."

I stared at her outstretched hand. She was never going to go away. She was right about something: she would pop up when I least expected her, screwing up my life. But I suspected I knew something. Something she hadn't anticipated I'd put together. I took her hand and smiled as we shook.

My smile unnerved her. I could see it in her face.

"My friend reminded me of something today."

"What's that?"

"Everything happens for a reason." I could feel her wanting to pull her hand away from me but not wanting to struggle.

Nicki giggled. "You're starting to sound like your mom. Are you telling me this is all destiny?"

"No. It's logic. You didn't choose that woman at random. You knew her house. You'd been there before." I let go of her and crossed my arms over my chest.

"Maybe." Nicki gave an elaborate shrug. "I like to go exploring sometimes — you'd be surprised how many people don't lock up carefully."

"It's not that. You act like you're some kind of scientist, that this is all about the pursuit of knowledge, but it's much sleazier than that, isn't it? You're not special or some type of above-the-rest-of-us kind of person. Your real motivation is much more banal. You slept with her husband."

There it was, a tiny twitch just above her eyebrow. A crack in her veneer. I'd been right. She said nothing. "This was never about a research project," I continued. "Or at least that wasn't the whole reason. It was about revenge. You were their baby-sitter, you slept with her husband, and when it all came out, you expected him to choose you, but he didn't, did he? He went back to his wife. And then when they got divorced, he *still* didn't want you — he moved away. That's what you really couldn't stand. That he didn't want you."

I locked eyes with her, enjoying the rage in her gaze. This wasn't the way this research project was supposed to turn out.

Research animals weren't supposed to bite back.

She'd never expected me to put it all together. And I might not have if I hadn't gotten Emily's letter. *Everything happens for a reason,* and if so, then there was a reason Nicki wanted me to kill that woman. When I thought it was her mom, then I figured it was because of her drinking or because Nicki wanted her money, but if it wasn't her mom, the reason had to be something else. Then the pieces fell into place: the relationship Nicki had mentioned on the plane with a married guy, the woman in the street talking about a scandal, the woman telling me at knifepoint about her cheating husband.

Nicki's lip twitched, almost snarled. "Well, aren't you a clever bunny?"

I tsked. "Now, don't be cranky. It's not my fault that the reason you did this was simple, common, basic revenge. It's not even original."

"Shut up," she said.

"You weren't in Vancouver visiting your dad, were you? You went there to find that guy."

There was a *whoosh* as a train went under the bridge we

stood on, disappearing around the corner. "Did you bring me here to remind me of Connor? To make me feel bad?"

"Do you? Do you feel bad?" I cocked my head. "I don't think you do, but you're right, being here isn't an accident. It's to make you remember. You went pretty far to get what you wanted, but it still didn't work. Connor's dead and that guy still doesn't care about you at all. Even now, when he's divorced."

Nicki's face cycled through a range of emotions. She jumped up so she was standing on the low bridge wall. She walked back and forth as if she were on a stage. I could see her wrestling her feelings back under control. She was up there because she wanted to be in power, but it was in appearance only. "Let's hear it for the girl genius, ladies and gentlemen." She gestured theatrically in my direction. "She finally figured out it wasn't all about her."

I stared at her as if she bored me. "Don't they say sarcasm is the lowest form of humor? Just be honest. Did you do something to that guy in Vancouver?"

The corners of her mouth curled. "Confessing to anything, even without you recording, strikes me as foolish. Let's leave it with the idea that he's not likely to bother me anymore."

I crossed my arms over my chest as I looked at her. "You have a way of getting rid of things that bother you." I wondered if the baby had even died of crib death or if there was another victim to add to her list.

Nicki kicked a loose stone, sending it flying into the empty space behind her, and watched it fall. "The good news is that you do seem to grasp what I'm capable of. I guess we'll have to leave it as a draw."

"What does that mean?"

She shrugged. "You go home. I stay here."

I shook my head. "I don't think so."

Nicki rolled her eyes. "Oh, now you've got some big plan? Now you're the one in charge?" She put her hands on her hips, but she didn't fool me. There was a slight tremor in her arms. She was scared.

"I was always in charge of what I chose to do — I'd just forgotten. I'm going to the police. I'm going to tell them about what I did last night. That woman will have made a report. I'm certain *she* knows your real name. The only way I would have known about her and her house is through you. The police will find a picture of you, Alex can confirm you pretended to be Erin, and if you were stupid enough to do something to the husband in Vancouver, then I'm pretty sure that will be the end of it for you."

"You aren't going to say a thing." She pinned me in place with her eyes, looking down her nose. "Unless you want to end up in your own world of hurt. I'll tell them that we bonded over stories of murder and mayhem. At the end of the day I still have no reason to have murdered Connor, but you do."

I felt myself take a deep breath. "I don't care. I'll take

my chances." It started to rain again. No one was out in this weather.

Her face was flushed an angry red. "Don't be stupid." Spittle flew out of her mouth. "You'll ruin it for both of us."

"Doing the right thing doesn't ruin anything."

Nicki kicked the wall in frustration, sending a spray of small rocks into my chest. "I can't wait to see you try to explain this." She dangled my list in front of me and I shrugged.

"I'll explain it the best I can and people can believe me or not. It doesn't matter anymore what people think of me. The ones who matter will know the truth."

She wadded up the list and threw it at me. It bounced harmlessly off my chin and skittered to the ground. Nicki looked disappointed, as if she thought it was a grenade that had failed to detonate.

"In case you're wondering," I said, "you aren't one of the people who matter."

I could see her drawing saliva. She lurched forward to spit on me, but the movement put her off balance.

Time seemed to slow down. *One Mississippi.*

Her eyes widened as she realized she was teetering. *Two Mississippi.*

I lunged forward and grabbed ahold of her wrist, pulling her toward me, away from the edge. *Three Mississippi.*

She snarled at me and yanked her wrist free, smiling as she tipped back. Nicki plunged off the bridge. Her scream was drowned out by the blast of a train as it shot out of the tunnel below.

Four Mississippi.

Then she wasn't screaming anymore.

I stood there, shaking. I crept forward and peered over the edge. The train was still going by, its brakes squealing as it tried to stop. There wasn't a single sign of her. It was as if she'd never existed.

Had she wanted to jump because she knew she'd been bested? Or had the idea of me helping her been that repugnant? Or maybe she thought I would feel guilty forever and that she'd win for all eternity.

I bent down and picked up the crumpled list. If she'd thought the guilt would crush me, she'd been wrong.

THIRTY-SIX

AUGUST 31
HOME

The plane bounced down the runway as we landed in Vancouver. I peered out the window to catch a glimpse of the North Shore Mountains as we taxied toward the gate. They marched along the horizon, thick and green.

Home. The sun was even shining.

My bag was one of the first to drop down the luggage chute. Once I turned in my customs form, I headed for the hall. I could see the crowd waiting in the arrivals lounge. Some were carrying flowers, and there was a big sign held by a toddler that declared WELCOME HOME, MOMMY! I searched the faces and spotted my parents standing toward the back.

I waved. My throat was tight with emotion and I hustled toward them. My mom took pictures as I walked up, then hugged me stiffly. My dad waited until she was done, which didn't take long, and then pulled me toward him. His hug smelled like fresh-cut wood and burned leaves. He must have been working in the yard before coming to pick me up.

"Good to have you back with us," he whispered in my hair. Then he held me at arm's length. "Look at you. I think you grew while you were gone. Doesn't she look older?"

My mom nodded. She took the handle of the suitcase from my hands. "Are you tired? Hungry? We thought we might get a bite to eat on the way. Then once we're home you can take a shower and go to bed early."

"I could eat," I said. "Listen, about the past couple of days . . ." I began.

"Let's not have an argument in the airport," Mom said, her voice tight.

Dad put his arm around me and tugged me close. "We can talk about it tomorrow. We were worried about you, and we were upset that you took off and caused trouble for the program, and there will be consequences, but most of all we're glad you've made it home safe and sound."

Mom nodded, but her lips were pressed into a thin line that let me know she had a lot more to say on the subject.

I followed them out to the short-term parking garage, past the totem poles and the smell of hot dogs from the Japadog food cart. My mom kept up a nonstop patter about the weather and what school supplies she'd already picked up at Staples for me. I tuned her out. It wasn't as if she wanted a response.

It had all gone smoother than I could have hoped. The detectives had been waiting for me when I got back to Metford.

For a second I wondered if they were there because of what had just happened, but then I realized Tasha had called them. I thought of telling them everything, but in the end, I kept my story simple. Told them what they expected to hear: The death of Connor had thrown me. Then Alex's allergic attack. I'd freaked out and I was so far from home. I had acted out. I let a few well-timed tears fall while telling my story, as if even I was disappointed in my reckless behavior. I'd just needed to be by myself. I knew I shouldn't have run off, but I had been upset. When the detectives pressed me for where I'd been all that time, I told them I didn't really know. I'd walked a lot.

At one point, I realized I really was crying. Detective Sharma watched me as if trying to read between each of my words. She seemed to know something was off about my story, but she couldn't put her finger on it. With luck, she'd never connect me to the home invasion across town. Or the body on the tracks. There was a chance the police might even recognize Nicki from the video of Connor's death. They might assume she killed herself because of the guilt of having killed him. But they wouldn't think of me—as far as they knew, there was no connection between the two of us. Nicki had been right about some things—without a motive, no one would suspect me. We were strangers. It made for a perfect crime.

Telling the police the whole truth would have only complicated things now. My mom believed in destiny. Maybe this time karma took its own justice.

The whole time I talked and apologized to the detectives, Tasha had stood there with her hands on her hips and steam coming out of her ears. She was probably biting back a sea of curse words. But that's all she eventually gave me: a lecture. How people had been worried. How it was a waste of police time. It didn't matter — I was home now. I'd be in trouble with my parents. Grounded, if I had to guess. But home.

I followed my parents through the parking garage while they bickered about where they'd left the car. I turned my phone on, letting it find the local network. I sent a message to Alex before I could think too long about it.

Back home. Would like to take you out to say sorry in person.

A second later he responded.

Sorry for what, exactly?

Everything.

World hunger? Wars? The declining number of bumblebees?

I smiled and my fingers flew over the keyboard. I do feel bad about the bees. Lunch Friday?

Sure. The block of tension in my stomach melted. Another ping a second later. Not Thai.

I laughed. Deal.

Dad raised an eyebrow. "That your friend Alex?"

I smiled. "Yeah."

Mom's mouth pinched. "I hope you're not letting things get too serious." Dad nudged her and she shut her mouth.

I didn't bother answering. Now that he was safe, that we were both safe, I was hoping it *would* get serious. Emily would be back home this weekend too. I wanted her to meet Alex. She would like him.

I could never tell either of them what had happened.

That was my real punishment. I was going to have to carry this on my own. I'd pushed Nicki into losing her temper. I'd wanted her off balance. I hadn't imagined how it would end, but I wasn't totally innocent, either. I'd wanted her to be scared, but I'd never wanted what had happened. Even if, in the end, that had been her choice.

My dad unlocked the car with a beep of his key fob and I hefted my bag into the trunk before he could do it. I opened the window as soon as I got into the car.

"Do you really want that open?" Mom asked. "It's going to blow your hair around."

"The air smells different here," I said. "Clean."

She shook her head slightly and stared out the windshield, her Coach handbag held tightly on her lap.

"Anything in particular take your fancy to eat?" Dad asked over his shoulder as we pulled out of the garage, merging with traffic headed toward the city. "We could stop for sushi, or head to Earls for some pub grub, or there's that barbecue place on Granville."

Sushi was one of my favorites and I'd missed it in London, where it had been so expensive. But I also knew my mom didn't care for it. She wouldn't admit it because she thought sushi was something she should like. If we ever went, she'd order a California roll and some vegetable tempura and then pick at the food as though it were something the waitress had fished out of the garbage for her.

"What about Secret Garden Tea," I suggested, listing my mom's favorite place. "Or is that too out of the way?"

Mom sat up straighter in the passenger seat. "That might be nice. We could get some scones to go for the morning."

"Secret Garden it is." Dad caught my eye in the rearview mirror. "I swear, you do look older." I could tell he was pleased I was doing my part to smooth the waters. He didn't know I wasn't doing it for my mom's approval. I was doing it because it was the right thing to do. "You know what they say: Travel changes a person."

I nodded and gazed out the window. He had no idea.

THE END

ACKNOWLEDGMENTS

I know all too well how many great books are out there (I have a stack sitting right here) so I appreciate you, the reader, for taking the time on this book. Thanks to all the readers, booksellers, librarians (special call out to librarian super-hero Rachel Joyce) and teachers for spreading book love far and wide.

I tend to write about friendships that are twisted, but in real life I have the best friends in the world. For being there for me when I needed you most, big thanks to Laura Sullivan, Jamie Hillegonds, CJ Hunt, Kelly Charron, Joelle Anthony, Robyn Harding, Naomi Anderson, Mary Robinette-Kowal, Donna Barker, Joelle Charbonneau, Jeanette Caul, Lisa Voisin and so many more. Also, a big call out to family who have to be nice to me, but I suspect would anyway. My family might be crazy, but they're my kind of crazy.

Writing is a craft, but publishing is a business. I'm lucky to work with some of the best people in the industry. Barbara

Poelle is a dream agent—the perfect balance of support and butt kicking. I'm grateful for her belief in me along with her willingness to share cocktail recipes. The entire team at HMH is amazing, but I have to give a special call out to my editor Emilia Rhodes who shares my love of murder podcasts and dogs. Thanks also to Tara Sonin, Sammy Brown, Lisa Vega, and Mary Magrisso for being so supportive and amazing.

Finally, a wag of the tail to my two dogs who can be counted on to sleep on my feet while I write, bark when I'm on the phone, dig holes where they shouldn't, shed on everything I own, and their ability to provide unconditional love.

TURN THE PAGE
TO READ THE FIRST CHAPTER OF
ONE LIE TOO MANY,

ANOTHER SHOCKING THRILLER FROM
EILEEN COOK

ONE

Destiny is like a boulder. Bulky and hard to move. It's easier to leave it alone than to try to change it. But that never kept anyone from trying. Trust me: I'm a professional.

Reading people is a talent. I've always been a good observer, but as with any natural ability, if you want to be any good, you've got work at it. When I talk to people, I size them up. I listen to what they say and, more important, to what they don't. I notice what they wear, what brands they choose, how they style their hair. I watch their body language to see if it matches their words. The image they work so hard to show off tells me what they're trying to hide.

I make guesses and let them lead me. It's easier than it looks. Then again, most people aren't paying that much attention when someone tells them what they want to hear.

"What do you think, Skye — will it work out?" Sara leaned forward, ignoring the rest of what was going on in our school cafeteria. She chewed her lips. There were sticky pink clots of Sephora lip gloss on her teeth. Nerves. She was worried about what I would say. She'd have been better off worrying about why she wanted to stay with a guy who was a class-A jackass. However, she wasn't paying me for love advice; she was paying for a psychic connection to the universe.

I shuffled the cards. They were worn and faded, more like fabric than paper. My official story was that my grandmother had passed down this deck of tarot cards to me on her deathbed because she believed I'd inherited her psychic ability. This was a complete lie. The only thing my grandma believed in was bourbon. However, no one trusts a psychic who works with brand-new cards. I ordered the deck from Amazon years ago. When it arrived, I soaked each card in a weak tea bath, then put them in the oven, set on low. It wasn't exactly a Food Channel recipe, but it worked. I'd shuffled them over and over until the cards took on the look and feel of a deck that had been in the family for generations. I held the cards out to Sara.

"Cut these," I said. "Make three piles and then stack them." I pulled back as she reached for the deck, holding them just out of her reach. "It's important that you focus on your question as you do this." I fixed her with a stare as if this were a matter of life and death. Sara nodded solemnly. Her hands shook as she cut the deck and then passed it back to me. Part of my secret was making the other person touch the cards. It made them feel complicit in whatever happened next.

I dealt six of the cards into a Celtic Cross spread on the table between us. The cafeteria wasn't the ideal place for a reading. It was hard to feel a connection to something otherworldly when the smell of greasy industrial sloppy joes and overboiled canned corn hung like a cloud in the air. On the other hand, there was no way I was inviting people back home with me. I'd take the overcrowded café and people's judgment that I was a bit of a weirdo before letting my classmates see our salvaged-from-the-dumpster furniture. No thanks. I may be a fake psychic, but I've got some pride.

I tapped the table. "The first card represents you and your question. The one over it is what crosses you — got it?" I waited for her to nod and then lightly touched each of the others with the tip of my finger. "This is the basis of your question, the past, what hangs over you, and the final card is the future."

Sara took a deep breath. "Okay, my question is, what's going to happen with Darren and me?"

I flipped over the first card. The queen of cups. This was going to be easy. That is, if I believed in any of this, which I don't. What no one seemed to realize was I could read the tarot any way I wanted. There was no magic. What I had was my ability to memorize the meanings of the various cards, years of watching my mom, and an ability to spin a story. "This card represents you. This is associated with women who are creative and sensitive."

Sara's forehead wrinkled. "I'm not really creative. I mean, I want to be, but . . ."

"You're in the band," I pointed out.

Her shoulders slumped. "Only because my mom made me. She thinks it'll look good on my college apps."

"I suspect you have a creative side that you haven't fully explored,"

I offered. "Don't think of it as just the arts. The queen represents creativity — someone who sees things in a new way." Her friend Kesha, who was practically seated in her lap, nodded. Her elaborate African braids bounced up and down.

"You're totally the most creative person in cheer," Kesha said.

"The squad always does ask me to do the posters," Sara admitted.

I fought the urge to sigh. Sara needed to broaden her horizons beyond being a good cheerleader. "There you go," I said, tapping the rest of the deck with confidence on the scarred and chipped table. "Now, the card crossing you is the six of swords. That often means a journey or a separation."

Her eyes grew wide. "Like a breakup?"

Only if you're smart enough to dump his ass.

I shrugged. "Maybe, but it could also be a journey of the mind."

Kesha's forehead wrinkled up like one of those shar-pei dogs. "What does that mean?"

"It means that either Sara or Darren is at a stage where their life could go in a different direction. That they're changing. Evolving."

"What if he changes so much that he doesn't want me anymore?" Sara's voice came out tiny and small. Kesha reached over and squeezed her hand. Sara's lip quivered. "He's going downstate for college in the fall. He says we'll date long distance, but . . ." She was unable to put into words what she knew was coming.

I turned over another card. "This is the seven of cups. It means opportunities and possibilities."

"Is that good?" Sara bit her lower lip.

"It's always good to have options." Like choosing a guy who doesn't sit with his Neanderthal friends and hold up a sheet of paper with a number rating girls as they walk by in the cafeteria. "You have choices coming up. You could see who else is out there." I saw her expression and switched my approach. She wasn't interested in advice about who to date. "Or another option is figuring out what changes you could make to your relationship with Darren."

"How can I do that?"

I turned another card. Death. The skeleton held his scythe at the ready. Kesha gasped. "That looks really bad," she said.

They're playing cards, I wanted to say, but I stuffed down the urge to ask if she was afraid of Monopoly or Chutes and Ladders. "The death card isn't bad —"

"Death card?!" Sara's voice cracked.

The effort to keep from rolling my eyes was giving me a headache. "It doesn't mean death, not like physical death. It means that there's a change coming. Something moving from one state to another. It can be a really good thing." I flipped the next card. "Ah," I said, and nodded knowingly.

Sara looked down and then back at me. "What does that mean?"

"It's called the hanging man."

"Oh Jesus." Kesha's hands twisted in her lap.

"See how he's suspended by his feet?" I pointed to the illustration. "His card represents seeing the world from a different perspective. It's not a bad card."

"I don't get it, Skye. What does that have to do with Darren and me?" Sara was leaning so far forward, her nose was practically on the table.

I smiled and spread my arms. "Don't you see? That card gives you the possible solution."

Sara exchanged glances with Kesha to see if it made more sense to her. Based on Kesha's expression, it didn't.

I sighed. "Tarot isn't about any one card. It's about how they work together. Look at what you have here, what cards you drew." It never hurt to remind the person that if they didn't like the outcome, they were partly to blame. "We started with you as a creative person. Then what's opposing you at this point is that Darren is undergoing a journey. That makes sense if he's going away in the fall. Then there are two forces — this card meaning change is coming. That tells me this can't be avoided."

Sara nodded. "I feel like I'm already losing him, and he hasn't even graduated yet."

"I understand," I said. "But how the situation turns out will depend on your ability to make him see you in a fresh way. Maybe change your look, or do something out of character that makes him rethink your role in his life."

"He always wants me to go camping," she mumbled. "It's usually not my kinda thing."

"There you go," I said, pointing at her chest as if she'd just solved a really tricky problem. "Doing stuff outside your comfort zone is exactly the kind of thing you should be doing if you want to keep him."

Someone a few aisles over tripped and dropped a tray with a loud crash and the shatter of exploding dishes. A cheer went up from the crowd in the cafeteria. Pain and humiliation is always amusing when it happens to someone else. Other psychics never had to work with these distractions.

"So, if I reinvent myself, then Darren and I will stay together?"

I shrugged. "That's what the cards imply. Not that he needs someone different—just that he needs to see you differently." At least I was giving her good advice, regardless of Darren. Everyone benefits from shaking up their routine once in a while.

The corners of Sara's mouth started to turn up. "You know what this means . . ."

Kesha let out a squeal. "Makeover!" The two of them hugged. "We'll go to the mall after school. When he sees you he'll already be planning his first visit home before he even leaves." Kesha's face was determined. The woman was on a retail quest to help her bestie.

"There's another way you could read the cards," I said, kicking myself for not just leaving it alone. "Your card is creativity and strength. You could also see this situation as change is inevitable, but you'll be fine no matter what Darren does. That you have the inner strength to move forward in a new direction on your own."

Her mouth pinched. "But there's still a chance for me to work things out with him, right?"

I gave up. If she wanted to waste all that energy on a boy, it wasn't my problem. None of their problems were mine. I had plenty of my own. "Sure."

Sara leaned back in her chair as if all of her energy had rushed out like air from a balloon. Now that she had a plan, she was exhausted.

I shuffled the cards back into a tidy stack. I took my time. Sometimes people decided once the cards were out that they might as well ask a few more questions. Fine with me. I charge for each deal, but after a beat I could tell Sara wasn't going to ask anything else. Now that the great Darren mystery had been put to bed, she wasn't interested. She was too busy plotting how to remake herself into Darren's ideal. She could do better, but that wasn't the question she'd asked.

That was always the awkward moment — when it came time for them to pay. I hated asking for the cash. It felt slimy, but not so distasteful that I was willing to do it for free. My mom made it easy with a sign by our door noting that she accepted both cash and PayPal. I cleared my throat and turned my hand palm up.

"Oh, sorry." Sara pulled a ten out of her wallet and slid it over as if she didn't want to touch me. "Thanks, Skye. That was awesome." I shoved the bill into my pocket. She watched me tuck the deck of cards into the small paisley fabric bag I kept them in. "That was pretty cool."

"The gift chose me," I said with a shrug. I didn't point out that the reason she thought I was amazing was because I told her exactly what she wanted to hear. I knew Darren well enough to know he followed his dick around like a dog on a leash. Sara wasn't done crying over him. I'd have bet money on it. No psychic ability required for that prediction.

Sara wasn't some cheerleader cliché. She was on squad, but she was also an honor student. I'd heard she was in AP chemistry and calculus, and she was only a junior. You would think someone that smart wouldn't be so stupid. But they were all like that.

She waved to me over her shoulder as she scurried across to her friends, and I smiled back. Another happy customer. With any luck, a few of those friends would decide they wanted their own readings. They tended to come in clusters.

My stomach rumbled. Even with the ten bucks, I shouldn't make a Subway run. I was still way short of my goal. I should have saved the money, but it wasn't like ten bucks was going to make a huge difference. Screw it. I could already smell that fresh-baked bread.

TWISTY, SHOCKING THRILLERS

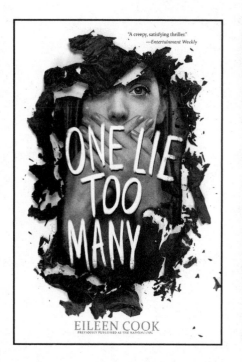

FROM EILEEN COOK